Bloody Twine #5
Twisted Tales with Twisted Endings
Matthew L. Marlott

ISBN: 979-8-9894444-9-6

This book is for all who just wish to sit back, relax, and enjoy some twisted tales with twisted endings. This book is dedicated to fans of traditional horror.
If you like this book, give it a good review and tell me what your favorite story was in this collection.

Table of Contents

Preface

These stories were originally published on my own personal site, bloodytwine.com. It's a little site that has received an equal amount of little attention, but it's mine, and I'm proud of it. I use this site to perfect my stories, and thanks to it, you have these bundles of fine short horror tales you can now peruse and enjoy at your leisure.

Imagine walking into an abandoned storage room filled with old newspapers and magazines, all articles stacked in bundles neatly tied with twine, but then you discover other bundles, bundles not so neatly tied, ragged bundles of yellowed and partially-charred paper tied in bloodstained twine.

You see, some stories are meant to educate, and some stories are meant to entertain, but some stories…some stories are simply looking for a victim.

Enjoy.

Bloody Twine #5

Definitely not uneventful.
He'd cased her for a week already, and now it was finally time to act. She was a pretty little thing, a sorority girl, short, about 5'2", pixie-cut dyed-blonde hair, hourglass body, button nose, round lips, decent boobs, cute face and smile…He hoped she wouldn't put up too much of a fight…
Average Read Time: 33m 19s

The call of the wild.
Pyotr followed the others into the abandoned house. Everything was abandoned now, or the owners were dead, like many others, but this was the new normal. There was nothing now but snow, just a blanket of it everywhere, and this was also the new normal…
Average Read Time: 26m 41s

Do you believe in the Man in the Moon?
There was a shadow in the moonlight, a shadow of a man, or maybe a woman; he couldn't tell. It was tall and gangly, an amorphous shape in rough-humanoid form with extra-long arms, long hands, and long, long fingers. He did not know why, but the primal fear inside him told him not to go near it, and definitely, *definitely*, not let his own shadow touch it. That was a no, no…
Average Read Time: 14m 22s

If it's too good to be true, then you've probably been had.

She was pale, so pale in her skin, but this accented the pinkish-red of her sultry lips. She had on a tight, burgundy, sleeveless one-piece with a miniskirt, the sections separated by a thick black belt with a gold buckle, and this really showed off her beautiful hips and legs…She was truly to die for. Dear God, was she something to drool over…
Average Read Time: 32m 55s

Girls just wanna have fun, right?
The beautiful, otherworldly shape in the center of the pentagram stopped and turned to stare directly into Cindy's dark eyes. There were two pinpoints of vermillion light in that smoke where its eyes should have been, and those two pinpoints of light burrowed into Cindy, burrowing into the very depths of her mind right down to her innocent soul…
Average Read Time: 39m 51s

No crisis is too big for the superior man.
Two burly security guards in grey shirts burst through the office door, guns drawn, ready to blast away, but they didn't make it five feet in before two beams of light speared through the roof to strike them both through the tops of their heads. They were babies in mere seconds, and then they were gone, mere infants drawn up through the roof to pass through solid ceiling as if they were ghosts…
Average Read Time: 31m 10s

Ah, spreading Christmas cheer.
He'd come across an old red fire axe, so he'd stolen a Santa suit right away, smashing through a

department store window to get it, and that stupid holiday suit fit him more or less. Now, with his suit and his axe, he was ready to start the bloodshed all over again…
Average Read Time: 22m 54s

Being unattached has its risks.
He continued his walk toward Alex's meeting place, but he did not have to walk for long. He saw Alex shivering in the cold, dressed in his dark-blue parka, standing right next to that "Jupiter Cola" machine the boy so loved…
Average Read Time: 45m 27s

Some things should remain forgotten.
In the middle of the room was a huge stone head, that head settled directly center within the winding stone slabs, a carving of a bearded, bald white man, that huge head resting upon its left cheek, the eyes closed, the "skin" bedecked with more concentric, circling swirls like strange, carved tattoos
Average Read Time: 1h 11m 2s

Sometimes there's a reason the unexplored remains unexplored.
Technically, none of them were supposed to be out here, not out here in the Forbidden Zone, an arm of space few travelers ever returned from, but the scientific discoveries just waiting to be…discovered…were far too tempting to pass up…
Average Read Time: 22m 39s

#1…BECCA'S NIGHT OUT

Definitely not uneventful.

Lester pulled into the lot and parked his red F-150 in an empty space. The bar across the street, the Tin Bird, had its usual crowd of college kids for a Saturday night, the same pack of vapid, barely-out-of-their-teens meat sacks that normally caroused such places.

He was a little out of place here, he being in his early thirties while dressed like a cowboy, but he knew what he was doing. He had a target in mind, and she was here…He knew it.

He'd cased her for a week already, and now it was finally time to act. She was a pretty little thing, a sorority girl, short, about 5'2", pixie-cut dyed-blonde hair, hourglass body, button nose, round lips, decent boobs, cute face and smile…He hoped she wouldn't put up too much of a fight.

He crossed the street and walked toward the bar entrance, the shaded double doors that led to this pit of hormones and booze.

This was a Midwest college town, so it wasn't like there were bouncers out front to pick and choose who got in. Nah, those dinks were actually in the bar, and their job was just to toss out the drunken toddlers that caused too much trouble for the night.

But all of that was irrelevant. He had something more important on his mind right now…He had to find his target.

He walked into the bar and gave a quick scan of his surroundings. There were a lot of college kids, just like he'd thought, so it was tough to pick out one individual, but he spied her, nonetheless.

She was dressed in a green college sweater with the Greek symbols of her sorority on it, blue jeans wrapped tightly around her heart-shaped butt, something attractive, true, but he could tell she was dressing down. She wasn't even wearing makeup.

She was laying her own bait. She was at the bar sitting on a stool, and she was laying her own bait.

She was selling that cute face, an innocence in her blue eyes that was an outright lie, but he was well aware of these tricks…It didn't matter…He'd make short work of her. After all, he had his own tricks.

The music was a little loud in this boozy arena of vapid speech and drunken hormones, but this wasn't a nightclub. No, the Tin Bird was just a bar, but that was about the best you got in a Midwest college town.

He made a beeline for her and sat right next to her, not even trying to put on a discreet show. No, he needed to look like a predator, to raise her alarms, her red flags, because he'd had her pegged the moment he'd laid eyes upon her. She was the kind of girl who wanted some kind of social justice, but she'd veered far from the normal blogging and vlogging diatribes that your average SJWs preached from their pulpits…Oh, she'd gone *way* dark.

This was the way Lester liked them, though. He didn't have to strain to come up with a reason to do what he liked to do to them, and what he liked to do wasn't very nice.

He really hoped he wasn't going to have to torture her to get what he wanted. He was good at breaking fingers, but sometimes, this wasn't enough. Often, it took direct but small cuts to the nipples and other erogenous zones—the ones with the most nerve endings—to get them to squeal…He kind of enjoyed that, especially the look of absolute terror in their eyes just before the razorblade touched their sensitive parts, but breaking fingers was usually enough.

His last had been a young Latina in the city. She'd been twenty-one, just old enough to drink, but she'd been a spitfire. He had broken all eight of her fingers and both of her thumbs, and she still hadn't talked. No, it had been the razorblade to her junk that had made her squeal. That had gotten her squawking.

He really didn't want to do that again. He kind of enjoyed the torture, but that last one had worn on him, so hopefully, it wouldn't come to that this time. True, there was a part of him that liked listening to their screams, but that got old, you know? He wanted to be on hiatus from that for a while.

Of course, he'd gone all the way before—six times, in fact—but it was a sick, sick thing to do. It was the fact that he enjoyed it that got to him, but to be honest, there were other ways to get the information he needed. That's what he should have done with the Latina, but…

Lester pulled himself inward and pitched out the memory of that last botched job. This time was going to be different. This time was going to run more smoothly. He wasn't going to collect *that* this time. He wanted to; he wanted to take *it* from this new mark and listen to her scream in pain and horror, but the truth was, he had enough of *those* already. He didn't need any more.

But back to the task at hand.

He turned toward his mark and flashed her a cocky grin. She had noticed him, of course, but he knew she was waiting for him to make the first move, so he did.

He pushed up slightly on his black cowboy hat and gave her a quick nod in recognition. He laid both hands on the bar in front of him and adjusted his black duster. He was a redneck this time, a good ol' country boy, someone that normally made sorority girls like this little thing nervous just to be around.

"Hey, what you drinkin'?" he asked.

"Oh…I'm…uhhh…" stammered the blonde. "I…"

Her cheeks flushed red as she turned slightly from his obtrusive gaze, but he did not take his eyes off her.

Either she was really good at this, or she was a straight-up newb. Either way, she was leaving in his truck tonight. He was going to make sure of that.

"I'm Red," lied Lester. "Let's start off with some beers…Hey, barkeep! I need a couple of beers over here!"

He did not give her time to object. This was always a mistake when dealing with new marks. You had to keep them flustered, on the defensive, or you'd back yourself into a corner, one marked with the word "rejection."

He paid the bartender and tipped the guy, and then he handed her one of the sixteen-ounce glasses of beer. She took it out of courtesy, a mistake on her part, so things were already going smoothly.

"Thank you," she said shyly.

It was time to pour on some aggressive obnoxiousness. How he'd caught her alone without some college dweeb on her was nothing short of a miracle, so he'd have to act quickly to get her in his truck.

"You're pretty, you know that?" he grinned.

He took a sip of his beer, and she took a sip of hers due to nervousness; he could tell. All he needed to do was lighten her up, get her talking, and then he had her.

"Th…Thanks," she said uncertainly.

Yeah, she was a newb. This was going to be easier than he'd originally thought.

"I like pretty girls," lied Lester. "I'm a purebred American country boy, though. I don't meet too many college girls."

"How do you know I'm a college girl?" asked the blonde.

Maybe she thought she was being coy, but the answer was pretty obvious. Either she was a serious pro, which he highly doubted, or she was just straight up new, like "first-time" new, a virgin at this kind of thing.

"You're wearing one of them college shirts," he smirked.

She looked down at her own green sorority sweater, and he immediately took advantage of that. He flicked up on her button nose with his right index finger, and her gaze popped back up to stare into his dark eyes, her own blue eyes wide with sudden alarm.

He laughed and then shook his head.

"Sorry," he chuckled. "Couldn't help myself."

She gave him a nervous chuckle in return and took another sip from her beer. This kind of drink wasn't nearly stiff enough for his tastes, but he could tell she was a lightweight, so it wouldn't take much to get her to loosen up.

"Whatchyou studying at the college?" he asked.

"Oh…uhhh…nursing," she nodded. "I want to be a nurse."

"I getchya," he replied. "Ain't nothin' wrong with that."

"Yeah," she said with a slight smile.

"I'm working as a mechanic," said Lester. "I mostly work on agricultural vehicles, tractors and the like, but it pays good money."

"Really?" asked the blonde. "That's interesting."

But he was on the clock, so this small talk wasn't doing him any favors…It was time to step up his game.

"What's your name anyway?" asked Lester. "I mean, you don't have to tell me your name if you don't want to. I can just call you, 'Sugar.'"

"It's Sherry," said the blonde politely.

That was a lie, of course. Her real name was Rebecca Roms, "Becca," for short. Her birthday was March 4th, her parents were Debra and Osmo Roms, she secretly liked horror movies, and her browsing history had some interesting tells in it…She had a penchant for monster-porn stories, some really hardcore stuff at that. He especially liked the one with the werewolf that ravished a young woman who was alone in a cabin in the woods.

She shared her apartment with three other girls, but all of them went to class during the day, so it hadn't been a challenge for him to pick the apartment lock and scope out her life's history, what he could glean anyway. From what he'd learned, she was the only one doing this…None of her roommates were in on it. However, what he did not have was the information he needed, but he'd get that soon enough. He just needed to get her in his truck.

He just needed to work on her a little more.

"Sherry…Sugar…Either one's fine with me," he shrugged.

She took another nervous drink of her beer.

"Sherry is fine," she said quietly.

Her blue eyes were suddenly downcast, her look sullen.

She was getting cold feet. He needed to lighten her up, not depress her. Unfortunately, alcohol could work both ways…What he really needed was a commitment from her. He needed to egg her on, get her to see him as the bad guy. Then she'd make her move.

"Sherry's a pretty name," he said matter-of-factly. "I knew a church girl by the name of Sherry. She was real nice to me, but she didn't want anything serious with me. Let me down nice and easy…You know, I liked Sherry. Wish more girls were like her."

"I'm sure she had her reasons," said Becca.

He would think of her as Becca. He'd call her Sherry, but he did not want to forget her real name. Real names were a weapon he often used when the timing was right.

"It's because I get a little angry at times," said Lester. "I think she knew that. Just can't seem to hold back, you know? I forget sometimes that you can't be rough with a girl. They're not tough like guys…You're not supposed to get angry like that with a girl…Next thing you know, there're a couple of bruises, and then you're the bad guy…

"Oh, I'm sure I'll meet someone someday that'll tame that beast, but it would have to be a pretty special girl…I can understand if you don't like that kinda guy…We can just talk if you'd like. We can talk and drink if you'd like, one-on-one…"

"Oh…" said Becca.

Her blue eyes flitted back and forth as if she were thinking of exactly what to say, which was exactly what she was doing. She was really new at this, and she probably hadn't received much in the way of instruction, just empty promises, but that was how this game worked.

"We can drink and talk," said Becca.

He'd known that would work. He'd seen her *Tumblr* account. She wasn't going to pass up an admitted abuser.

But it was time to set the bait.

"We can go talk one-on-one somewhere else," grinned Lester. "It don't have to be here…You got a boyfriend? A girlfriend?"

Her cheeks flushed red as her eyes widened slightly. She lowered her head, her blue eyes flitting back and forth, and then she made a silent nod to herself, silent but subtle, a tell that Lester still noticed. She downed her beer in quick gulps after that, emptying the glass before setting it back down upon the bar top.

"Doggone, little lady," said Lester in slight surprise. "Here…You can finish mine."

He slid her his barely tasted beer.

She placed both of her small hands around the glass, and then she downed that one as well. She placed the empty glass back upon the bar top, looked up at him, and grinned.

"We can go talk somewhere else," she said in a weirdly-happy voice.

Yep, there was no more cold feet here. She had made a snap judgement about him, a not-so-happy one, and what she was planning really ticked him off, but he was careful not to show it.

"Sure thing," he grinned in return. "My truck's just outside…You walk here? You need a ride?"

"Yeah," smiled Becca. "I could use a ride."

"Great," said Lester.

And that was that. They left the bar together, crossed the street, and Lester escorted her into his red F-150.

She buckled up and gave him a strange look, but he already knew where she wanted to go, the place he wanted to go as well, though where she wanted to lead him was the information he was missing, so naturally, he had to ask.

"Where to?" he asked.

"Oh…ummm…" said Becca as she shook her head for a second.

Yep. Alcohol was kicking in.

"I'm going to my sorority house," she nodded. "My sorority sisters would definitely like to meet you."

"They would, would they?" asked Lester. "I don't know about that. I thought we would just talk one-on-one."

"Oh, you don't understand," said Becca as she shook her head no. "They love guys like you."

He knew what he was doing, of course. He had to play a little hard to get, or she'd get suspicious.

"Are they pretty?" asked Lester. "I can't imagine a girl being prettier than you."

"Oh, I'm the plain one," smiled Becca. "I'm kind of jealous of them. Ravina, for instance, is drop dead gorgeous. She makes me look like trash."

Bingo. "Ravina" was the name he was looking for. He was definitely on the right track. He had been 99.99% sure beforehand, but there was always that doubt…Now there wasn't any.

"Is that right?" asked Lester.

It was time to pour it on thick, make sure she was devoted. This was a little too easy, and the easy ones made him paranoid. He didn't like it when things were too easy. It didn't sit right with him.

He hit the lock button, and the doors locked with a loud click.

"I'll tell you what," he nodded. "I'll meet your friends, but I want to know if they're fun. Are they fun, Sherry?"

"Yeah," nodded Becca with wide eyes. "Oh, yeah. They're really fun."

Lester pursed his lips, pushed up his black cowboy hat, and leaned his head to one side as he studied her. This was his redneck-audacity pose, something he rarely used, but it was a lot of fun when he did.

"Okay," he nodded. "I'll go…but I need to know how fun they really are."

"How so?" asked Becca, a look of stark confusion upon her cute face.

"You show me your rack," he grinned.

"What?" asked the young blonde in surprise.

"Show me your ta-tas, and I'll meet your friends," he shrugged. "The way I figure it, you're the shy one, so pony up, and I'll go. I wanna have some fun, not be bored by girly talk."

The young woman looked out of sorts for a moment, the scarlet in her cheeks noticeable even in the dim light of the parking-lot lamps, but it was the swift decision that crawled across her face, that telltale look of commitment that convinced him she was following through with what she had started.

She reached down, pulled up her sweater and bra, and showed him her bare breasts. He grinned like an idiot in return, but this was part of the act. There was no actual surprise here. He'd seen a million of these already.

She lowered her sweater and adjusted her bra from beneath that article of clothing.

Her face was flushed, some slight sweat across her brow, so her adrenaline had kicked in, the thrill of the hunt, and she was probably feeling it between her legs, too. These newbs were all the same as far as he could tell.

"Nice," grinned Lester. "You got a beautiful rack, Sugar."

"Thank you," grinned Becca in return. "Now, let's go to my sorority. You promised."

He hadn't promised anything, but whatever.

"Yepper," said Lester. "Can't wait to meet the girls. I can tell this is gonna be lots of fun."

"Oh, it definitely will be," nodded Becca.

Her blue eyes were wide again, crazed. She knew what was going to happen once he got there, and she was following through with it anyway. True, he'd given her the idea that he was an abusive piece of dog doo, but that didn't justify what she *thought* was about to happen…Of course, he *had* actually done some truly terrible things, but she didn't need to know that…Not yet anyway.

At least he wasn't going to have to resort to torture this time in order to get directions. No, she was too new and naïve to hide anything from him. A more seasoned girl would have picked up on his BS a mile away, but then he would have had to get creative, and whenever he did that, the pay wasn't as good.

Still, Becca was a cutie. He definitely wouldn't have minded adding her sweet piece to his collection.

He started the truck and pulled out of the lot, and she gave him directions to somewhere on the outskirts of town, nowhere near the university, but this was to be expected. They weren't going to a sorority anyway.

Nevertheless, he had to stay in character, and that meant a little suspicion was in order, especially when they had driven far enough out of town.

"This don't look like no way to a sorority," he said.

They had pulled off of a back highway and onto an equally back gravel road. Out here was nothing but trees, trees on each side of the road, something he was well used to, but still…this was not a good place to be for any normal guy. Luckily, he wasn't normal in the slightest.

"That's because…uhhh…they…the sorority got a good deal on a house out here," said Becca. "It's a pretty big place. You'll like it."

She was lying, of course, but he already knew that. They both knew they weren't going to a sorority, but she didn't know he knew that.

"Okay," shrugged Lester. "If you say so."

"Oh, yeah," nodded Becca.

They drove up to a large three-story house, something completely out of place amongst the trailers and white-trash homes that normally bedecked this area.

He parked on the other side of the road, as there were already a number of cars in the driveway and along the house-side of this backwoods gravel stretch.

"We're here," grinned the young blonde. "Come on in and meet the girls."

"Are you sure?" asked Lester. "Can they have guys over?"

"Oh, yeah," nodded Becca. "Come on in, and we'll have some fun."

They were going to have fun all right. Well…he was.

He unlocked the doors, they both exited the truck, and Lester grabbed his black duffel from his back seat before shutting his driver's-side door. He walked around his truck to escort his "date" to the front door of the house, but she eyed his bag for a second.

"What's that?" she asked in audible confusion.

"Beer," he lied. "Can't have a party without beer."

"Oh," she said, and she questioned him no further on it.

He shook his head at her obliviousness. Good grief, she really was a newb.

They walked up to the "sorority" door, Becca unlocked it with a key she produced from her right jeans pocket, and they walked right on in.

The place was well lit, there was a lot of well-cared-for old furniture strewn here and there, an old wood floor beneath that furniture, and the walls were garnished with a goodly number of old paintings and decorative tapestries. It was more like a bordello than a sorority, but this was not surprising at all.

Five unbelievably hot women rose from where they were lounging upon various couches, but Lester didn't bother to study them. No, he set down his duffel and went straight to unzipping it.

He needed to make this quick…He needed the edge of surprise.

"Look what I brought!" said Becca in excitement.

She turned toward him with a wave of her hand just as he pulled out his crossbow from his duffel. Her expression changed to one of confusion at first, but this incertitude changed to surprise and pain as he planted his right boot right between her legs with one swift, well-placed kick.

He'd learned a long time ago that if you kicked a girl hard enough in the baby maker, it didn't matter whether she had danglers or not. She would bend right over for you, and that position always gave you a better target to kick.

He brought that same leg up in a crescent after that, striking across her right cheek with that same right boot as she bent over from his previously sudden and brutal attack. She shrieked as she spun and fell to her stomach upon the old wood floor below, but he let this momentary violence give him an edge in time, because he needed every advantage he could get while inside a nest.

Lester brought up his crossbow and fired with both experienced precision and a distinct lack of hesitation. The bolt in question lodged itself in one particularly-hot black girl's chest, right underneath her left breast, right in the heart.

This "young" lady with an afro was dressed in something from the late 1960s, a paisley button up with tan bellbottoms, something very outdated but still somehow hot.

Her lips opened with a gasp of surprise as she lit up from the point of impact, turning to ash within seconds, those outdated clothes burning up along with her.

His bolts were silver-plated, blessed, and dipped in holy water. He didn't take any chances when it came to the undead.

A debutante-looking blond of the group was on him in a heartbeat.

She had long, curly blonde hair, and she wore a summer dress with flower print, something from the 1940s. She was drop dead gorgeous in the face, but it was her speed and dress that tipped him off about how dangerous she really was. The older *they* were, the deeper in the manure *you* were.

This particular bloodsucker hissed, bared her fangs, and was suddenly in his face. She was a speedster, and that was dangerous, but he knew how to handle her. He had a defense against this sort of thing.

Her clawed right hand reached forward to tear through his black T, her intent to plunge that hand into his chest and rip out his heart, but he had a crucifix taped there with duct tape, because he knew this tactic. It was vamp-protection 101.

She drew back her hand as it smoked and popped, and she let forth a short shriek as she bent over and backed away from him, but that was all the time he needed to deal with her.

He dropped his crossbow, pulled forth a flask of holy water from one of his duster's inner pockets, uncorked the glass container, and doused her in the face with it.

The blonde debutante screamed as her face simultaneously melted and lit up in a blaze. She staggered across the old wood floor before falling to it, but her burning head lit up the side of a couch just before she turned to ash.

Yep, the place was going to go up, and it wouldn't take long for it to burn to the ground once it did.

"Ravina!" screamed one of the remaining three vampiresses.

So, he'd already gotten her, target eliminated, and it had been out of sheer reaction…Well, c'est la vie.

The other three vamps came at him in unison, like enraged hornets from a smashed nest, rushing him all at once, a redhead, another blonde, and a brunette. The redhead and the blonde were dressed in modern fashion, young ones, so to speak, probably turned no longer than a decade ago, but the brunette had the clothes and hairstyle of the '80s.

The brunette was still hot, but Lester never did understand why vamps never changed their styles…It was weird to just keep an outdated fashion like that. He'd only ever known one vamp that had changed her original style, but she was unique as far as he was concerned.

Lester pulled forth his silver-plated Bowie knife and threw it as the redhead came at him first. The shaft of the blade buried itself in her forehead, right between her green eyes. Her head went up in flames after that, and he planted his right boot in her solar plexus, causing her to explode into ash just as she struck the burning couch behind her.

He was probably going to have to replace some of his gear, and that wasn't going to be cheap. Good thing he was getting paid well for this job, because he never went into a nest without the proper gear.

He ducked underneath the new blonde's swiping right claw, snatched up a crossbow bolt from his open black duffel, and rammed it into her stomach. The new blonde screamed as her torso lit up, and she was a walking pyre for a few seconds, but then she turned to ash as she fell to the floor, puffing away in a cloud of black soot and flaming specks to spill all over the wood floor below.

The last vampiress, the brunette with '80s fashion, dropped into a wrestler's stance, charged, and grabbed him by both arms just below the shoulders, but her expression changed from one of anger to one of shock as he stopped her charge by impaling her upon the consecrated wooden stake he'd quickly pulled from his duster. She disappeared in smoking ash after that, and his job was done for the moment.

If there were any more vamps in this place, they were on different floors, but the house was quickly going up in flames, so there was no more time to waste. He wasn't going to be able to track down any more for the time being. He'd just have to hope they went up with the house…Besides, he'd already nailed his target.

He picked up his crossbow, dropped it in the duffel, turned, opened the front door, and tossed the bag outside. He then yanked up a very shocked, terrified, and surprised Becca from the floor and threw her outside the house like so much trash.

He slammed the door shut behind himself as he roughly pulled up his new hostage with his right hand while carrying his duffel with his left.

"Get moving!" he yelled.

The young blonde shrieked and stumbled forward as Lester dragged her to the truck.

"Don't kill me!" screeched Becca, but Lester ignored her.

He threw his duffel into the bed of his F-150, pulled her around to the passenger side of the truck, and forced her inside. He trotted around to the driver's side, got in, and quickly locked the doors.

"I'm not one of them!" cried the sorority girl. "I swear, I'm not one of them!"

Lester pulled out a pair of handcuffs from his duster and quickly snapped them over her thin wrists. These were basic cuffs, so his employer had the keys to them as well. Even so, he was only using them to dissuade his new hostage from jumping from the truck while it was moving.

"Shut up," he said gruffly.

"Please!" begged the girl. "Let me go! I'm not one of them! I swear!"

He reached over, grabbed her restrained right hand with both of his, and then bent back her pinky until the digit broke with an audible "CRACK!"

The young woman screamed from the pain, but Lester ignored her pitiful cries. Mercy was something he no longer had.

"You are going to shut up," he said firmly. "If you don't keep quiet, I'm going to break another finger. If you keep it up, I break more fingers. If I run out of fingers, I cut off a nipple…Understand? Nod your head if you understand."

She nodded her head as fat tears rolled down her flushed cheeks. He could tell she was already in intense pain, horrified, and terrified at the same time. Also, her jeans were soaked between her legs, a large dark stain there that spoke volumes.

He started the truck and drove after that, occasionally checking the mirror to see the enormous forest fire he'd just started. That house had really gone up, so if there were any more vamps in the area, they weren't happy.

He drove back to the highway and headed toward the city. It was about an hour drive to get there, but he had an appointment to keep, and he needed to get paid.

It took about thirty minutes, but she spoke again, this time in a much more rational tone. She was trying to bargain, but he'd already known she would. It was always the same…They never could keep their mouths shut once he had them in custody.

"You don't have to do this," she said quietly. "I don't know where you're taking me, but you can let me go now. I won't tell anyone…I…I'm just a normal person. I'm not one of them. I haven't even done anything wrong."

"You tried to feed me to a bunch of bloodsuckers," grunted Lester.

"Th…That's what they wanted me to do," sputtered Becca. "They…They threatened to kill my family if I didn't."

"That's a lie, Becca, and we both know it," he said firmly.

She stared over at him in both surprise and fear…Yep, real names had power.

"How do you know my name?" she asked.

"I know a lot about you," said Lester. "I cased your place and got a real close look at your life. Your name is Rebecca Roms. You wanted to be a vampire after you met a real vampire. She convinced you she'd make that a reality if you played the part of bait and lure. This was your first time bringing someone in. I ruined all that for you. Now they're destroyed, and you're screwed. End of story."

"I…It's not…I don't think it's that simple…" stalled out the girl.

"Doesn't matter now," said Lester with a shake of his head. "You don't have to worry about any of that anymore. Just be quiet."

She didn't say anything for a few minutes before she started up again, but he'd already known she would. He didn't hunt male vampires; he only hunted the women, and these girls, these thralls, these little honeybees that brought in the guys?...They were all the same beggars, liars, and blood-junkies looking for that next vamp hit. They couldn't keep their mouths shut to save their lives.

"You're a vampire hunter, right?" she asked.

"Yep," he said in firm reply.

"Are vampire hunters supposed to attack normal people?" she asked. "You hurt me, Red. You kicked me and then broke my finger. I'm…I'm in a lot of pain. I need a hospital."

"Yep," he said again.

"Well?" she asked.

"Don't care," he replied.

"Why not?" asked Becca, but her tone was desperate, whiney.

"Because you're a slave, Becca," replied Lester.

She winced at the sound of her own name, but he had expected this. It was clear she was not used to being on the defensive.

"I wasn't a slave," she said quietly. "I was working for them as an equal. They were going to make me one of them…I…I don't want to do that anymore, though. I just want to live a normal life now."

"No, you don't," said Lester.

"Yes, I do," nodded Becca. "They were evil…I see that now. I was blinded by all of the glamour and power and eternal youth, but I see the truth now. Vampires are evil. I see that now."

"No, you don't," said Lester. "You've been drinking their blood."

"What?" asked Becca. "How did you…? What?"

Her expression was one of genuine shock, but he knew a vamp junkie when he saw one.

"In fact, you're shaking right now because you need another hit," continued Lester. "You could heal that finger on your own if you could just get one more hit…I can always tell. You injure a thrall, and their body reacts. That's how you can spot a vamp junkie."

"Well, if you're so smart, then you can help me," said Becca. "Is that why you broke my finger?...You were being cautious, weren't you? I really do need to have some more blood, but if you can help me get off of it, then I'd never be able to repay you. You'd be saving my life…

"I can tell you're actually a good person, Red. I can see now that you were trying to save me. In fact, I know you'll help me. If you help me, I'll give you anything you want. I don't have much, but I do still have something I can offer…You…You can have my body if you want. That's what you want, isn't it? You don't have to take it by force, you know. I'll give it to you."

The bargaining again. It was annoying, true, but there was no reason for him to be overly cruel. He didn't have to break more fingers to deal with this. Of course, he did enjoy that torture to some degree, especially if it would shut her up, but…nah. He still wanted to be paid in full. He had bills to pay.

"Just shut up," he said firmly.

"I can't," said Becca. "I don't know where you're taking me, and I'm scared, Red. Wouldn't you be scared if a stranger was holding you hostage?"

"You're lucky I haven't killed you," said Lester. "Unfortunately, I need you alive. So here's the deal…I'm going to get very creative with a razor blade and what's inside your panties if you don't shut up."

"You wouldn't do that," said Becca. "I know you wouldn't, Red. You're actually a good person."

"Uh, huh," said Lester. "You actually think I'm a good person…Uh, huh…Look…I want you to open the dash box there in front of you and take out the length of twine inside."

"Okay," she said quietly. "But I know you're a good person, Red. I know you'll help me and let me go."

She reached up with her bound hands, opened up the dash compartment, and pulled out the length of bloodstained twine he had stashed inside it. This was his "shut-the-hell-up" card, though he didn't play it very often.

"I know you won't do anythi…" she said, but her voice trailed off as she stared at the length of bloody twine in her hands, her breath sucking in at the sight of it, her face twisting in horror upon its comprehension.

He had a line of cured and dried lady parts strung along it, a total of six to be exact, all cut with precision from his victims, the full flowery bits complete with petals and stem, because he was an artist in some respects.

She dropped the disgusting line of feminine trophies to the truck floor and gave a slight wail, her cuffed hands shaking from realization, her whole body trembling in response to this revelation.

"Now I want you to shut up for the remainder of this trip," said Lester. "If you don't want me to add to that collection, you won't say another word. Keep talking, and I *will* go straight to the razor blade, and I'll take it right inside your panties. No more broken fingers…You won't die when I cut it off, but you sure won't be happy about it…The other girls sure as hell weren't."

The young woman silently wept as she took in saliva-gulping breaths…Yep. It was sinking in, but more importantly, he had finally shut her up.

They drove to the suburbs of the city, but Lester took a turn toward the well-to-do district. There was one particular residence he was driving to.

He pulled up to the gate of a large mansion, rolled down the window, and stared at the security camera for a few seconds. A light flashed green under the camera, the gate opened, and Lester drove through that gate and onto a long gravel driveway.

He parked his truck in a small paved lot, got out, nodded toward one of the large and burly security guards dressed in black, and then pulled his prize from his truck, though she was still weeping and definitely not happy to be with him.

A couple of security guards armed with submachine guns walked them to the front door of this huge and opulent building, and then they were escorted inside.

Lester sat a silent, sullen, sniffling, and terrified Becca upon a small couch in the foyer and waited for his employer to arrive, all while a couple of security guards watched over them as they waited.

"Stupid thing to hook up with those bloodsuckers," said Lester quietly. "Did you honestly think that would work out?...I got news for you, Sugar. Things aren't what they're like in the movies...Never are."

The double white doors that led into the grand hall opened up, and a tall, pale woman in a sparkling red dress walked into the foyer.

"Ahh, Les, my favorite little psycho," smiled the woman.

She was at least six-foot-two, in her late thirties, very slender, and she had small boobs, a gorgeous face, dark and flashing eyes, and straight, raven-black hair that dropped down almost to the top of her shapely bottom.

"So it's done, then?" asked this mysterious woman.

"Yep," he said firmly. "Got Ravina. Killed four more of them."

"That's confirmed?" asked the woman.

"Yep," he replied.

"Excellent!" said the tall lady with a clap of her pale hands. "That was all of them...Excellent, excellent, excellent...Ah, and I see you've brought in little Becca."

The tall and slender woman leaned over the young blonde and smiled, but that smile quickly turned into a frown. She gingerly held up Becca's right hand, inspected the girl's broken pinky, and then ran her left index finger along the bruise on Becca's right cheek.

"She's bruised in the face, and her finger is broken," said the woman unhappily. "I told you to bring her in untouched. I wanted her undamaged, Lester."

"Couldn't be helped," shrugged Lester. "She's still alive, and she's mostly there."

"Oh, really?" asked the woman in an accusing tone. "Are *all* of her parts intact?...I know your vices, Lester."

"She's in one piece," grunted Lester.

The tall woman stared down at him with an angry glare, but that glare softened after a few seconds.

He'd already known it would. She could always tell when he was lying, and this time, he wasn't lying.

"Oh, good," smiled the woman. "Well, in that case, you get extra pay. I can forgive what little damage you've already done, because I know what a monstrous struggle it had to have been for you to leave her in such a pristine state."

"Mighty grateful, Eliza," nodded Lester. "Thank you for the payment, but I'll be taking my leave now. I have bills to pay with that money and other matters to attend to."

The tall and imposing woman smiled, nodded once at him, and then nodded over at one of her guards.

"Hand the man his cash," ordered this "Eliza." "He's earned it."

She looked back upon Lester and smiled again.

"I'll give another call when I need you," she said happily. "You always pull through for me, Lessie."

Lester tipped his hat, happily received a briefcase full of cash that one of the guards handed him, and then took his leave. His job was done for now.

*****

A security guard undid Rebecca's handcuffs, and the tall woman with the dark hair beckoned the young blonde to follow her further into the mansion.

Becca did not know where she was or who this woman was, but she was just glad that she was no longer being held hostage by that psycho that had just left.

"Follow me, dear," ordered the tall woman named Eliza.

Becca followed her through the grand hall, that hall a shining example of opulence that one only saw in movies. The floor was all pristine-white tiles, there were twin looping staircases rising to the higher floors, there was a grand piano down here with guest divans for relaxing, and there was even a small bar with its own bartender, the man dressed in a white shirt, tuxedo vest, and black slacks.

Becca felt as if she needed to say something, if only to break the ice, because this woman was like royalty to her anyway.

"Thank you for saving me," she said quietly.

"Saving you?" said Eliza with a light and bubbly laugh. "Oh, my dear. You have no idea, do you?"

"Idea?" asked Becca. "Idea of what?"

The tall, pale woman in the sparkling red dressed grabbed Becca's right arm with her left hand and yanked her forward toward a side door. The woman's grip was like a steel vice, her physical strength on an insane level.

"Ow!" cried Becca. "OW!"

The tall woman threw open the door and dragged Becca down a flight of stone steps.

"What are you doing!" screeched Becca.

She was dragged against her will to stand before a large, dark wooden door carved with bat, wolf, spider, and snake motifs.

"Did you honestly think there was some mysterious organization that hunts vampires?" asked Eliza. "You can't be so naï—Oh, disgusting…You have Ravina's stink all over you…I'd say 'stench,' but that's far too nice…It's a stink…Ugh…That tart was a thorn in my side for far too long…Young people and their pretentious stupidity…Anyway…Anyway, let me ask you a question, Becca. Who do you think hires vampire hunters? Who could possibly want to get rid of an encroaching nest of them?"

"I don't know," said Becca. "I don't even understand what you're talking about!...Let go! You're hurting me!"

The tall woman stared down at her and smiled. Her eyes shone a bright red, and then her fangs dropped down, glistening white in the pale luminescence that lit this dark, descending hallway.

Becca's heart nearly stopped at the sight of Eliza's transformation, but then she pulled up her courage and spoke in her own defense. She was already used to the vampire-transformation show, and she would not be intimidated by it now…Besides, her goal of becoming a vampire was once again within arm's reach.

"You're a vampire?" she asked in audible surprise. "I didn't know…I…I would have come to you if I'd known…I wouldn't have gone to Ravina…Now…Now wait. We can make a deal…I…I can be your servant, you know. I can bring people to you. I can be your…your thrall…or you can make me a vampire, too…That's what I really want anyway…I'll be an excellent vampire…I'll be loyal to you forever."

The tall woman with raven-black hair laughed and shook her head no. She stared down into Becca's blue eyes, but there was no love in this woman's own flashing red eyes, none at all, in fact. There was only a sadistic lust in those eyes, but it was not a lust for anything sexual…Becca was certain of that.

"Do you know what Lester and I have in common?" asked Eliza.

"Lester?" asked Becca. "Lester…Do you mean Red?"

"Oh, Lessie's still using that name," grinned the tall woman. "How quaint. I suppose it's an homage to me…Yes, dear, I mean Red. Now answer my question. Do you know what Lester and I have in common?"

Becca could not think of a single thing that this woman, a vampiress at that, would have in common with a psycho—probably a serial killer—vampire hunter.

"No," said Becca with a brisk shake of her head. "I…I don't know."

The tall lady in red grinned, her fangs still menacing and glistening beneath her glowing red eyes.

"I'll say it slowly so that you understand, dear," said Eliza.

She opened the dark wooden door before them, and Becca's eyes widened in horror as her mind processed what lay in wait in the underground chamber within her field of vision.

"We both *hate*…young…pretty…girls," finished the tall woman in red.

In the underground chamber were four separate young women, all around Becca's age, all nude, all upon various torture tables or in torture devices.

The closest young lady was laid out on a table, and she had been shaved completely bald, bald all over, but that was not what was disturbing. This young woman had no limbs; they had been removed, fresh sutures at the stubs. Her nipples had been removed and the wounds sewn shut, and her lady parts were sewn shut, as were her lips and eyes. Worst of all, much worse, though, was the fact that this poor young woman was…she was…she was still *alive*.

Becca's eyes glanced over the other three girls, but they were not in any better shape, all of them alive, all in a state of this…this *horror*.

"Ravina was a young and pretentious fool that needed to be dealt with," said Eliza. "She actually thought she was going to stake a claim in *my* kingdom…*my* kingdom…Now you? You are nothing but a loose end, a blood bag I'll feed on until I tire of you, just like these other young harlots, these thralls that Lester dragged in for me."

Becca could not speak. She shook in place at the sight of this, her mind finally broken.

"He has a terrible penchant for mauling my prizes, but he brought you in intact," said Eliza. "Now *I* get to remove and keep the best parts for myself, dear, and I will…Oh, I most certainly will…You see, I've been doing this for a very long time, so begging for mercy will not help you, little Becca…Welcome to *my* house…Welcome to the House of Báthory, my little morsel."

Becca begged for mercy anyway as the ancient vampiress slowly relieved the young blonde of her clothing, one article at a time, the sadistic queen remarking with each removal how flawless and delicious Becca's body and skin truly were.

#2…THE WOLVES OF THE END

The call of the wild.

Pyotr followed the others into the abandoned house. Everything was abandoned now, or the owners were dead, like many others, but this was the new normal. There was nothing now but snow, just a blanket of it everywhere, and this was also the new normal.

All of them were bundled in heavy coats and thick undergarments, whatever they had found and grabbed at the last minute before all hell had descended upon them. Pyotr's thick parka was a dark-blue, much like his mood, but he had always been in a dark mood, something he had come to identify and accept.

Life had never been right for him, so the end was not so much a grief as it was just a fact. He had never felt right in his own skin, had never felt right around people in general, so he had fallen in with a bad crowd, though even that had been more happenstance than anything else.

Viktor was their leader, the leader of what was left of their little gang, the Concrete Wolves. He called the shots, what little decisions were left to be made. It was

Viktor who had led them all here, because this house was still standing by some miracle, by some miracle of the same angry god that had destroyed everything in the first place.

Pyotr did not care anymore. He was tired, he was hungry, and there was little left to believe in or stand for. The world was over. There was no other end to this story. All of them should have laid down and died with everyone else, but the Concrete Wolves were nothing if not survivors, so here they were, and here they would be for a while yet or until the very end.

Yes, Viktor was their leader, and the big man with an even bigger black beard had led them here. Viktor made the tough decisions for the group, and some of those decisions had been both bloody and cruel, but their little group could only survive if they had unity, so Pyotr had stood by and watched the others as they had done unspeakable things, but he had never partaken, nor would he ever. He was not like that.

Yes, he was Pyotr, but he did not like to think on himself. He was not like the others, as he was not willing to do the things the others had been willing to do to survive, but he believed in family, and the Concrete Wolves were the only family he still had. His own family were beneath his thoughts; he had abandoned them long ago.

Then there was Rodion. Rodion was stuck to Viktor like glue. He was Viktor's yes-man, if it were possible for a gang to have as such, but he would do anything for the big man with the big black beard. He had slit that old woman's throat at the behest of Viktor, and he had done this without even batting an eye. Rodion was one that Pyotr did not trust. Pyotr did not trust Viktor, either, but Viktor had some sense when it came to decision-making, so Viktor was a step above Rodion.

Leonid was the fierce one. He was always ready to fight. He had many scars, many scars that could have been avoided. Pyotr had been dragged into more than one of Leonid's drunken brawls, and those small battles had always ended in blood. Leonid had once killed a man by caving in his skull with nothing but a brick. Pyotr was always careful around him.

Vadim was the handsome one, but only on the outside. He was a womanizer, and he got what he wanted one way or another, if not by charm, then by force. Pyotr had been too late more than once to keep some young woman from being defiled by Vadim. Pyotr did not like him at all.

Last, but not least, was Rurik, the thief. Rurik stole anything and everything, but he did not like to share. Viktor was constantly disciplining him, if only to get something from Rurik that they needed that Rurik may have picked up. Pyotr kept his eyes on his own things whenever he was around Rurik.

And that was all there was to tell. It was just them left, six men, six wolves at the end.

"Everyone, inside," ordered Viktor.

They entered the two-story home via the front door, though Rurik had used his lockpicks to open that door. Once inside, Rurik shut and locked the door behind them. They could never be too careful, especially now that the world was a wasteland.

This house was more of a shrine to the dead than anything else. The rotting old couple upon a flower-print couch were too frozen to attract flies, but Pyotr did not like them being there. They would have to throw these bodies outside soon. None of them wanted to sleep near the dead.

First, though, they needed heat. All of them were chilled to the bone, but this place had a wood-burning stove for heating, so all they needed was some firewood, and they would be fine. One of them would probably have to chop wood if there was no firewood ready, but that was also fine.

"There may be food here," said Viktor. "We will get a fire started, but in the meantime, Pyotr and Vadim will search for food."

"Aye, Viktor," said Pyotr, though he had no desire to search for food with Vadim.

"Leonid and Rurik will drag out these bodies," ordered Viktor. "Rodion and I will get to work on the stove."

Well…at least Pyotr did not have to move the bodies.

He stared off to his left through an open archway that led to the kitchen.

This old couple must have had money, because most people had lived in apartments, but this couple had owned a house, a two-story at that. This was also probably the reason they had been located in an isolated area. They would have avoided thieves and other ne'er-do-wells that way.

At least they had already been dead when the Concrete Wolves had arrived. Viktor would have ordered their execution, and Pyotr had no stomach for death anymore.

He walked into the kitchen along with Vadim. There was bound to be something in here, but it was canned goods they were looking for. Those kept the longest and could be carried for long journeys.

Pyotr opened up a cabinet above the sink and found cans of tushonka, shproti, soup, canned sorrel, and even some condensed milk. This would most certainly do.

"Here they are," he grunted.

Vadim lifted up a burlap sack of potatoes and grinned.

"These are still good," he said confidently.

"Then we will eat those first," nodded Pyotr.

"There are also two bottles of vodka here," said Vadim.

He placed the two full bottles of the strong spirit upon the kitchen counter next to Pyotr.

"Viktor will want those," said Pyotr.

"So will Rurik," chuckled Vadim.

"Unfortunately," said Pyotr, but Vadim only laughed once more.

Vadim slung the bag of potatoes up on the stovetop and took one out.

"Time to cut these in half," he said. "Once we have firewood, we can bake them, and then we can eat."

That sounded good to Pyotr. A warm place to sleep, a belly full of food, and the heat of vodka may be the simplest of pleasures, but it was more than enough for him, more than enough for a wolf at the end.

＊＊＊＊＊

They sat around the heat of the living-room stove as Viktor passed the vodka bottle to Pyotr. Pyotr took a swig, shook his head from the strong burn of it, and then passed the bottle to Leonid.

"Here is to the end, men," said Viktor. "If we don't die of the cold, we die of starvation. If we don't die of starvation, we die of radiation sickness. Such is the nature of life. To the end, men! To the Concrete Wolves!"

"Aye!" they all said together.

It was a depressing toast, but Pyotr was glad for it. He was glad that Viktor understood the futility of it all, the sad function that was waiting for death, but it was a blessing in disguise, because there was comradery here, a last spout of honor before the last gasp of breath.

At least there had been a stack of firewood in a small shack out back. This was good, because they were currently using that wood to heat themselves, and they had used it to bake the potatoes they had eaten.

They had all stuffed themselves with as much as they could possibly eat, devouring the bag of potatoes with gusto. There was no telling when they would eat again, and the canned food they'd found, though plentiful, would not last forever.

"We will stay here for the while," continued Viktor. "A couple of days at the most, though. Then we will move on."

"Aye," said Rodion.

It would be back into the cold soon, but Pyotr did not care. There had to be someplace, somewhere, that was better than here. This country was lost.

"Let us enjoy the heat for now," said Viktor. "Rurik, go out and get us more wood for the fire."

"Aye," said Rurik.

The skinny thief snatched up the bottle of vodka from Leonid, took his drink, and then passed it on to Vadim.

"A warm place to sleep is all I want right now," said Rurik.

The others gave him a resounding "aye," but Pyotr was just grateful that Rurik was being useful for once.

The thief walked to the back of the house to leave via the backdoor. Once he had left the living room, Vadim spoke up, asking a question that Pyotr figured had no meaning anymore.

"Where are we going next?" asked Vadim.

"The cities are a wasteland," replied Viktor. "The countryside is nothing but snow, so we will head to the border, maybe south. Perhaps the Chinamen are in a better state. I do not know. I know that we cannot survive in this nuclear winter. There must be someplace where food can be grown."

Pyotr thought about saying something, perhaps throwing in his meager suggestion. It occurred to him that maybe they could take a boat to some tropical island somewhere, but he never got to voice his opinion. No, he was interrupted by something far more pressing.

Rurik's loud scream was heard by everyone.

Pyotr hopped to his feet along with everyone else.

Nothing was said as the rest of the Concrete Wolves rushed to the backdoor. Viktor flung open the back entrance and bolted outside, Rodion and Pyotr right behind him, Vadim following last.

There was no sign of Rurik. There was only a trail of blood that led out into thick forest, drag marks of a body in the crimson-stained snow.

"What?" asked Viktor in an almost reverent hush.

Pyotr looked around and noticed the drag trail of where the dead old couple had been.

"The bodies of the old people are gone," he said quietly. "It looks like something dragged them off, too."

His observation was met with a loud howling, a lugubrious song of the wild, mournful and poignant, echoing from every direction.

"Back inside," commanded Viktor. "We are not the only ones to have survived the cold."

Viktor stepped forward toward the wood shack, grabbed the axe from inside it, and backed away toward the house, never taking his eyes off the line of thickly-clustered trees stretched out before them all.

All of them stepped back into the warmth of the house, and Viktor locked the door behind them.

"Wolves," said Leonid.

"Death," said Viktor. "We will have to find a way to kill enough of them, or we'll never leave this place."

"We'll be trapped here," said Vadim.

"That sounded like…a lot," said Pyotr. "There are a lot of them…Where did they come from?"

He had not wanted to say it, but he had voiced his thoughts anyway.

"It does not matter," said Viktor. "It only matters where they will be going, and that is to Hell. They took one of ours, so we will take half of them. Once we thin out their pack, they will find prey elsewhere."

"We have no weapons except for the axe," said Vadim.

"Then we will search the house for some," said Viktor. "Everyone, spread out and look for something to arm yourselves with. I will keep watch at the backdoor. Pyotr, you watch the front."

"Aye, Viktor," replied Pyotr.

He did not like being unarmed in this situation, but someone had to watch the front door, and his eyes were as good as any.

He walked into the warmth of the living room, brushed back the curtains of a window next to the front door, and stared out into the cold. He could see dark shapes moving in the tree lines on either side of the dirt road that led to this out-of-the-way house, but he could not tell what those shadows were from this distance. Nevertheless, he had a good idea of their identity anyway.

He stood there for a good twenty minutes until the rest of the Concrete Wolves gathered in the living room.

"This is all we have," said Leonid from behind him. "Make it work."

The big brawler pressed a large kitchen knife into Pyotr's right hand, the very same one Pyotr had used to cut the potatoes…It would have to do.

"They are out there," called Viktor from the backdoor. "I can see them moving in the trees. We are going to need more wood soon. We'll have to send two of us out to get more."

"Aye, Viktor," called back Rodion.

"These beasts must have been attracted to the warmth of the house," said Leonid. "There must be a lot of them, but I can't understand where they could have come from."

"Who knows?" said Vadim. "All I know is that we have to kill them. We can skin them and eat them for all I care."

"Sounds good to me," grunted Leonid. "We can kill them all as far as I am concerned."

Pyotr shook his head in dark realization. Their chances of surviving this pack were slim at best, but at least the others were ready to fight. They were ready to lay down some vengeance for Rurik's sake. Pyotr had not particularly liked the skinny thief, but Rurik had not been so bad as all that, and the man had certainly not deserved that fate.

Leonid left them after that, walking out of the living room to the small sitting room that housed the backdoor, probably off to chat with Viktor. Viktor would have Leonid relieve him of his post if necessary anyway.

Pyotr didn't care. He had his own post to watch, and watch it he did.

Pyotr stared out the window and rubbed his eyes in denial of what he saw at that moment.

A young woman, nude and beautiful, was walking toward the house.

This young lady could not have been older than twenty-four, twenty-five maybe, slender, with small breasts and long, straight, raven-black hair that hung down to her bare shoulders, gorgeous in the face with wild blue eyes…Pyotr was not sure if he was hallucinating or not.

This woman was completely naked, nude in the biting cold, something that should have killed anyone else from hypothermia.

"I must be going mad…" said Pyotr, but Rodion heard him.

"What?" asked Viktor's right-hand man.

Rodion pushed Pyotr aside and stared out the window, his dark eyes goggling at the sight of the young woman in her birthday suit methodically walking in a straight line toward the front door.

"What in the hell?" said Rodion in audible confusion.

He stared at Pyotr, his dark eyes flashing in sudden comprehension, and then he shone a wide grin.

"Fresh young meat for the taking!" breathed Rodion. "We can pass her around!...And so beautiful, too…Aren't we lucky!"

He pushed Pyotr all the way aside, flung open the front door, and dashed out there to meet the young and beautiful naked woman.

"Rodion!" barked Pyotr.

This stooge was a fool for simply walking out there unprotected and without backup.

Pyotr rushed out there, knife in hand, just as a large grey wolf took Rodion off his feet, ambushing the man from his blind right. Pyotr would have helped him immediately, but he was too busy defending himself as another beast jumped at him from his own left.

Pyotr stepped lithely to his own right and swiveled as he stabbed downward with his knife. The blade cut into thick fur and skin, but not deeply enough to fatally injure the animal. It growled and continued running, only to turn and face him as three more wolves approached from the right.

Rodion's screams were drowned out by a howling from all around them.

There was no time to think, only react.

Pyotr reached forward and gripped the nude young woman's bare right arm with his empty left hand, and then he dragged her through the open doorway into the safety of the house. He could see the trail of blood in the snow just before he slammed shut the front door, that trail of blood that marked the dragging of Rodion toward the tree line, that fool's screaming growing fainter by the second.

Pyotr did not feel sorry for the man, not like he had with Rurik. Rodion had brought that fate down upon himself, not to mention that he had never liked Rodion, but that was beside the point.

Pyotr locked the front door just as Viktor and the others gathered around him.

"What happened!" demanded Viktor.

"This girl appeared, and Rodion rushed outside without protection to get her," said Pyotr. "The wolves took him. I got to her, but I was almost taken, too."

His story was as simple as that. There was nothing else to tell.

The young woman in his grip did not shake from fear. She merely shivered from the cold, and her blue eyes gazed upon them all with a strange wariness, something primal that Pyotr could not define.

Viktor stepped forward and clenched the nude young woman's jaw in his big right hand. He held the axe in his left, though he raised it slightly as a show of force.

"Who are you!" demanded the big man. "Where are your clothes, you little fool!"

The young lady said nothing, but there was a defiance in her blue gaze that was undeniable, a defiance that immediately enraged Viktor.

He smacked the mystery woman across the left cheek, letting go of her jaw in order to smack her with an open palm hard enough to turn her head.

"This fool got Rodion killed!" hissed Viktor.

He was truly angry; Pyotr could tell, and if Viktor was angry, then this young woman's fate was sealed.

Pyotr did not know why he spoke up in defense of her, but he felt compelled to. There was something about her that called to him, some kinship he could not define.

"She is not right in the head, Viktor," said Pyotr. "Only madness would cause someone to strip and march through this wolf-infested hell."

"Then she is of no use to us," said Viktor.

"Oh, I can think of a use," grinned Vadim. "She most certainly has a use…Look at her!...She is luscious…We can pass her around."

"Yes," scowled Viktor. "Take her, Vadim. And when you are finished with her, bring her to me. Once we've all had our turn, I will slit her throat and throw her to the wolves for Rodion's sake."

"Rodion made his own choice to rush outside like a fool," frowned Pyotr. "How is taking this girl's life justified for that? It's clear she is ill in the head, defenseless. I don't even think she can speak."

Viktor stared at him with a fury in his brown eyes, but Pyotr would not back down, not this time.

The big man with the even bigger black beard reached forward and snatched Pyotr's knife from him. He used the blade to slice into the bare skin of the woman's right shoulder before Pyotr even had time to react.

The woman grimaced and squeezed her eyes shut at the bloody line that appeared across her once-flawless peach skin, but she said nothing, did nothing. She did not so much as breathe out a whimper to express her pain.

Viktor handed the bloody knife back to Pyotr and scowled down at the nude young woman.

"Perhaps you are right," he said in slight anger. "She will do as a toy, then. We've lost two of our own, and there is no guarantee we will find any more women, certainly not one so…enjoyable…Fine, then. Since you are so bent on keeping a pet, you are in charge of her, Pyotr. You will watch her, feed her, and wipe her clean after she uses the toilet. You can be her nursemaid from now on."

Vadim and Leonid laughed at this, but Pyotr did not find it funny. For one thing, he did not like what the others had in store for her.

"Find something for her to wear and then hand her over to Vadim," ordered Viktor. "We don't want our new pet freezing to death before we get to play with her."

"Aye, Viktor," frowned Pyotr.

Pyotr pulled the new prize of the Concrete Wolves toward the narrow set of wooden stairs that led upwards toward the second floor. He did want to find her some clothes, but he did not feel good about the fate that was in store for her. There was supposed to be some honor amongst wolves, but he was not feeling it now.

"Come on," he said quietly as he marched her up the stairs.

He turned his head to view Vadim following them, a wide grin on the man's square, if handsome, face.

Pyotr shook his head and led the nude young woman via pulling upon her right arm. He clutched the bloody knife in his right hand, a sick nausea sifting and settling down upon him, unsure as to what to do.

He could always slit her throat. He was not a murderer, but perhaps it was a mercy killing. Yes, Viktor would be angry with him, but he did not like the thought of this stranger, a mentally-ill one at that, being defiled by the rest of the men.

He shook a little as he led her into a short hallway and through an open door, a door where he could see the previous old couple's small bed.

The bedroom was the best place to find her some clothes. Perhaps he could get her dressed before he ended her…It was the decent thing to do.

He pushed her into the bedroom, walking in after her, and he was going to close the door behind him, but Vadim followed him in and closed the door for him.

Vadim forced the young woman onto the bed where she sprawled out upon her back, her legs spread, her head slightly lowered, her blue-eyed gaze fixed upon Pyotr rather than her would-be rapist.

Vadim stared at Pyotr and then back at the young woman on the bed.

"Let's get this started," grinned the lascivious man. "Don't put any clothes on her yet. She is perfect the way she is."

The young woman's sapphire eyes bored into Pyotr's own, and he could not help but stare back at her, study her for what she was, something alien and beautiful, something wild and wholly apart from anyone he had ever met.

He could smell her scent, the tangy scent of woman, but it was wild, untamed.

His eyes viewed the thick black hair of her pits, and then they wandered down over the small bulbs of her bare breasts, her pert brown nipples erect in the cold upstairs chill. His eyes continued to wander down to view the tufts of curly black hair between her open legs, those slender legs unshaven, a fine coating of black hair over them as well.

She was like a wild creature in the shape of a human, completely nude like this in front of strangers, men at that, wholly uncaring of what they thought in their civilized minds…

The howling outside picked up in a symphony of mournful wailing, a song that seeped into Pyotr's bones. He could smell the young woman on the bed, hear the notes in the howling, the longing sounds of the pack…

"You hear it," said the young lady.

"Oh!" said Vadim. "It speaks!"

The lascivious man unzipped his coat and pulled it free from his arms, tossing the article of clothing to the wood floor. He then turned and gave Pyotr a puzzled look.

"So, are you going to watch or what?" asked Vadim. "I don't really care if you watch, but you will have to wait your turn. I don't share with other men…Now sharing with other women? Absolutely."

Vadim turned his attention back upon the woman.

Pyotr's eyes fluttered as he listened to the lugubrious howling outside, drawing in the scent of this woman through his nostrils, that powerful smell of both sex and animal, of both hunger and freedom…

"He does not hear it," said the strange mystery woman. "He does not heed the call."

Pyotr knew she was talking about Vadim and not about him, though Vadim did not understand this.

"He's always like that," said Vadim as he unzipped his pants. "Don't worry, though, beautiful. I'm heeding the call right now."

Pyotr had thought about killing her, had thought about ending any suffering for her before it could truly begin, but now his thoughts ran in a different direction. He wanted her now, fully and truly wanted her, but not like Vadim wanted her, not like a toy to be used and then thrown away.

She was something more than that, much more, much more than any other woman he had ever known, and Pyotr wanted that, wanting what she had, her animal presence, that connection to the wild, and he wanted it more than anything.

He wanted to run with her, to be like her, to be wild and free, untamed, to completely abandon this ridiculous notion of society he had somehow been born into.

"You feel it," said the young lady on the bed. "I know you do. I can smell it on you."

"Oh, you think so?" asked Vadim. "Well, you'll be feeling it too in a moment."

But Pyotr knew she was not talking to Vadim. She was talking to him, to Pyotr, and he knew this with one-million-percent certainty. He had never been so sure of anything else in his entire life.

"Come with me," said the woman.

"Oh, we'll be doing that together," said Vadim. "I think that's a great idea. Loud and pleasurable is how I like it."

Pyotr gripped the bloody kitchen knife in his right hand. Yes, he had honestly thought about killing her, but this was no longer a possibility, nor would it ever be, not now, not now that he truly wanted her, not now that he truly wanted what she had.

Still…he knew what to do. This was abandoning everything he had been, but…he wanted something strange and alien, something he could sense just below the skin, but not his skin, no. He could sense this wild freedom beneath the skin of the world, beneath the skin of the end. He sensed it in her, and he knew she would lead him to this destiny, so he was taking her, and he was taking her now.

No, he had no stomach for death anymore, but death was necessary now, or he would not be leaving this house with her.

The wolves outside howled in a longing and forlorn symphony as Pyotr stepped forward with the knife. He gripped Vadim's short black hair and pulled back hard, pulling the man's head back enough to expose the throat, and then he quickly slit that throat, a red line erupting in hot blood as that sanguine lifeforce spilled from Vadim's ruined jugular.

Vadim struggled for a brief few seconds as Pyotr covered the rapist's mouth and held him firmly around the chest. It did not take long for Vadim to bleed out, and then the man died, expiring in Pyotr's arms, though Pyotr felt nothing for him, no twinge of loss or regret over Vadim's murder.

He laid Vadim upon the bed at the woman's bare feet like an offering. She stared at the fresh corpse for a moment, but that brief attention was an acceptance, an acceptance of Pyotr and what he was, the first time in his life he had ever felt such acceptance.

The young woman arose from the bed and stood before Pyotr, and he drew in her scent, that wild and tangy scent that fit like an interlocking piece with the song of the wolves outside. His eyes fluttered again from it, the song and the scent, and he stood there, shaking from the power of it.

She closed her eyes and breathed him in too, breathing in his scent, his musk, and he could tell she was feeling it as well, that connection, that electricity that bound them both to something so primal but also so natural.

"Come with me," said the woman in a quiet voice. "Run with us."

Pyotr stared down into the depths of her glacial eyes and breathed out one word in response to her request.

"Aye," he said.

Oh, yes, he knew what to do now.

He turned and opened the door of the bedroom, and she followed behind him, walking softly on the soles of her bare feet on cold wood. They made their way down the stairs after that, stepping into the living room together.

Leonid was at the front door, peering out the window, a kitchen cleaver in his right hand, the curtains of the window pulled back in his left. He turned his head once to view the arrival of Pyotr and the mystery woman, went to looking outside again, and then turned his gaze back upon them as realization kicked in.

"What are you doing down here?" he asked in audible suspicion. "I thought you were finding her clothes to wear…Wait…Where is Vadim?"

Pyotr gripped the bloody kitchen knife in his right hand. There was blood on the sleeves of his dark-blue parka, difficult to see within the blending of those darker tones, but it was not difficult to see the fresh blood on his hands or the deadly resolve in his eyes.

"We are leaving," he said firmly.

"You are not leaving," growled Leonid. "Where is Vadim?"

"It was not a request," threatened Pyotr. "Step aside, Leonid, or you will end up like Vadim."

Full comprehension swept across Leonid's eyes, and then a rage burned within them, a small flame that stoked to a blazing fire within the span of seconds.

"You son of a…!" choked out Leonid.

He rushed Pyotr, and they grappled, each gripping the other's weapon wrist as they jockeyed for position. Leonid was both strong and tough, an experienced brawler, but Pyotr was also strong and tough, and he also had experience.

Pyotr smashed his forehead down into Leonid's nose, breaking the man's nose in a brutal strike of bone on cartilage. Leonid staggered backwards from the pain, and then Pyotr was on him, gripping him around the waist, only to pick him up and slam him to the floor a moment later.

The nude young woman with the raven hair and sapphire-blue eyes appeared on her hands and knees behind Leonid's prone form, and then the brawler cried out in gurgling anguish as she bit into his exposed throat, taking a bloody chunk of skin and muscle as she ripped up and away with that torn flesh in her mouth.

She spit out the chunk of raw human meat in her mouth as Leonid struggled to stand, only for him to fall to the floor again, his throat ripped out, his eyes glazing over with the finality of death.

Pyotr felt some regret over Leonid. He had not wanted to kill him. Leonid had been a violent man, but he had also been the closest one of the others with any semblance of honor.

At least he had died a warrior's death. At least he had died fighting.

Pyotr had no more time to think on the matter before he was beset by an angry shout from behind.

"What have you done!" cried Viktor.

Pyotr turned to face him. The others had been one thing, but Viktor was truly deadly, especially with an axe in his big hands. This was the real battle, but Pyotr had to win it. He had to win for both his sake and the woman's. He had to win this fight in order to start his new life.

He reached down and snatched up Leonid's kitchen cleaver, switching his knife to his left hand. Now he had two weapons, and though they were kitchen utensils, they would have to do.

"Fool!" yelled Viktor. "You killed Leonid over this pet! She's an animal! Look at her! You killed your comrade over a pair of bare breasts! Are you mad! You have killed Leonid!"

"And Vadim," grunted Pyotr, though he mentioned this fact with some bit of pride.

Viktor was all fury over this confession.

"I'll butcher you, you swine!" shouted the big man. "Betrayer! I'll cave in your skull, you traitor, and then I'll flay the girl alive and wear her skin as an overcoat!"

He swung the axe in a side arc with the intent to bury the head in Pyotr's gut, but Pyotr danced backwards to avoid the strike.

But Viktor was an experienced killer.

The big man with the even bigger black beard thrust the metal head of the axe up and into Pyotr's jaw, and then Pyotr was on his back, stunned, stars in his eyes.

He watched in slow motion as Viktor raised the axe, both of the big man's arms raised above his head, the height of the axe just below the ceiling, the weapon ready to come down with the maximum amount of force necessary to cleave Pyotr's skull in twain.

"WAIT!" shouted the young mystery woman.

Viktor paused just long enough to turn toward the young lady, the axe still raised, his face still a mask of rage and hate.

"You will have your turn, witch!" he yelled.

"I will have it now," said the young woman in a matter-of-fact tone.

The nude young woman with the raven hair and arctic-blue eyes stood by the front door, her lips and chin covered in Leonid's blood, a wild and untamed expression of defiance upon her beautiful face. The knob of the door was in her right hand, the door already unlocked, and she simply turned that knob, pulling backwards upon it to open the door wide.

The wolves poured in after that, a wave of fur and fangs that crashed into the living room with all the fury of the snowbound wilderness behind them.

Viktor shouted and screamed as he was pulled to the ground by gnashing fangs and the heavy weight of bestial muscle and fur, and then he was torn apart, a bloody carnage of meat and bone and blood.

Anyone else would have been afraid. Anyone else would have been terrified, but Pyotr simply stood up and watched the bloodbath that ensued. He no longer cared for this world, this world of men that deserved such an end, and that was all there was to say and think about that. Viktor had been the last symbol of such, and that symbol was now nothing more than a pile of bloody meat.

There would be no more of man's world.

Pyotr unzipped his coat, pulled it from his arms, and tossed it to the floor. He shimmied out of his clothes as the wolves before him tore into the bodies of Viktor and Leonid, the blood and gore everywhere, some of it spraying onto Pyotr's bare skin, the blood hot and steaming, but he did not care.

He stood there now, naked with the animals, but he did not feel the cold as he should have. He did not feel the bitter chill or the biting wind from outside. No, he only felt freedom as he strode through the wild pack and toward the woman he had killed for.

"Run with me," said the woman. "Be my mate. Leave this world behind and run with me."

Her voice was hushed, her breath steaming in the cold air, her scent a heady aphrodisiac in his nostrils, stirring the call in his blood.

He followed her outside, and they ran in the snow, barefoot and naked and free, and then she was on all fours in front of him, her hind end suddenly slender with black fur, her tail in the air, a marker for him to follow.

He ran after her with all the joy of the wild within him, and then he was on all fours, his once-peach hands now dark-brown paws, his new fur protecting him from the terrible chill around them.

They were the real wolves of the end, and they had been waiting a long time for the last vestiges of humanity to burn out, for civilization to die in the fading embers of man's final winter, and now that end was here, and now the world was theirs.

He reveled in the call of the pack, his new brothers and sisters, reveling in the crunch of snow beneath his quick and treading paws, reveling in the husky scent of his new mate before him…Yes, Pyotr had found his real family at last, the wolves of the end, the wolves of a new beginning.

#3…SHADOW IN THE MOONLIGHT

Do you believe in the Man in the Moon?

𝕯𝖆𝖛𝖊𝖞 𝖘𝖙𝖆𝖗𝖊𝖉 at the shadow on the light-blue wall of his bedroom.

There was a shadow in the moonlight, a shadow of a man, or maybe a woman; he couldn't tell. It was tall and gangly, an amorphous shape in rough-humanoid form with extra-long arms, long hands, and long, long fingers. He did not know why, but the primal fear inside him told him not to go near it, and definitely, *definitely*, not let his own shadow touch it. That was a no, no.

Davey was only six, but he wasn't stupid. He knew when the hairs stood up on your skin that you were in danger. He knew this thing in the moonlight was no ordinary shadow, and he also knew it was out to get him; the goosebumps on his arms told him so.

The shadow marked its dark blot upon the southeast corner of his east wall, the moonlight shining in through his window on the north wall, his bed parked firmly at the west wall, so the shadow would have to cross onto the south wall in order to reach his own shadow tucked in the southwest corner of the south wall.

Where it had come from, he did not know. It had risen with the bright white of the moon outside his window, rising up like some phantom from a scary story, a boogeyman that could not be reasoned nor bargained with, only defeated.

He wanted to get out of bed and go to his parents' room, but that meant his shadow would cross its shadow, and that wouldn't do…No, it would not.

He was in his favorite PJs, the ones with the space shuttles and astronauts on them, but this gave him no comfort, no comfort at all.

What he needed was protection. He needed to hide somehow, but he feared that hiding beneath the covers would do him no good. Maybe he could turn on the light, and this had been his first thought, his first plan of action, but the light switch was also way across the room, so there was no way for him to reach it, no way at all.

He had been scared of the moonlight ever since Jason had told him about the man in the moon during recess yesterday.

"There's a man in the moon," Jason had said. "He will get you at night. He'll get you in your sleep."

Jason had tried to push down Davey, but Davey had done a cartwheel and had avoided the attack entirely. If he was anything, he was resourceful.

Of course, his little evasive maneuver had only angered Jason, and that's when Jason had taunted him with the man in the moon story.

"The man in the moon will get you," Jason had said. "He comes after little babies like you. There's a full moon tomorrow night, and you know what that means. He'll come for you in your sleep, just you wait."

Well, Davey couldn't sleep. There was no way he was going to sleep now, not with that shadow on the wall.

He stared at the dark shape on the wall and pondered what to do. There wasn't much he could do, but he was not giving up. He was not going to let that thing get him.

The room went dark for a brief few seconds as something, probably the wisp of a cloud or the swaying of a tree, interrupted the moon's wicked light, and then the bright of that pale light shone back in through the window, but the shadow had changed.

It had turned.

It had turned and was facing toward the south wall…It could *see* his shadow. It could see Davey's own shadow, and that was not good.

He could always scream. He could always shout, and then his parents would come running…and normally that would work for other kids, but he knew his mom and dad quite well. Both of them could sleep through a freight train rumbling through a thunderstorm, so waking them up with a shout was never going to work, not in a million-bajillion years.

Plus, they never listened whenever he had a problem. They had always just shrugged off anything he had tried to tell them. Oh, he had told them about Jason at school, but they hadn't done anything about that big jerk, so it was up to Davey to solve his own problems, and he had for the most part, but this shadow on the wall?…There had to be something he could do to get rid of it.

The light of the moon dimmed again, and then it came blazing back in, blazing like a torpid facsimile of the sun, ironic in that description, but more than bright enough to cut out the shape of the deadly shadow he suddenly so hated.

Davey pulled his covers closer to him.

The shadow had moved again.

This time it was buried in the corner of the southeast wall, but the long, long arms and long, long fingers were stretched forth, stretching forth with a tangible malice that Davey could feel all the way down to his soul.

He had to do something.

He stared over at the dresser that was placed right beneath his north window…Yes…Yes, that might work.

His box of toys was next to the dresser, in the northwest corner of his small bedroom. His bat and glove were also next to the toybox in the corner, but he didn't care about them. No, he knew what he needed, and what he needed was in his precious box of toys.

He slid from his bed, pattered over to his toybox on bare feet, and quietly opened the container, the wooden lid creaking forth on old metal hinges. Inside were many things, many valuable things, but he was looking for his soldiers, specifically his soldiers.

He quickly dug around the large wooden box until he found the small cloth bag containing his precious militia. He also pulled forth a plastic castle wall, a block of a thing that had gone to a castle set he had owned a long time ago, way back when he was four.

He quickly turned to view that shadow, and he nearly dropped his toys as he did.

He had not been keeping an eye on it.

It was past the southeast corner, just at the beginning of the south wall. It was standing straight and tall, fragments of wispy hair around its head, but it was the blob of darkness that made up that head that terrified him.

It was staring at him, not his shadow, *him*.

There were two white circles of light-blue wall within that rounded face where no shadow touched, and beneath it was a wide smile, a wide smile with the shadowy outlines of blocky teeth, a grate of inky-darkness that spread from one side of that face to the other, a strange casting of moonlight that made up a terrifying image that Davey could not deny…

Its long arms drooped down below where a waist would be, the hands elongated, the fingers stretched forth, and Davey knew he could not let those shadowy hands reach his own shadow.

He had to hurry.

He stepped backwards until he felt the stiff wood of his dresser, never taking his eyes off the deadly shadow. He reached backwards and placed the castle wall up and upon his dresser top, placing it so that the moon's own terrible light cast a shadow of the toy barrier upon the south wall, creating an umbral blockade against the evil that lurked upon the light-blue of his bedroom's plaster.

The shadow of the castle wall was quite large in the moonlight, a barrier that rested above the shadow of Davey's bed, a barrier that came up to the moon-thing's chest.

Davey then set up three soldiers, one after the next, each with pointing rifles and protective helms, each waiting to take their shot at the creature that lurked in the moon. Their shadows also came up to this thing's chest, but that was good enough. There were three of them and only one of it, and three was more than one.

Of course, it would have to get past the shadow of his bed, but that would not be much of a barrier. It could just crawl up onto his bed. That's what Davey would do.

The light of the moon dimmed once more, and then it came flooding in again, only this time the shadow was standing at the end of the shadow of Davey's bed, one elongated arm up and reaching for the castle wall, the barely-recognizable shape of a leg and knee moving up and onto the bed itself.

Davey kept his eyes on the moon-thing. He would not let it out of his sight again.

He shimmied to his own right and stepped backwards until his legs touched his wooden toybox. He reached behind himself, bent down, and dipped his fingers into the box. He had never closed the lid, so he grasped the first thing his fingers touched, his Captain Cosmo action figure. This was his favorite toy of all time, but more importantly, Captain Cosmo could do things his soldiers could not, so if they failed, his beloved action figure would do in a pinch.

The moonlight faded yet again. He hated when it did that, because that meant he could not see the shadow, and if he could not see the shadow, then…

He heard the cracking sound of breaking plastic, terribly loud in the silence of his small bedroom, and then the light returned, that terrible pale light of the moon, and he held his breath as he studied the scene that had unfolded upon his wall.

The shadow had moved forward onto his bed, and his plastic wall of defense, his castle wall, was broken in two, the shadow of it halved, that halved shadow on top of the first of his soldiers, that soldier down and crushed beneath the wall, the arm and rifle bent upwards in a strange way.

Davey resisted the urge to look at his dresser top. He already knew what he would find on it anyway.

The light dimmed again, that evil light waning until there was nothing, and then it waxed to its former brilliance, and he could see the shadow again, but this was of no comfort.

He had heard plastic hit carpet, so his suspicions were confirmed when there was no shadow of the second soldier. No, there was the creature in its place, the malevolent moon-thing that was bent on destroying him, bent on choking the life from him like the evil thing it was.

Its long arms and spindly fingers were up, reaching for the next soldier, the last of his trio of defenders.

Davey shook in place. This was not working.

The moon's light receded once more, and then came the sound of breaking plastic, and then came the light, and then came more fear.

The shadow on the wall had its long fingers wrapped around the third soldier's top half, but there was no head on that soldier, just the light-blue of untouched plaster in a head's place.

But Davey still had his Captain Cosmo figure, and that would have to do.

He shimmied over to the dresser top again and set his action figure up without looking at it or the dresser itself, his eyes ever on the malevolent shadow upon his wall.

He accidently pushed Captain Cosmo farther back than the superhero needed to go, but the action figure's shadow grew larger, and this gave him hope. He made Captain Cosmo's shadow big, bigger than the moon-thing on his wall, and this would certainly stop the evil that lurked in his room. It had to.

The waning moonlight pushed the room into darkness yet again, but this time Davey watched carefully for any changes, which there would be. Of that, he was certain.

The shadow of the moon-thing was before the large and looming shadow of Captain Cosmo, but this time the evil on his wall cringed before Davey's own protective action figure, its long hands up as if to ward off the superhero.

"Yes!" whispered Davey. "It's working!"

His voice was loud in the silence of his room, but Davey didn't care about that. He needed this moon-thing stopped before it could get to him.

But saying anything had been, of course, a mistake and a serious one.

The pale light of the moon swathed over in darkness, and then the light returned, but the thing on his wall was looking straight at him again, straight at Davey, the eyes two circles of light-blue plaster wreathed in pitch, that bracketed smile of big teeth a mocking grin that Davey could not stand.

It had heard him…It *knew*.

"No," said Davey quietly as his face paled. "Oh, no…"

He should not have said anything. He should not have spoken at all. He had tricked it, but he had said something, and now it knew, and now it was going to get him.

The wind picked up outside, the panes of his window rattling, but the effect upon the light in his room was instantaneous as the clouds traveled in rapid speed across the moon, the light in his room going in and out in a flickering dance, a macabre stop-motion parade that played out a disturbing scene in front of him.

The shadow of the moon-thing rose on its knees from upon the shadow of his bed, the long arms snatching forth to grasp the Captain Cosmo shadow around the waist, and then there was a cracking sound as Davey's beloved action figure snapped in half, the pieces tumbling from his dresser to hit the carpet below, the bouncing of plastic something that Davey could hear quite well, even with the wind blowing outside.

The wind died down, and the shadow of the thing in the moon stared at him once more, its smile a taunting and deadly praise of its own foul deed.

"You!" hissed Davey.

Now he was mad. That had been his favorite toy.

Davey stumbled backwards toward his toy box. He had one option left, the only option left, and it had just come to him, mainly because he was angry as all get-out.

His fingers wrapped around the handle of his wooden baseball bat, that bat leaning in the corner of his wall in-between his toybox and the wall itself.

"I'll kill you!" screeched Davey.

His own shadow loomed as he stepped forward into the moonlight, stepping forward just as the wind began to blow again, the shadow of his bat raised high in his small hands.

The light wavered in and out, in and out, the final battle raging, a last hurrah before the end, whatever end may come from this terrible showdown of boy and shadow.

Darkness struck Davey as the moonlight blacked out again. He felt a cold chill burn into his left cheek, lines of wet blood opening up across his clammy skin, and then he slammed down the bat with all his might, feeling the bat strike something soft and squishy, striking solid and fast even though there was nothing in front of him.

The shadow on the wall bent backwards as if struck, its long arms up in defense of the blob that made up its head.

The moonlight continued to waver as the wind blew, and blood dripped down Davey's face where he had been sliced open.

There was no light for a brief second, and Davey was pulled forward a bit as his favorite PJs ripped open at the chest, more sanguine lines of blood opening up across his formerly untouched skin.

Anyone else would have screamed from terror and pain, but Davey was lost in his own rage, a rage that was amplified now that his favorite PJs with the space shuttles and the astronauts were ruined, ruined just like his castle wall and his soldiers and his beloved Captain Cosmo.

"I'll kill you! I'll kill you! I'll kill you!" screamed Davey.

He brought down the bat with one swing after the next, each swing in time with his own battle screech. He could feel the wood impacting something with each hit, and the shadow in the moonlight receded with each hit, shrinking in on itself, one of its long hands bent in a strange way as if the wrist were broken, splatters of black across the wall like blood, a cold wash of something that hit Davey but was invisible, splatters of invisible moonblood he could not see.

The pale light of the moon flickered in and out, and the shadow on his wall was driven back as it struck out in simultaneous fashion, but Davey would not relent in his assault.

No, he had definitely had enough.

Davey's PJs were sliced open at the legs, the cloth in tatters, blood running down to his ankles, the injuries set with a burning cold, like ice from the South Pole, but Davey swung his bat again and again with all the might of Captain Cosmo.

"Get…out…of…my…room!" screamed Davey.

He struck the moon-thing, shadow on shadow, again and again as the shadow of the wooden bat drove the malevolence from the moon back and off his bed, back and down in splatters of cold black shadow that spread across the light-blue plaster of Davey's bedroom wall, splatters that disappeared an instant later, splatters of moonblood to match Davey's own real blood that ran down his face and chest and legs.

There was a brief howl on the wind, a cry of both anger and anguish, and then the wind stopped blowing, the clouds outside ceasing to move at top speed.

The wan light of the orb that had tormented him so shone brightly into the room, but there was no more shadow on his wall, nothing to prevent Davey from making his way to his parents' bedroom.

It was a good thing, too. He was bleeding all over the carpet.

*****

Jason's mother tucked him in as she kissed him on the forehead.

"Goodnight, honey," said the woman, but Jason did not want to look at her fat face.

She angered him every time he saw her pudgy face, mainly because she had taken his remote-controlled car away from him. All he had done was chase the cats with it, nothing big, but she had taken it away from him anyway, and now he didn't want her attention at all.

The woman stood up, walked to the bedroom door, and flipped off the light. She closed the door behind her as she exited his bedroom, and with that closing, a finality of sentence that Jason could not ignore.

He would have to find his car tomorrow. Of course, he would have to pay back his mother for her own indiscretion, and that meant flushing something down the toilet in order to clog it. That would show her not to mess with him.

He stewed over this as he thought upon yesterday's encounter with Davey, something else that drove into him with a nail of spite. He would not have thought about Davey at all, but this nonsense with his mother had reminded him of Davey, and this made Jason even angrier.

Davey was a little worm of a kid that he hated, mainly because Mrs. Wren, their teacher, liked Davey better than Jason, and Jason had no tolerance for that. Teachers weren't supposed to play favorites, but Jason knew they did. There were some kids they liked, and some they didn't like, and Jason knew, just *knew*, Mrs. Wren didn't like him.

Yes, he had failed to push down Davey yesterday, but he would get ahold of that worm on Monday when school picked up again. He would make sure of that. He was going to hold him down and twist his arms behind his back until the boy squealed for mercy.

That would be fun.

He smiled as he closed his eyes at the thought of it, but he opened his eyes again as the pale light of the moon waxed over his bed, lighting up the sepia overtones of his bedroom wall.

He blinked twice, smacked his lips, and then yawned, taking a moment to stare at something that had caught his sudden attention, something he had not noticed until just now…

There was a shadow on his wall.

#4…ZENOBIA

If it's too good to be true, then you've probably been had.

She walked up and sat down next to me at the bar.

"Hi," she said in a friendly, easy voice.

I was well familiar with that tone. I had used it myself. Even so, this woman was gorgeous, far, *far* out of my league, but she made my heart jump; she made it flutter. It was the sound of her voice really, for there was a mysterious note to it, something strange and fay, alien yet beautiful all the same.

"I'm Zenobia," said the gorgeous lady.

She was a little taller than me, about five-foot-eight minus her black high heels. She was blessed with an hourglass body and green eyes set like emeralds in her beautiful face, that face ringed with raven-black curls that she had tied back into a bun decorated by loops of tightly-braided hair.

She was pale, so pale in her skin, but this accented the pinkish-red of her sultry lips. She had on a tight, burgundy, sleeveless one-piece with a miniskirt, the sections separated by a thick black belt with a gold buckle, and this really showed off her beautiful hips and legs…She was truly to die for. Dear God, was she something to drool over.

"Hello," I said politely, though my voice wavered a bit. "I'm River."

"*Ooo*, River," nodded Zenobia. "That's an unusual name. I guess we have that in common, huh?"

"I guess we do," I replied.

"Aren't you a little young to be in here, River?" she asked.

"No, no," I said quickly. "I'm twenty-two."

"Oh, really?" asked this beautiful woman. "You're very boyish for an adult. You look sixteen. Even your voice is...you know…a little immature."

"I get carded all the time," I shrugged. "It's in the genes."

That was a pun, a little joke on my part, but she didn't need to know that.

She nodded once, smiled, and looked me over as if I were some work of art she was studying.

"You're cute," said Zenobia.

Those two words really sank into me. I had heard "you're cute" so many times that I'd lost count, but I had never been interested, not like, *interested*, in the people who had spoken those words before, not like I was with this goddess.

I decided to play it cool. I didn't want to chase her off, but I had heard guys liked to be nonchalant, ambivalent, that sort of thing. I was a newb when it came to hooking up with anyone anyway. Comes from living a sheltered life with strict parents.

Anyway, I was going to play it cool. Knowing my luck, she was simply trying to get me to buy her drinks, but that was okay. I didn't mind.

"I try," I shrugged. "I don't know if I'm cute or not, but I do try to look presentable."

"Good enough for me," smiled Zenobia. "Let me buy you a drink."

Of course, this shot an arrow through my heart. A woman who buys you a drink? How amazing is that?

Needless to say, this flustered me.

"I…Oh…I…Okay," I stupidly replied.

She giggled a bit, and that mild laughter was like a simple melody that sang to my soul. Oh, I felt so flushed and warm inside, and I had just sat down not more than a few minutes ago. I hadn't even ordered anything yet.

"You're so cute," giggled Zenobia. "You're just a little angel…You're bite-sized, you know that? I think I might actually be taller than you…How funny…You know, you're not like the others in here…You're…something different. Are you gay?"

That was abrupt and kind of rude...Not to mention that I didn't want to answer that. That wasn't something I fully understood myself. Besides, I…No. I'd only just recently changed my style, and I really didn't understand what was going on with me lately, but she didn't need to know about any of that anyway.

"That's…kind of a personal question," I said after a second of thought.

"That's okay," she said. "I understand…Are you from around here? You look like a college kid."

"Aren't you?" I asked.

"Oh, honey, I'm everything," chuckled Zenobia. "I asked because of the choice in your clothing…white dress shirt…forest-green sweater vest…tan slacks…good brown dress shoes…Honestly, you remind me of one of those little private-school teens."

"I'm twenty-two," I nodded. "I assure you. I'm not lying about that. My ID is real."

"Well, you're slender, well-dressed, neat haircut…" continued Zenobia. "I do love that whole '50s straight-arrow style of your hair…Are you sure you're not gay?"

"Let's say I was," I shrugged. "Would that turn you away?"

She chuckled, shook her beautiful head, and grinned.

"Oh, no, precious," she said slyly. "It just means some experimentation is in order."

"Experimentation?" I asked. "Who's experimenting? Me or you?"

"Both of us," grinned Zenobia.

I had to admit…I was smitten. She was so gorgeous, like way, *way* out-of-my-league beautiful…and she was right, of course. I did look like a sixteen-year-old boy…Maybe she was one of those weird perverts who was into kids or something?…I don't know.

You know, upon further thought, this had to be a trick.

"I don't know, Zenobia," I frowned. "I have a hard time believing you would be interested in talking to someone like me. We don't really mesh in the looks department. You're way out of my league, and that kind of makes your motivations suspect."

"Oh, come now, River," said the beautiful woman as she gave me a light push. "Don't be like that."

"You've asked me if I'm gay," I said warily. "That's a really forward question, so I'll ask you a forward question now."

"Fire away," shrugged Zenobia. "Go for it. I might not answer it, though. You didn't answer mine, but go right ahead and ask anyway."

Fair enough.

"Are you a predator?" I asked.

"Mmmm…more like a huntress," she replied.

This was not the answer I'd been expecting. I'd actually thought she was going to deny any kind of predatory behavior, but I was wrong. Hmm…how funny.

"How so?" I asked. "I mean, what's the difference?"

"Predators are bestial in nature," said Zenobia. "They're ruled by instinct…The huntress is intelligent.

She lures in her prey and then strikes when the timing is right.”

“Am I your prey tonight?” I asked.

It was a coy little question to throw out there.

“You could be,” she shrugged. “The truth is, I could have any man in here, but look at these louts. They’re all the same ridiculous frat boys that only think with their other heads. Same cheesy pick-up lines every time…Hey, beautiful, you got a nice rack…Nice butt, babe…We’re having a party over at blah, blah, blah fraternity…Come with us…

“Blech…I’m so tired of them…They have no class, no spark, and they all taste the same...So bland and blasé. Now you?...You’re delicious in a different way…I suspect you’re gay, and you’re not telling me the truth about it…but you know what? I could go for a little gay…Like I said before…you’re something different.”

“Well, I’ll agree to that bit,” I said with a slight smile. “I *am* different.”

I couldn’t help myself with that upturn of lips. Zenobia was the first woman I could think of who had actually noticed me, and she was…well…dear, God…

She gave me another gentle push and giggled.

“Look at you!” she chuckled. “Is that a smile I see!”

I couldn’t help but grin. She was infectious that way.

“So tell me, River,” said Zenobia as she cocked her head to one side. “Have you ever been with a woman?”

I immediately knew what she meant by that because I wasn’t born in a barn, but I didn’t want to answer that question. The truth was embarrassing…No, I had not been with a woman, but I really, *really* wanted to be with one. I’d had sex on the mind for far too long now, and my mind was currently wondering what she looked like naked.

Was that wrong? Was it wrong to fantasize about a real person who was right in front of you?...Whatever the case, Zenobia was very flirty, and I wanted to capitalize on that.

I decided to lie.

"Sure," I said in an easy tone. "I've been with lots of women."

She snorted out a stark laugh and then gave me another light shove.

"Liar," she chuckled. "Here, I'll change the subject, but first…let's get some drinks."

This was truly exciting. I'd never felt like this before, so energized, so wired over someone I had just met. I was happy for once, and I hadn't been happy in a long time.

She ordered two tall mugs of beer for us, and I was carded again, but she only found that amusing. I thanked her for my drink after she tipped the bartender, and we went right back to talking again.

"So what do you think about the Y2K problem, River?" asked Zenobia.

Well, true to her word, she *had* changed the subject.

"It's a thing," I shrugged. "I don't really understand it."

"It's going to be the turn of the century at the end of the year," said Zenobia. "Aren't you scared everything's going to fall apart?...Heck, I've seen so many people buying up supplies, building bunkers…"

"Eh," I said. "People are always saying the world's going to end. It never has."

"True," said Zenobia, a thoughtful look on her face. "Still…doesn't it scare you even a little?"

"Not really," I said.

"Aren't you scared of death?" she asked.

There was a strange sheen to her emerald eyes to match the equally strange connotations behind that question.

"I…well…" I said as I gave it some thought. "I think everyone's scared of that. I just…I'm just trying to discover myself, so I…haven't really thought about it…I haven't given it much thought. I've been preoccupied with other things. Let's put it that way."

She looked me over, looking me up and down as if inspecting every part of me, and I blushed a little under her obtrusive gaze. She found my shyness amusing, of course, and she spoke as much.

"You *are* a little darling," she chuckled. "So tiny and precious…I could just eat you up in one bite!...Now, that's an idea…How about I show you *my* secret treasures, huh?...The night is young…Come on, let's get out of here."

"What?" I asked.

I was a little confused over this. That was an extremely sudden and blunt come on.

"You're not deaf, hon," she said firmly. "Let's get out of here…Come with me. We'll go to my place and have a *really* good time…Oh, come on, you're not stupid, River; you know what I mean…Oh, and I'm rich, you know. Just throwing that out there."

I should have questioned her further as to why she would want *me*, *specifically* me, to come with her and have you-know-what with her, but I stupidly asked about her money instead.

"You're rich?" I asked. "How much?"

"Oh, I'm worth about forty-two million," she said matter-of-factly. "But that's not important…What's important is what's under this dress…Don't give me that blank stare…Good, grief, could I be any blunter, River?...I'm asking you over for sex, silly. Come with me."

This shocked me right down to my good dress shoes. She wanted *me*? This gorgeous, incredibly-rich goddess wanted *me*? Little tiny me?

"I…I…uhhh…" I stammered.

She shone me an amused grin and shook her head.

"I'm beautiful, I'm rich, and I'm interested," she said firmly. "You're coming with me, hon. I'm going to show you a good time, loosen that stick shoved up your butt. You look like you need to get laid, babe. Just saying."

I felt weird inside over this. This was…unexpected. I really, really wanted this, to be with her, even if it was only for one night, but, I mean, she had to know, right? She had to know, but she was asking me over anyway?...Wow. She really did want something different.

Screw it. I was doing this.

"I…I…Okay…" I complied.

"Good," she said firmly, and that was that.

We left the bar and headed down the street to a small lot where her car was parked, and upon seeing that car, I knew right then that she hadn't been lying about being rich. Her car was a brand-new, devil-red Lamborghini Diablo.

"Told you I was rich, baby," she said with a laugh as we got in. "Welcome to 1999, River. This is the end of the millennium, so let's go have some fun before the world ends!"

Hear! Hear! Oh, my God, was this going to be a night! I was finally going to have sex, and it was going to be my first time, and it was going to be with this gorgeous goddess…

No, no. I needed to calm down. I was losing focus. Okay, so we were going back to her place to have sex…Maybe after that we could hook up on more than just a temporary basis? I mean, she was obviously the kind of girl who goes barhopping, but maybe there was a chance I could actually snag her as my girlfriend…

It was a thought.

We drove on for a while as I hoped and dreamed that I could make her mine. In fact, it was all I could think about.

Also, riding in that car was something I could check off my bucket list, not that I had a bucket list, but if I did have one?…riding in a Lamborghini Diablo would have been on it.

"You really are fun-sized," said Zenobia. "How tall are you, hon?"

I winced at this. My size wasn't something I was proud of.

"I'm five-six," I said, but I couldn't hide the disappointment in my voice.

"Well, I've had all kinds," she replied. "There's nothing to be ashamed of, love. I can tell you're nervous and unhappy about your body…You know, it's not what's between the legs that counts anyway…I'll have fun with it; don't worry about that. I'm quite experienced…

"I've done this before, if you haven't figured that out already, so don't worry about what's down there. I know I'm not what you were expecting, but you'll have fun with me, too. I already know I'm going to have fun with you."

"I really hope you mean that," I said unhappily.

She laughed and shook her head over my self-deprecation.

"Don't be so hard on yourself," she grinned. "Experiment a little! I can tell you're trying to figure yourself out, so I'm going to help you with that…You're just a darling little thing anyway, a real cutey-bear. Oh, trust me, I'm definitely going to have fun with you."

This made me feel really weird, a twisting inside, a knotting in my stomach, because I wanted this more than anything, but there was always that fear of rejection.

There was always that fear that someone will take one look at you and just say, "No." I was scared she was going to be very disappointed upon seeing the real me, but…

Zenobia reached over with her right hand and massaged the back of my neck. She steered with her left, barely looking at the road as she drove with a preternatural sixth-sense.

"Loosen up, baby," she said. "You're tense and scared…It'll be all right…That's better. This is difficult for you, isn't it?...I don't think you know what you really want in life."

Her touch turned me to jelly, and I felt like melting into the passenger-side seat of her Lamborghini.

We drove out of the city, driving for a good forty minutes until we went off the highway and onto some side roads that led into thick woods. I had no idea where we were going, and the truth was, I didn't care.

It didn't take long before we drove up to a large estate, a big plantation-style mansion with an old-Southern feel. She drove through a large, black, wrought-iron gate and parked the car in a huge garage that lay apart from the main building.

You know, this place was gigantic, like big, big, like nothing I was used to. Even the garage was bigger than my entire family's house, that garage filled with expensive car after expensive car.

"Here we are, darling," said Zenobia.

She turned off the engine and proceeded to turn on mine. She leaned over, grabbed the back of my narrow head, and kissed me, her lips embracing mine, her tongue in my mouth, and I went with it, but I could tell she knew I had no experience…like none, zero, nada.

She pulled back after a few seconds and gave me a sly look.

"You're a very light kisser," she said gently. "You were even gentle touching my breast, no squeezing at all. You know, I'm really beginning to think you're a blossoming gay…You're at least bi. You're too darned gentle to be fully straight."

I blushed, feeling the hot burn on my cheeks as she grinned over at me.

"It's okay, baby," she said softly. "You don't have to be macho for me."

"Good," I said unhappily. "If it's one thing I'm not, it's 'macho.'"

She gave me a strange look, something I could not define, but I could see a disturbing shine in her green eyes, something predatory, and I felt the hairs on the back of my neck stand on end.

It was a stupid feeling, and I didn't want her to get offended, but I had to ask. I had to.

"Are…Are you sure you're being honest with me?" I asked. "You're not planning anything bad, are you?"

"Bad?" asked Zenobia. "What does that even mean?...I offered you sex, silly. Is that bad?...Don't answer that…Look, you got me. I do have an ulterior motive. I didn't just bring you here for fun. I brought you here to offer you something."

Was this some kind of a con?...No, it couldn't be. Zenobia already had money; that was clear. What little money could she gain from me?

Still, I wasn't stupid. I decided to fish a little, play dumb.

"Offer me something?" I asked. "What are we talking about? This isn't about sex?"

"Not that," she said as she waved me off. "We'll get to that, honey. No, I'm referring to something else."

"Something else?" I asked. "Like what?"

This was the moment of truth. Was she going to be upfront with me or not?

"Aren't you even a little bit afraid of dying?" she asked.

Oh, boy.

There was something sinister about that question, and I had to reply to it with all honesty, even though I knew she wasn't going to like that reply. It had just now occurred to me that she might be a serial killer and not just a wild flirt hunting for some action, and stupid me had followed her out here like a dumb animal looking to mate.

"Well, I wasn't afraid of dying before, but I am now," I said nervously. "You're not going to kill me, are you, Zenobia?"

She gave a tremendous laugh and shook her head no.

"Oh, no," she chuckled, that wicked gleam in her green eyes. "Quite the contrary…I want to offer you the opposite."

"And that is?" I asked anxiously.

"Okay, baby," she smiled. "Let me ask you something. If you could stay young and beautiful forever…would you?"

I had no idea where this was going, so I answered the best I could.

"I don't know," I shrugged. "I've never really thought about it…My life is…*complicated*…right now. I don't really know what I want or what I'm doing in it or where I'm going or anything…I'm just…*experimenting*…right now."

"So am I," grinned Zenobia. "You're not the typical lover I like to bring over. I want you *because* you're different…I want you to be my special one."

"Your special one?" I asked.

In spite of all of my previous misgivings and internal warnings, my heart was flying around in my chest like a World War I biplane.

Honestly, though, this was way too good to be true.

"But you don't know anything about me," I said in marked uncertainty.

"That doesn't matter," said Zenobia with a shake of her beautiful head. "No one knows anything about anyone when they first meet…but you never really answered my question, hon…No, you danced around it…Now…answer my question and be honest with me…If I could give you eternal youth and beauty, would you take it?"

This sounded…weird…but I was used to weird, because I was weird, so…

"Would that make you happy if I did?" I asked.

"It would make me very happy," smiled Zenobia.

Okay, I could play along. I knew how to answer these types of questions anyway. You answered these questions with more questions. That's how you knew if you were being played.

"Okay, would I die?" I asked.

"No," said Zenobia firmly. "You would not die. Not in the normal way anyway. You would outlive any normal person."

There was actually a question I had wanted to ask for a while now, and though it was kind of a stupid question, I still wanted to ask it. With her pale skin, her unnatural beauty, her vast wealth, and her strange line of questioning, I was beginning to think, impossible as it sounded, that she was a vampire.

"Are you…like…a vampire?" I asked.

"What if I was?" asked Zenobia.

My heart skipped a beat. Could she really be…?

"I…don't…know…" I drawled out.

"You don't know?" asked Zenobia.

"Are you going to make me into a vampire, Zenobia?" I asked.

"No, honey," chuckled Zenobia. "And, if you're wondering, no, I'm not a vampire, so you don't have to worry about that. I'm not going to kill you, and you'd have to die to become 'undead,' so there's that."

"Oh, thank God," I breathed out.

This was a giant relief. I wasn't sure if I wanted to be a vampire anyway. That was something for the Goth crowd, not me.

Zenobia laughed and shook her head.

"Oh, you are so precious!" she said. "You are going to fit right in!...I know exactly what to do with you, too."

"And what's that?" I asked nervously.

She leaned over and kissed me again, and this time I kissed her back. We kissed in a passionate heat for a few seconds, and I even took some initiative and squeezed her ample breasts. After those few hot seconds, she let me go, fanning her own face with her left hand, and I could tell she was flushed.

"Whew!" she said excitedly. "I'm getting worked up!...Okay, okay…I was being serious when I said I could offer you eternal youth and beauty, so let me explain, okay?"

"*Okaaaay…*" I said warily.

"Every twenty years, I bring someone here to partake in a ritual with me," continued Zenobia.

"Every twenty years…" I repeated.

Well, one of two things was happening here. Either Zenobia was crazy, or she was the real deal. Whatever was going on, I needed to find out and deal with it. The odds were pretty darned good that she was just nuts, in which case, I still wanted to sleep with her—don't judge me—but if she wasn't crazy…if she was the real deal…hoo, boy.

"How old are you, exactly?" I asked.

"I just turned a hundred and sixty-seven," she replied matter-of-factly.

Yep, she was crazy…Oh, well…I'd just play along with it. There was still the matter of hot sex with this gorgeous, if crazy, goddess.

"You look gorgeous for your age," I nodded.

"Oh, honey, I was always gorgeous," shrugged Zenobia. "Look, every twenty years, I bring someone here to bask in the glorious presence of my goddess. She bestows eternal youth and beauty to my guest, but as her priestess, I already have that, so I get other rewards, like money, for instance. It's the reason I'm filthy stinking rich, baby. It's kind of like one of those 'referral' bonuses you get whenever you refer someone to a company or something. Think of it that way."

Okay, this was really weird. Nevertheless, I knew the right questions to ask.

"I see," I nodded. "So, if I bask in your goddess's presence, I'll live forever, too? Because eternal youth and beauty aren't the same as eternal life."

"You'll live until you die of…unnatural means," said Zenobia. "In other words, you won't age, so you won't die that way. Someone has to end you, or you have to have a fatal accident, or nature does you in, or whatever."

"Do I have to sell my soul?" I asked.

"*Yyyesss*," drawled out Zenobia. "You're giving your soul to my goddess. That's how it works. It's a pledge-of-allegiance kind of thing."

There it is, the catch.

"So I'll be, like, tortured by the Devil or something after I die?" I asked. "I don't want to go to Hell, Zenobia."

"You won't go to Hell," said the beautiful woman with a shake of her head. "You'll actually be admired by my goddess for all eternity. You'll be treated like the priceless work of art you are, darling. I only choose the best for my divine lady, and she only accepts the best…Doesn't that sound like a great alternative to Hell?"

Uh…huh…Well, as far as afterlifes went, that wasn't such a bad deal.

"Who is your goddess, then?" I asked.

"Her name is Artemis," said Zenobia. "Have you heard of her?"

I shook my head no. Unfortunately, my ignorance was showing on this one. I didn't know much about anything like that.

"My parents are very strict Christians," I said sheepishly. "Southern Baptists, actually. I'm afraid I'm a little sheltered when it comes to that sort of thing. Is that a Pagan goddess?"

"Ancient Greek," said Zenobia. "Look, if you turn yourself over to her, she'll grant you eternal youth and beauty, and even better, she'll take you under her watch for all eternity. And when all is said and done, I'll get my referral bonus, so to speak."

At this point, I didn't care about that. As far as I was concerned, Zenobia was a goddess unto herself, and she had taken an interest in me, so I just decided to go with it, go along with her brand of crazy.

The facts were—and I wasn't ashamed to admit it—that more than just my hormones were at play here. My heart was burning like a furnace…I wanted to please her, but more importantly, I wanted her for myself, and I was willing to do whatever crazy thing she wanted in order to achieve that goal.

"Okay," I said. "I'll do it, but only if you promise to be with me afterwards. I want you and I to be together."

Zenobia grinned, held my face between her hands, and kissed me on the nose.

"Oh, honey, I'll be with you every day from now on," she said happily. "You won't have to go to school anymore, and you'll live here with me…every day…here, right here with me, and I'll adore that precious little body of yours every…single…day…How does that sound?"

My breath caught in my throat.

"Too good to be true," I said in a wavering voice.

"Out of the car, sweet heart," grinned Zenobia. "Let's head to the shrine. We'll do the ritual there."

I nodded yes with my head still in her hands. This whole thing was really weird, but this beautiful, beautiful, crazy woman wanted to be with me, little tiny *me*, and I was all for that. Dear, God, was I for that.

There was nothing else to be said. She let me go, and we exited her Lamborghini.

We left the garage via a side door, and Zenobia led me around the grounds. There were huge lights on poles lit around the area so that we could see, and we walked around her mansion grounds until we entered a large hedge maze. After traveling through the hedges for a couple of minutes, we entered a clearing that was paved over with white marble, and in that clearing was a ring of statues, seven total, seven statues of nude young men in various artistic poses.

"Here we are," said Zenobia with a wave of her hands. "This is my humble shrine to Artemis. Do you like it?"

I nodded out of amazement. I knew she was crazy, but good *God* did she have the money to really accent that crazy.

"That pedestal over there?" said Zenobia. "The empty one in the very center of this big circle? I want you there."

"Okay," I said.

I walked over to the pedestal, stood upon it, and waited for further instructions.

"Give me a moment while I get ready," said Zenobia. "As you can see, I have a little locked box over here. This has my scroll in it…Oh, and that scroll is for the ritual…Let me just get into my box here…"

She took to fiddling with a large metal black box that had been placed upon a white dais, so I took that time to look around.

This clearing we were in was surrounded by hedges, of course, and the floor below us was all white marble as I'd mentioned before, but I just now noticed the large mosaic of a nude young woman with a bow and arrows surrounded by various wild animals, her right bare foot upon the head of a prone naked man. I could only assume that within this mosaic within the marble was Zenobia's goddess, Artemis, so Zenobia's previous description of herself as being a huntress now made much more sense.

The mosaic gave me a strange feeling, however, as I did not know what to make of the prone naked man beneath the goddess's feet, but I figured Zenobia would just explain the meaning of that later.

But something else caught my eye.

The circle of statues around me was odd, very odd. There were at least twenty or so stone pedestals in this "shrine," but there were only seven statues to adorn those pedestals, and those statues were unevenly placed, an almost random placing on pedestals that didn't align with each other in a symmetrical sense.

I could see the statues well enough due to the lighting on various poles around the hedge maze, but every statue was very different in the way that individual people are very different…They didn't have that uniform "Greek style" I was so used to seeing.

These men were all nude and attractive, but they were, first of all, very well detailed in *all* of their parts—if you know what I mean—but even those parts were of different shapes and sizes. It was like Zenobia had commissioned a completely different artist for each statue, and each one of those artists had brought with them a very different vision of their art.

Something pulled at me, an omen of sorts, a warning that all was not right here, but I brushed it off because I was stubborn. I just took it that Zenobia was nuts, and okay, this was the real catch. Zenobia wasn't just crazy, she was *really* crazy, but I still wanted her. Stupid me still wanted her, and if this kind of thing was what she did, then who was I to judge?…*especially* me. I certainly wasn't one to judge someone else for being "different." I had no room whatsoever to talk there.

This crazy gorgeous woman I so wanted in my life turned around and had what looked like a very, very old scroll of parchment that was stretched out between two golden rods she held firmly within her beautiful hands.

"Undress for me, baby," she commanded.

My heart practically stopped beating. I had not been expecting that command.

"U…Undress?" I stammered.

"Yes, hon," nodded Zenobia. "Get naked for me."

"I…I'm not sure I want to do that yet," I said in a shaky voice.

I didn't think I was ready for that. I wanted that to happen while we were in the heat of passion, so to speak. She might reject me otherwise…I mean, I didn't think she would, but there was always that fear, you know?

"Don't you want to be with me?" asked Zenobia.

"I…I do," I said nervously. "It's just…my body…I'm just not comfortable with showing it off yet…"

"Look," sighed Zenobia. "I'll turn around, and you get undressed, and then I'll turn around when the ritual is finished so I can see you in all your naked glory…You're beautiful, River. You shouldn't be ashamed of who you really are. You can show me your true self."

Yeah, yeah, okay, that really resonated with me. I really did want to show her my true self, so I caved.

"I…Okay," I nodded. "Okay. You turn around, and we'll do this, and then you can turn around after it's finished, and I'll…I'll show you myself…*all* of myself."

"Good," grinned Zenobia. "First, though, I need to know if you really are going to pledge yourself to my lady, Artemis."

"Only if I get to be with you," I said firmly. "I won't do it unless you promise me that."

I had to throw that in there. Yeah, she was coocoo, but I still wanted her, and…I didn't want her to reject me. I needed that promise.

"I promise you," smiled Zenobia. "You'll be here with me forever, okay?...Now, I'm going to turn around, and you get undressed. You tell me when you're ready to start."

"Okay," I nodded, and this time I was the one who grinned, because this was my dream come true.

She had promised, so I felt like I had some leverage, some hope. Maybe she really was going to be with me now. She was rich, beautiful, and built like an hourglass…Oh, God, I really wanted this…It was like holding a lottery ticket and getting all but one of the numbers right, but that last number hadn't yet been announced. I was just waiting on that last number.

She turned around to give me my privacy, so I kept my end of the bargain and undressed, throwing my clothes to the side of the center pedestal I was standing on. It felt weird and unnatural being naked like this in the open air, but I had kept my promise, so I was hoping she would keep hers as well.

Zenobia stood at the edge of the circle of pedestals and statues, spread out the scroll in her hands upon a marble dais in front of her, that dais lit up by two small braziers on each side of it, and she read from the ancient parchment, though she translated the words into English, because I was pretty sure it was written in another language, probably Ancient Greek.

"Do you, River, give unwavering worship to our goddess, Artemis!" called out Zenobia.

"I…I do!" I called back.

This was exciting. It was like getting married at a really bizarre wedding.

"Do you, River, give your eternal soul to our goddess, Artemis!" called out Zenobia.

"I do!" I called back, this time with more confidence.

"Repeat after me, then," called Zenobia. "I, River, pledge my unwavering worship and eternal soul to the Goddess of the Hunt! My lady, Artemis, take me as your prize! I am yours to collect and to own for all eternity!"

"I, River, pledge my unwavering worship and eternal soul to the Goddess of the Hunt," I repeated. "My lady, Artemis, take me as your prize. I am yours to collect and to own for all eternity."

The confidence I had previously shown vanished in the wake of what happened next. Something I had never even thought possible happened, something absolutely horrifying, and it was a betrayal of the highest order, something I will feel the grief of till my dying day.

A brilliant light shone down from above, and I was yanked up a bit by an invisible force, almost to the point where I was standing on my tippytoes.

I couldn't move. My arms were at my sides, my chest puffed out a bit, and I was forced to stare up into that light, an unearthly light that shone down directly from above me, no light source to reveal its origin.

"Oh, Goddess of the Hunt!" cried out Zenobia. "Goddess of virgins and enslaver of men! Grant this mortal man his everlasting youth and beauty in the way he deserves! Trap him in your prison of stone to look upon his arrogance and hubris at your whim! Protect the sanctity that is woman!

"Oh, Goddess of the Hunt! Defy the oppressors that deny us our freedom! Punish those who would harm your sisters in arms! Take this man as your gift from me so that I may be your faithful servant forever! Reward my diligence with your unending benevolence!...May this mortal man decorate your temple for all eternity!"

My skin tingled as I felt my bones stiffen, and my previous elation turned to shock and horror. I started to cry as I suddenly realized what was happening, as all of the pieces of this warped puzzle, this terrible farce, came together, but it was too late. There was nothing I could do at this point.

I was turning to stone. I was becoming a statue. That's what was going on. That's why all of the statues here looked so different from each other and why they all looked so masterfully sculpted.

"Stop!" I choked out. "I trusted you!"

"It's too late, babe," chuckled Zenobia. "You're already my centerpiece. Besides, you just wanted to plow me...Men are all the same, you know. You should think more with your top head rather than with your lower one. Guess you'll have the rest of eternity to think that one through."

I felt myself change entirely to stone. The light above me stopped shining down upon me, and the weird thing was, I could still see and hear, but I couldn't feel anything, or breathe, or smell, or notice the temperature, or anything like that. I mean, obviously I couldn't move because I was a statue now, so immobility was a given.

But worst of all—and this was truly worst of all—I was still *alive*. I was a statue now, but I was still *alive*. That meant those other statues had been actual men, and they were still alive too, so that meant they'd been standing there for God knew how many years…unfeeling…unmoving…

I wanted to cry. I wanted to scream and shout and do anything but be like this, but I had stupidly screwed myself over by trusting a complete stranger because I had wanted her as my own prize. My own selfish desires had screwed me over…No, there was no other feeling inside me now but *horror*, just pure, unadulterated *horror*.

"I kept my word, baby," I heard Zenobia say. "You'll live here with me forever, and I'll adore that precious little body of yours every single day, just like I said I would. You're just the cutest little thing anyway, let me tell you…You wanted to be here with me, and you got your wish, but nothing is free, honey…Nope, not a thing. Even I had a price to pay…I've never had sex, and I never will. I must remain a virgin. That was my price to pay."

I should have been seething inside, but all I could feel was the agony of a broken heart. Zenobia was supposed to have been my first, and she was also the first woman I had ever felt that pull for, that tug of the heart toward someone special.

How could she do this to me!

"What's different about you, River, is that you're my special one," continued Zenobia. "You're not like these other men. They were all used, but you have purity. That's why my lady, Artemis, has put you in the center. My goddess *loves* virgins, and I could tell you were one the moment I—"

Her sentence ended in an abrupt gasp.

The stone flaked and fell from my cheeks and face as I took in a deep breath. This curse or whatever it was?...It was being undone. Something was up…Something had gone wrong for Zenobia, but it had also suddenly gone very right for me.

I stared down into the wide and shocked emerald-green eyes of my betrayer. Zenobia had finally turned around, and she was finally looking at me, at my naked body, although most of it was still stone. Only my head was flesh, but the rest of me was quickly turning back to the beautiful peach color I was so familiar with.

However, Zenobia's expression did not stay locked in surprise. It quickly changed from shock to pure liquid rage, a Jekyll and Hyde transformation that was obvious to anyone with eyes.

"You're not a man!" she screeched. "You're not even a boy!...*You*!...You lying little pixie Tom! How dare you deceive me!"

Okay, that hurt. I had honestly thought she'd known, but apparently she had not...It was probably the hair that had thrown her off...I mean, I didn't really know what I wanted out of life, but I did know that this was the real me. This was how I felt about myself.

"I thought you knew!" I choked out.

"Know!" screeched Zenobia. "Of course, I didn't know, you vile, demented little camel toe! What is wrong with you!...Oh, by my lady, Artemis, do you know what you've done! Do you have any *idea* what you've done! You've defiled this holy ground!"

The stone surrounding me flaked and cracked off as I was freed from my eternal prison. I fell to my bare knees upon the pedestal, and that hurt, but that was nothing compared to the hit I was about to take.

"I'll kill you!" shrieked Zenobia.

She rushed me, and before I could react, her right fist impacted my left cheek. I cried out as I was knocked backwards off the stone pedestal, rolling across the hard marble flooring as I did.

I was naked, afraid, and completely out of my depth with all of this. I started crying again, because what I had thought was a dream come true was now a nightmare, and it was unfair as well. I had honestly thought I'd met someone who understood me, who wanted to be with the real me, who wanted to see me as I truly was, but I had been betrayed, and I had been betrayed in the worst way, and that broke me.

I screeched as she kicked me in the ribs, and I felt something break. There came a swift and sharp pain after that, and then my tears were really flowing.

"I trusted you!" I sobbed. "I thought you really liked me!"

I looked up into her gorgeous face, but that face was nothing but sheer animosity directed solely at me.

"You noxious, lying little slit!" spat Zenobia.

"You said I was beautiful!" I choked out. "You said you wanted…to see… the real me…"

I couldn't talk anymore. The only thing I could do was sob.

"You're a fool!" hissed Zenobia. "The real you! The real you is a sick, perverted little gutter-slide with a phallic fetish!…Ugh…You are unworthy of my lady's protection…I should beat you to death for this insult!"

Her flashing green eyes were nothing now but madness. She stood tall and proud upon the center pedestal where I had just been standing, her vengeful presence a beacon of unholy, if beautiful, fury, and my grief over this situation was suddenly replaced by fear, just good old-fashioned fear for my own life.

She kicked me again in the ribs, and oh…my…God, that hurt.

I squeezed my eyes shut and sobbed even louder, but this only angered her more.

"Please, stop!" I begged. "I'm sorry! I didn't do anything wrong! I thought you knew! I swear, I thought you knew! Please, please, stop! Please!"

"Don't beg, little Tom," grimaced Zenobia. "You're a disgrace to your own kind, and my lady, Artemis, has no place for you in her sacred temple…She would never kowtow to a phallus…Disgusting…No, you'll get no mercy from me, you dirty little ditch. I'm going to beat the heathen out of you until there's nothing left to beat."

She pulled back her right foot to kick me again, but she stopped and looked up as a brilliant light shone down upon her from above.

"No, wait!" cried Zenobia. "I didn't know!"

I watched in morbid fascination as Zenobia's burgundy one-piece disintegrated into specks of light, and suddenly she was naked, revealing all of her glorious body to me, all of it, every beautiful feature of that incredible body I had so desperately wanted to hold in my own slender arms.

"Have mercy, please!" begged Zenobia. "Please! Please, I didn't—"

My beautiful betrayer stiffened as she puffed out her chest, pulling her arms back at her sides, and then she began to turn to stone, starting with her perfect bare feet.

She choked out one last sentence, the last sentence she would ever speak.

"I didn't know River ..." choked out Zenobia.

Her beautiful legs greyed over to stone, that stone moving up across her wide hips to her narrow waist.

"Was..." she spat out.

The petrification process journeyed up her chest and across her ample breasts, upwards across her large nipples, up and up, all the way up to her flawless and slender neck.

"A woman..." she finished, and then she was gone.

The light from above vanished. Zenobia's beautiful face was permanently set in stone, that face staring upwards into the night sky, and it was right then that I realized I had just been in her position, locked in that unfeeling stone, but by some miracle of fate, I had been the one to walk away from this terrible travesty.

I gathered up my clothes and took some time to dress because of the injury to my ribs, but I was still crying, because though I was still suffering from the heartache of Zenobia's betrayal, hatred, and bigotry toward me, I had finally realized something about my own life, something I had needed to accept for a long time…

I was free. I had needed to accept who I was, and now that I had, I was free. I had broken free from more than just a stone prison; I had broken free from my own denial, and now that I was free, I was going to stay that way.

I ran my right hand down the smooth stone of Zenobia's beautiful stomach, running my narrow fingers over her exquisitely detailed belly button, and I sucked in a tear-filled breath.

I had to admit that I was still heartbroken, but if there was one good thing that had come from all of this, it was the fact that I wasn't ashamed of myself anymore. Zenobia had at least given me that.

#5…SLEEPOVER

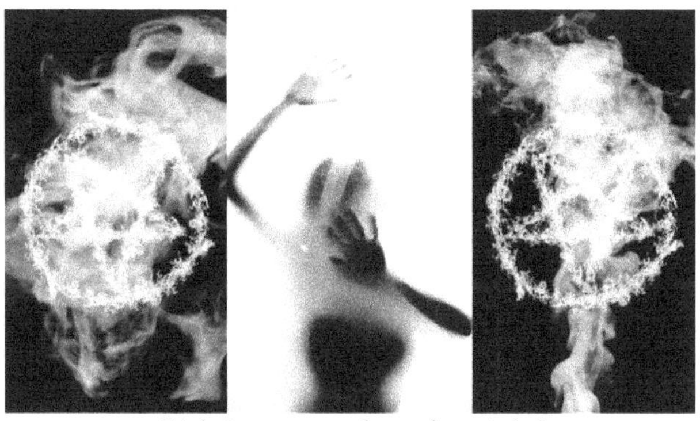

Girls just wanna have fun, right?

Cindy could overhear the others talking as she listened through the bathroom door. She had just changed into her grey sweatpants and white T-shirt in this upstairs bedroom bathroom, so she was ready for the party to begin, but now she was regretting accepting this invitation.

"Why did you invite her again?" asked Melissa.

Melissa was Misty's right-hand lackey, and both of them together were the terror of the eleventh grade. Cindy knew this—everyone did—but she had accepted their invitation anyway.

"Because we need a sixth," replied Misty. "We have the whole gang here, but that's only five of us, and to complete the circle, we need a sixth."

Misty was the unofficial boss of their high school, and she wasn't even a senior. No, only a fool would cross her, but that was the problem, because Cindy really didn't want to be here, but she was afraid to tell Misty "No." You didn't tell Misty "No."

"What's with that stupid old book anyway?" asked Melissa. "Why are you so obsessed with it?"

"Obsessed?" asked Misty. "Isn't that a big word for you?...Look, the only thing worthwhile my crazy old grandma ever did for me was leave me that book. The ritual is going to work, and it's going to give us power."

"We're sixteen," scoffed Melissa. "What are we going to do with power?"

"Anything we want," said Misty. "I don't know about you, but I want a million dollars."

"Even if that's true, you're just going to share this 'power' with a dork like Cindy?" asked Melissa.

"If that's what it takes," replied Misty.

Cindy frowned as she looked at herself in the mirror. She did not think of herself as a dork...She did not like that word. She was skinny, she had long curly black hair surrounding a gawky face, and she wore thick square glasses just so she could see, but she was not a dork.

She liked the same music the others liked, like Madonna and Cyndi Lauper and Michael Jackson. She liked the same magazines the others liked, like *Bop* and *Seventeen* and *Teen*. She even liked the same shows the others liked, like *Family Ties* and *The Facts of Life* and *Square Pegs*. It wasn't fair that she'd been pushed into a corner just to be the butt of a joke.

No, life had definitely not been fair to her. She wanted to sing and dance like the stars, but she knew she never would. The stars were beautiful...For one thing, she didn't even have any real boobs yet. The other girls had grown in theirs, but hers were still M.I.A. She was just so flat, and that was really frustrating.

She wanted a boyfriend, too. All of the other girls had boyfriends, but none of the boys liked Cindy. They didn't like her at all. Misty was dating Brandon Marsh, the most popular boy in school, and Misty was a terrible person. Misty didn't deserve anything like that...It was just so unfair.

But that wasn't the worst of it. The others had been mean to her, terribly mean, in fact—Misty and

Melissa and Becky and Janet and Donna…well, maybe not Becky—but Cindy wasn't stupid. Maybe they would treat her a little better if she was in their circle…Anything was better than being at the bottom.

Still…what was this about a book?

She grabbed her overnight bag and opened the bathroom door. Misty and Melissa immediately swiveled to stare her down, but that was okay. Cindy had already expected this kind of treatment.

Misty was the tall and popular redhead, with Melissa being short and dark-haired. Both of them were the prettiest girls in school, so Cindy could not help but want to be in their circle. It was survival of the fittest when it came to being a junior in high school.

She decided to ignore the open hostility their gazes imparted upon her. She dropped her overnight bag in the corner of the bedroom where the other girls had put theirs, and then she turned to address her temperamental host.

"I heard something about a book?" she asked.

"Were you eavesdropping on us!" asked Melissa in a hostile tone.

"No, I was just—" began Cindy.

"It's fine," said Misty as she waved off Melissa. "I do have a book, a very special book, and I'll be revealing it shortly."

"Oh?" asked Cindy.

"Just shut up and gather round," ordered Melissa.

"That's right!" smiled Misty. "We're all going to get in a circle tonight."

"What for?" asked Cindy.

"We're going to summon a demon!" giggled Becky.

Becky had straight brown hair and a plain face, yet she had somehow made it into the popular circle. She was kind of stupid, but people liked her anyway. It really was unfair.

Still…they were going to summon a demon?

"S…Summon a demon?" stammered Cindy.

"Oh, don't tell me you're chicken," said Janet.

Janet was a natural blonde and kind of mean, especially to the boys, but that meanness just made her more popular for some reason. It was kind of unfathomable.

But yet again…they were going to summon a demon?

"I…I…I'm not chicken," stammered Cindy once more. "It's just that, isn't this kind of thing dangerous?"

"Only if it's real," scoffed Donna. "This is just for fun, stupid."

Donna had straight brown hair like Becky, though she was better looking in the face. She was a skeptic that didn't believe in anything supernatural. She was probably only here because Misty had demanded Janet come.

Janet and Donna were always together, and Donna was Janet's yes-girl. They were the off-brand version of Misty and Melissa, which made them doubly annoying, because they were just as terrible to Cindy as Misty and Melissa were, if not more so.

"I'm not stupid," frowned Cindy. "I was just asking a question."

"Yeah, a stupid question," said Donna.

"I'm just saying—" began Cindy.

"That we're all going to have fun," said Misty. "My parents are out of state for the weekend, which means us girls get to play while they're gone…Cyndi Lauper is right, you know. Girls just wanna have fun."

"Uh, huh…" said Cindy.

But her reticence was not welcomed.

"Why did you have to invite her?" asked Donna.

"I know," frowned Melissa. "What a dork."

"Because she's going to be one of us now," said Misty. "Isn't that right, Cindy?"

"Y…Yeah," said Cindy.

Still…she was really unsure about this. Summoning demons? What was that about?

This was irrelevant at the moment, of course. The other girls were just as unhappy about the current situation, but not for the same reasons.

"Great," said Donna. "Now we have a dork hanging around. Hopefully, we're not all ostracized by the time '84 rolls around. I don't know about you, but I don't want to be in the same category as this dork and Lauren Grouper."

"Let's not get testy, girls," said Misty. "We need Cindy with us, especially for tonight. There has to be six…Now, no more arguing with me…We have our fun to get to…This is a sleepover, right? We're supposed to have fun…Now, everybody gather round, and I'll show you my crazy old grandma's book."

"Yeah!" said Becky. "Let's see it!...Is it a book of spells?"

"Something like that," smiled Misty.

The popular redhead was all smiles, but there was something sinister in her green eyes that Cindy did not like. It was hidden there, a maliciousness, a malign force just beneath the surface, that surface a thin veneer of legitimacy that Misty always wore like so much makeup.

Misty rolled back the sleaves of the knit pink sweater she was in, got down on her hands and knees upon the short blue carpet of her bedroom, and pulled out a large tome from beneath her bed.

The tome in question was a relic to be sure. It was fairly thick for such an old book, as it was surely made long, long before even Misty's grandmother's time, as the covers were made from some unidentifiable dark leather and the bindings were large stitches of old crimson thread. On the cover was a symbol that Cindy had seen before, the reverse five-pointed star in a circle, a blood-red pentagram etched into the book.

Misty waved everyone forward as they all gathered around her. The popular redhead sat up on her knees as she smiled and tapped the front cover of the monstrous book.

"My grandmother told me this book is—" she began.

Cindy blurted out the first thing that came to mind, a private fear she held, one in which she knew *exactly* what this book was.

"*The Necronomicon*?" she asked. "Is that what it is?"

Misty let forth a disturbing laugh and shook her head no.

"The Necro-what?" asked Melissa.

"*The Necronomicon* is Lovecraft's invention," replied Misty.

"Lovecraft?" asked Becky. "What's a Lovecraft? Is that like *The Love Boat*?"

Everyone else laughed, but Cindy did not find Becky's ignorance particularly amusing.

"Uhhh…no," chuckled Misty. "H.P. Lovecraft was an author from the 1920s. Cindy, here, is a bookworm, so she would know that name."

Of course, Cindy did not like being relegated to the "nerd" corner.

"If I'm a bookworm, then how do you know it?" asked Cindy.

"Because I've studied this book," said Misty. "I went to the library and looked up anything I could find out about it, but there's nothing I could find that *didn't* deal with Lovecraft. It was really annoying."

"So it isn't *The Necronomicon*?" asked Cindy.

"No," said Misty with another shake of her head. "*The Necronomicon* isn't real. Lovecraft made it up…but he may have based it off of this book…*The Pentagony*."

"*The Pentagony*?" asked Becky. "That sounds ominous."

"It should," smirked Misty. "Only a few copies were ever made, and they all belong to crazy old women like my dear, departed grandma. Thanks to her, this one belongs to me…It's valuable beyond words."

"So what's so special about it?" asked Melissa.

"I was getting to that," smiled Misty.

Her smile was condescending, something Cindy picked up on immediately and something Melissa had not. It occurred to Cindy that Melissa was too trusting and too stupid to figure out that her best "friend" was nothing more than a wolf in sheep's clothing…Cindy was not about to trust Misty in any way, shape, or form, but she needed the popular redhead in order to become popular herself, or at least, less hated.

"This book is so old that its original name, if it had one, is lost to time," said Misty. "The title is called *The Pentagony* because it's a mix of 'penta,' the Ancient Greek word for 'five,' and 'agony,' which is an Old French and Latin derivative of the original Greek word."

"None of that made any sense," said Janet.

But it had made sense to Cindy, and this sounded like they were playing with fire. Furthermore, Misty had just proven herself to be very smart, far smarter than Cindy had originally given her credit for. Cindy had not known the popular redhead was so educated…

Now it really wasn't fair. If she didn't even have the brains to compete with the likes of Misty, then what did she have?

"It stands for 'the five agonies,'" smirked Misty. "The five agonies are ambition, seduction…which includes deception…defilement, pleonexia…or greed, for lack of a better word…and estrangement."

"None of those sound good," frowned Becky.

"Thank you, Becky," whispered Cindy, but Misty heard her.

"What was that?" asked the popular redhead.

"N…Nothing," stammered Cindy.

"Mmm, hmm, right," said Misty. "Just be quiet and listen, Cindy. You're lucky I'm even talking to you, much less inviting you over."

"Exactly," snorted Melissa.

Cindy winced over this admonishment. She really needed to keep her mouth shut.

"Anyway, the five agonies are centered around the five types of demons," continued Misty.

Of course, Cindy could not keep her mouth shut over this. She did not want to play around with demons regardless of whether they were real or not. She didn't know if the supernatural was real, but she really didn't want to find out. Nevertheless, if they were going to summon a demon, she did have *some* standards. She did not want to end up summoning anything absolutely horrifying to the eyes.

"These aren't like the weird horrors with writhing tentacles and lots of eyes like in Lovecraft?" she asked.

"No," said Misty. "No, that was Lovecraft's fantasy. This is more the 'traditional' type of demon…You see, what people don't know is that a demon can be summoned in order to gain mastery over them, and once you have that mastery, you have power…*real* power."

"Okay, whatever," snorted Donna. "So, what are we talking about here? What's this 'power' you keep mentioning?"

"Like anything you can think of," said Misty. "But what I have in mind is a little different. What I have in mind is more subtle than just an outright wish."

"What's that?" asked Janet.

"The demon I want to summon is actually a *demoness*," continued Misty. "I know, because my grandmother translated a lot of this book from Latin to

English—Latin, which, I might add, none of us can read—and that Latin had been translated from Ancient Greek, and that had been translated from an older language, probably an ancient language that originated out of the Middle East."

"That's a lot of translations," said Cindy.

"Yes, but the rituals still work, even from the English," said Misty.

"So who are we summoning, then?" asked Cindy.

She had a strange premonition that this was indeed a very bad idea. Even so, she wanted to know the name of who or what they would be summoning.

"Very perceptive, Cindy," replied Misty. "We're not just summoning some random no name…No, we're summoning Allerakth the Dancer. She's what's called a 'succubus.' With her influence, we can get people to do what we want, especially men, and therefore, we can get whatever we want…

"More powerful demons can grant big wishes that rewrite reality, but they're much harder to control. What we're going for is more subtle…It's influence. It's the difference between opening a locked door with a lockpick or with a sledgehammer. Both work, but the lockpick is the less obtrusive route…We're taking the smart route that doesn't alarm the powers that be. That's why we're using Allerakth. As far as demons go, she's the 'safest' to summon."

From what Cindy understood, there wasn't really any kind of a "safe" demon, but Misty was calling the shots here.

"We're going to use a pentagram as a trap and trap her in it," continued Misty. "I've already drawn the pentagram in the basement, and I've drawn all of the matching symbols from the book inside the pentagram. All we have to do is light the candles at the five points of the pentagram and say the words."

"And then what?" asked Janet.

"And then we make her give us what we want," said Misty in a smug tone. "I've studied this book extensively. I already know how to force her to give us what we want. As far as demons go, succubae aren't exactly at the top of the command chain. They're not really even middle management."

Cindy did not like this at all. She knew what a "succubus" was, and the connotations attached to that word were dirty and gross. She was human, of course, and she had those kinds of feelings like anyone else, but she wasn't one to obsess about them…Thinking about sex disturbed her a little anyway…

To be honest, she didn't like any of this, not the succubus part, and certainly not the summoning part.

"Isn't this really dangerous?" she asked without thinking.

"What are you, chicken?" sneered Melissa. "Just shut up and follow along."

"You want to be one of us, right?" asked Misty.

It was Misty's almost-sincere gaze that trapped Cindy into acquiescence. She knew in her heart that the deceitful redhead could not be trusted, but still…to finally be accepted into their group?…She could not simply pass this opportunity by.

"I…uhhh…Okay…" said Cindy meekly.

"Good," smiled Misty. "Then let's head to the basement."

The popular redhead led them downstairs, through the living room, into the kitchen, and then through the basement door into the basement. Misty flicked on the basement lights, and they all walked down the creaky wooden steps into the basement until they were in a large open space, a void of anything but a concrete floor and walls.

"It's empty down here," said Janet.

"It floods down here, and Misty's parents haven't fixed that yet," said Melissa dryly.

"They're getting around to it," shrugged Misty. "It's expensive to just rework the entire bottom of the house."

"Is that why there's nothing down here?" asked Becky.

Misty gave the slightly-stupid girl a rather frustrated, if not downright insulting, look.

"Yes, Becky," sighed Misty. "There's nothing down here because when the basement floods, anything down here would get ruined."

"Duh, dummy," scoffed Melissa.

"Oh…" replied Becky.

Cindy shook her head at all of this.

First of all, the basement wasn't entirely empty because Misty had been busy. There was a large pentagram drawn in white chalk that spanned a good eight feet in diameter, that pentagram filled with weird symbols drawn in said white chalk, and at each of the five points of that pentagram's star was a single red candle ready to be lit…No, Cindy did not like this at all.

"Everyone, sit at one of the five points of the star, right in front of a candle," ordered Misty. "You're going to have to light your candle when I say so…Melissa, remember that notepad I told you to hold?...Hand out the notepad paper, one sheet to everyone, including yourself. Don't give me one, though. I have to read from the book."

Misty's yes-girl tore off five sheets of paper from a notepad and handed one page to each of the other girls, save Misty, who held her precious old book in her own slender hands. Melissa then kept one page for herself.

Cindy reluctantly took her slip of paper and then sat down, legs crossed, in front of one of the star points in-between Becky and Janet.

Her anxiety grew as she sat there in strange anticipation of whatever was to come. She had a terrible feeling that Misty's ritual was going to work, and this scared her on a deep level, but she was even more scared of being ostracized, so she kept her mouth shut against her better judgement.

"Everybody, take the small matchbox in front of you and light your candle," ordered Misty.

They all complied without argument, lighting their candles without further coaxing.

Cindy removed a single match from a tiny matchbox on her right and lit the large red candle before her.

Once all of the candles were lit, Melissa asked a very insightful question.

"Where are you sitting?" she asked as she looked up at their unofficial "leader."

"I have to stand and read from the book," smiled Misty. "Now, everyone, be quiet. Put the sheet of paper Melissa gave you in-between your legs, close your eyes, and hold each other's hands so we can complete the circle."

"Eww!" exclaimed Janet. "I have to hold hands with this dork?"

Cindy knew that insult was directed solely at her, and this bothered her, but Becky, surprisingly enough, stood up for her in that single moment.

"Cindy's not that bad," said the slightly-stupid girl. "At least she's not Lauren Grouper."

"Yeah, yeah," said Janet.

Lauren Grouper was another ostracized girl at school, someone Cindy now felt infinitely sorry for.

Misty and her friends really were mean, but…Cindy wanted to be a part of their group anyway. She did not want to be at the bottom anymore. She had said it to herself before, and she would say it again: It was survival of the fittest when you were a junior in high school.

Cindy took Becky's hand and then Janet's, though Janet treated her touch as if she were a victim of the black plague.

"Everybody, close your eyes," said Misty. "It's time to read from the book."

"Okay!" said Becky happily. "This is going to be fun!"

Cindy wondered if Becky was really all there or not, and apparently, so did Janet.

"We're summoning a demon, doofus," scoffed the blonde. "I don't think it's supposed to be fun. It's supposed to be scary."

"Well, I think it's fun," said Becky, a frown etched across her plain face.

Cindy shook her head and closed her eyes. Whatever was going to happen was going to happen, so…

"Okay, everyone's eyes are closed," said Misty. "Now it's time for the incantation…I need absolute quiet for this, and whatever you do, do *not* open your eyes. You'll ruin the summoning. Those are the instructions in the book. Just don't do it."

"Yeah, yeah," said Janet. "Did you hear that, Donna?"

"Yep," said Donna. "I'm not the one to worry about, though. You should worry about Becky. She's the one with cheese for brains."

"Hey!" protested the slightly-stupid girl. "I'm not going to open my eyes."

"N…Neither am I," stammered Cindy.

She was afraid to open her eyes anyway. She was afraid she would open them and see something horrible standing in the center of this large pentagram. She most certainly did not want to experience that, but she knew herself quite well, and she had a habit of staring directly at whatever terrified her, ensuring she would have nightmares for weeks. This always happened to her whenever there was a horror movie on TV. Nevertheless, she would try to keep her eyes shut this time.

"Good," said Misty. "Now everybody, shut up and sit quietly while I read from the book…and remember, whatever you do, *do not* open your eyes until I say so…One more thing…After I read a line, everyone has to repeat it. I'll read one line at a time so that everyone can follow along. Be quiet until after I've read a line, then repeat it. Understood?"

"Yeah, yeah," said Janet. "We'll repeat after you."

"This is fun!" giggled Becky.

"Just shut up and do as she says," said Donna.

"Quiet, everybody!" hissed Melissa.

"No matter what happens, don't open your eyes," warned Misty one last time. "I mean it. Anyone that breaks the circle is kicked out of the club…Am I clear? I already know Melissa won't screw it up, so none of you others had better screw this up for me."

"Tell that to Dork, here," said Janet.

Cindy winced at that insult. She was really getting tired of the blonde's caustic mouth.

"I'm not worried about Cindy," said Misty nonchalantly. "She's too much of a coward to open her eyes, but in this case, that's a good thing, because I already know she won't screw up the ritual."

Cindy winced yet again at that insult, but it was also a compliment, if not a backhanded one.

"So don't screw this up for me, Janet," warned Misty. "Things are about to get hairy down here, and I don't want you freaking out and ruining it."

"Yeah, yeah," muttered Janet. "I'm not going to freak out…Are we going to do this or what? Let's get this done. I don't want to touch Dork's hand any longer than I have to."

Cindy really wanted to rip out the blonde's naturally golden hair, but she kept her temper in check for her own sake.

They sat there for a few seconds of silent and uncomfortable handholding, and then Misty began to read.

"Let the Black Gate open," chanted Misty.

"Let the Black Gate open," said everyone else, including Cindy.

"Let the Starless Void swallow," chanted Misty.

"Let the Starless Void swallow," chanted everyone else.

A breeze picked up, a slight gust of wind, which was weird, really weird, considering they were all down in the basement and none of the tiny basement windows were open. What was even stranger was that Cindy could only feel that breeze around her head and shoulders and not on any other part of her.

"We traverse the Hollow Sea," chanted Misty.

"We traverse the Hollow Sea," chanted everyone else.

"Five are we, for five is the number of Man," chanted Misty.

"Five are we, for five is the number of Man," said everyone else.

The breeze around Cindy's head and shoulders turned into a whipping wind that flung her curly black hair back and forth, and she struggled not to open her eyes.

The other girls cried out a little, but Misty shushed them.

"Don't break the circle!" hissed the popular redhead. "Something bad will happen if you do! We have to complete the ritual! Don't open your eyes!"

The wind died down a little, as did the girls suffering through it.

"Five are we, for five is the number of Man," chanted Misty again.

They repeated the line as before, and the wind picked up again in time with their chanting.

Cindy felt a cold chill grip her heart…This summoning actually seemed to be working. Her private fears were being realized.

"Let the Sixth fetter," chanted Misty.

"Let the Sixth fetter," chanted everyone else, including Cindy.

She did not want to engage in this madness any longer, but she felt compelled to, a strange calling she could not resist, a calling that was infernal in nature; she just knew it.

"We open the Black Gate," chanted Misty.

"We open the Black Gate," chanted everyone else.

"We pull forth Allerakth the Dancer," chanted Misty.

"We pull forth Allerakth the Dancer," chanted everyone else.

Cindy trembled and clutched Janet and Becky's hands as the wind blowing past her head and shoulders continued to whip around her long, curly, black hair. She could hear a whispering in the back of her mind, a sultry voice that spoke to her in a wanton tone.

"Look at me, Cindy," said the voice.

She opened her eyes without meaning to, that terrible habit she had coming forth to play, but once her dark eyes were open, she could not shut them again.

She could see that the others had their eyes closed as Misty read from the book. The popular redhead was thoroughly engrossed within the pages of that cursed tome, so Misty did not see what Cindy saw, or she may have stopped reading.

Cindy could see a humanoid shape in the center of the pentagram, a wispy, shadowy form of a nude woman, the candle smoke gathering in the center to form that image, and that image spun and danced as the wind picked up all around them to blow everyone's hair to and fro.

"We pull forth Allerakth the Seducer," chanted Misty.

"We pull forth Allerakth the Seducer," said everyone else.

"We pull forth Allerakth the Deceiver," chanted Misty.

"We pull forth Allerakth the Deceiver," repeated the group.

The wind whipped around Cindy's head and shoulders as she held tightly to the two girls' hands. She wanted to get up and run, but the whispering in her mind told her to stay, and she was too scared to ignore it.

"Stay with me, Cindy," came the voice at the back of her mind. *"We can dance together."*

The shape of smoke in the center of the pentagram was beautiful, a dancing, naked woman of perfect proportions, and that shape spun and twirled with otherworldly grace. Cindy could not take her eyes off it.

"Let Allerakth cross the Hollow Sea," chanted Misty.

"Let Allerakth cross the Hollow Sea," chanted everyone else.

"Let Allerakth cross the Starless Void," chanted Misty.

"Let Allerakth cross the Starless Void," chanted the group.

The beautiful, otherworldly shape in the center of the pentagram stopped and turned to stare directly into Cindy's dark eyes. There were two pinpoints of vermillion light in that smoke where its eyes should have been, and those two pinpoints of light burrowed into Cindy, burrowing into the very depths of her mind right down to her innocent soul.

She felt cold inside, and not because of the wind whipping around her. Her skin felt hot as if touched by flames, but her insides felt ice cold, a chill that wrapped around her very essence of being.

"We pull Allerakth through the Black Gate," chanted Misty.

"We pull Allerakth through the Black Gate," chanted the rest of the girls.

"We fetter Allerakth," chanted Misty.

"We fetter Allerakth," chanted the girls.

The weird form of smoke danced in a circle again, only this time its wispy hair turned thick and curly like Cindy's own, and it swung its wide hips in a circle until it stopped to stare at Cindy again with those bright pinpoints of crimson light, those twin beacons of strange, unholy desire.

Cindy felt an abnormal heat building up inside the cold within her. It was faint at first, and then it grew little by little, making her sweat, even as the wind continued to whip around her. Her body felt strange, excited, something private that was not for the company of these girls, and she did not like it.

She did not like the weird feelings this vision of smoke brought down upon her, but the tingling in her skin, the electricity that ran through her, was very powerful. She had visions of herself with attractive men, strange desires too graphic for her own normal imagination, and this disgusted her, making her tremble as she resisted those unnatural urges.

"The sacrifice shall be made," chanted Misty. "The pact shall be sealed."

"The sacrifice shall be made," chanted the girls. "The pact shall be sealed."

Cindy repeated the lines along with the others, but she did so against her own will. She was not in control anymore, not while having to fight off the raging flames of desire within her. It was taking everything she had to fight these unwanted feelings, and this frightened her like nothing else.

The smokey, otherworldly dancer in the center of the pentagram twirled a few more times before staring one last time into Cindy's wide and horrified eyes.

"We can dance together," came the voice in Cindy's mind. *"Don't you want to be a star?"*

"Let the order be written," chanted Misty. "Let the pact be sealed."

"Let the order be written," chanted the girls. "Let the pact be sealed."

As soon as the group had finished that last line, the wind suddenly stopped, and the dancer in the center of the pentagram turned into formless candle smoke.

Cindy's logical, rational mind came to the surface of her brain, and that logical self tried to explain away the mysterious, otherworldly dancer as a weird coincidence of light and smoke, or maybe the strange image had been a hallucination caused by anxious hysteria, but whatever the case, she did not want to believe in it. She did not want to believe that thing in the center of the pentagram could possibly have been real.

Cindy took in a breath and shook her head a couple of times, because she felt whole again, her normal self, unviolated by whatever dark force she had *thought* had threatened to grip her immortal soul.

Janet ripped her hand away from her and gave her a deep and unforgiving scowl.

"Are you *trying* to break my hand, dork?" she asked.

Cindy ignored the volatile blonde. She was simply trying to recover from…whatever had just happened. She felt heated, flushed, a leftover of whatever strange hysteria had tried to violate her, and she shook a little as she tried to bring herself down from that strange and excited physical high. She could feel it all the way down between her legs, and she did not like it. She did not like it at all.

"That was wild!" grinned Becky. "Wasn't that crazy!"

"Y…Yeah…" stammered Melissa.

Even Misty's right-hand yes-girl was freaked out by what had just happened.

"Okay, everyone," said Misty. "Look at the paper you have and tell me what's written on it."

Cindy stared down at the slip of paper between her legs. In spite of all the wind that had whipped around them, not one piece of paper had blown away from any of them.

The other girls picked up their papers and studied them.

"Mine says, 'first,'" said Melissa.

"Mine says, 'fourth,'" said Becky.

"That's weird," said Donna. "The writing is in big red cursive, like from a pen, but it's turning brown and leaking through."

"It's blood," smiled Misty.

"Ha, ha," sneered Donna. "I don't know how you set up this trick, but you're pretty good at this, I'll give you that. You should go on stage."

"Uh, huh…" smirked Misty. "Just tell me what's on the paper, Donna."

"It says, 'third,'" shrugged Donna. "So? What's that supposed to mean?"

"Yeah," said Janet. "Why does mine say, 'second'? Shouldn't mine be first? Why does Melissa get to be first?"

She stuck out her tongue at Melissa.

"Because I'm number one, doofus," replied Melissa as she returned the gesture.

"What's on your paper, Cindy?" asked Misty.

Cindy picked up her piece of paper and stared down at it.

"Well?" asked Misty.

To be fair, Cindy was still simply trying to recover from the harrowing violation she had just experienced, so what was on the paper did not quite register in her own mind at first, so it took her a few seconds to comprehend what she was reading, but by the time she did comprehend it and her lips parted to speak, she was interrupted.

She was about to speak aloud what was on her slip of paper, but the paper in her hands burst into flames, as did all the other slips of paper. The girls squealed and threw the burning bits away from them out of reflex, but Cindy was too stunned to do anything but stare down at the empty space where her piece of paper had been.

"Oh, well," sighed Misty. "I already know Cindy's number then. It must be five."

But that was not what had been written on Cindy's paper…Not to mention that Misty's nonchalant reaction to the spontaneous combustion was not normal at all, not in the slightest.

But Cindy's fearful pondering was interrupted yet again.

"How long has that been there?" asked Melissa.

The yes-girl's voice drew Cindy's attention toward the center of the pentagram.

In the center of the large encircled star was a black knife made of what looked like some heavy metal, something Cindy could not identify. The blade was deadly sharp and wickedly serrated, and its handle looked like it was made from bone…human bone…Cindy just knew this morbid fact for some weird reason. In fact, she was strangely sure of it. There was no "looked like." The knife in the pentagram had a handle made of human bone; she just knew it.

"*Ooo*," said Misty as she clutched her own arms through her pink sweater. "This was what I was waiting for. Just looking at it gives me chills."

"What is it?" asked Becky.

"It's a knife, stupid," said Janet.

"It's not just any knife," grinned Misty. "It's the Sacrificium Daemonibus. Allerakth must have sent it…It's part of the ritual."

"Uh, huh," said Donna. "Look, your cheap dime-store tricks were fun at first, but now this is getting old."

"You wanted to have fun tonight, and this is fun," shrugged Misty. "You think this is theater, right? You think I'm playing a show for you, do you? You said I should be up on stage, so this is just a show, right?"

"Yeah, obviously," said Donna.

"Good," smiled Misty. "That's really good, because I have more, but only if you're not chicken, because now it gets really scary. You have to sit tight, though, and watch the show. Don't be a chicken and run."

"You think I'm chicken?" scowled Donna. "I'm not scared of anything; you know that."

"Okay," shrugged Misty. "Let's continue then, shall we?"

"Yeah, lets," scoffed Donna. "What does the knife have to do with any of this?"

"Let me show you," smiled Misty.

She picked up the large and deadly-looking blade from out of the center of the pentagram, that black knife long and sharp, its shape gleaming in spite of its ebony makeup and the soft, dim glow of the basement lights. She held it with almost loving grace within her right palm for a few seconds, and then she gripped it tightly, a wicked smile on her red lips.

"What are you gonna do with that?" asked Donna.

The popular redhead grabbed a chunk of Melissa's short black hair and pulled the yes-girl's head back. Cindy sucked in her breath in horror as Misty slit her own best friend's throat with ease, the sharp blade running across the girl's bare neckline to spring forth a spraying fountain of bright red blood.

The other girls shrieked and screeched, but unbelieving Donna simply laughed as Melissa choked out a bloody death gurgle.

Misty simply smiled in return, dragged the dying Melissa toward the center of the pentagram by her own short dark hair, and then dropped Melissa's bleeding body in that center like so much trash.

Melissa's blood spurted out of her gashed throat in a red waterfall as everyone simply stared at the murdered girl choking in her own death throes.

"It's very simple," shrugged Misty. "I kill you one by one, I let your blood spray around the room, I drop you in the center here, and then I step into the center of the pentagram to seal the pact. It's that simple. That's how the ritual works."

"Ha, ha," said Donna as she rolled her eyes. "Very funny…How lame. I've seen better effects at the drive-in."

Cindy could not move. She stared in wide-eyed horror at Melissa's own lifeless eyes…This was not some joke or trick. Misty had just murdered her own best friend, and she had done it right in front of everyone.

"Look at this dork next to me," chuckled Janet. "She's about to pee her pants."

Cindy ignored her as she trembled in place. This was beyond horrific, and her mind was temporarily in a happy place, someplace that definitely wasn't down in this terrifying murder basement. Her lips parted to let forth a short gasp, yet everyone else simply stared at her.

"Geez, you're as white as a sheet," scoffed Janet. "It's not even real blood, stupid. It's just corn syrup. Melissa's such a hack, even her death is hammy…God, you're such a dork, Cindy. Stop acting like you're going to have a heart attack…Look, stupid…"

The mean blonde shuffled forward on her hands and knees to the center of the pentagram where Melissa's body lay. Her right-hand fingers reached forward to touch fresh blood as she held those crimson-stained digits up to the light.

"See?" she said. "This isn't real…Wait…What the—"

Misty grabbed Janet's naturally blonde hair, pulled her head back, and quickly slit her throat as well. She forced Janet's head over the center of the star as the blonde's life's blood spilled over Melissa's dead, lifeless face.

Janet gurgled out a dying choke as her own blood sprayed out everywhere, including all over the chalk pentagram, yet that chalk did not wash away, nor would it. Cindy knew this permanence of chalk for a fact, though she did not know how she knew such a thing.

Misty dropped Janet's body, looked up, and smiled.

"Who's next?" she asked. "What was the order?...Oh, right…"

Donna stood up and cocked her head to one side as she studied Janet's body.

"What is this!" she cried in angry disbelief. "You didn't tell me you were in on it, Janet!...Unbelievable…Get up!"

She walked forward to pull up her clearly dead friend, but Misty was on her in a flash, the knife in the redhead's right hand stabbing upwards and inwards through Donna's throat and directly up into the nonbeliever's brain.

Donna turned and staggered in a circle for a few seconds before falling to the concrete floor after that, her brown eyes rolling up in the whites, and Cindy knew right then that the young woman had died before she had even hit the floor.

"W…Wait…" said Becky in a shaky voice.

As stupid as she was, the girl was finally beginning to realize what Cindy already knew.

"H…Hey, wait a minute," continued Becky. "Are…Are they dead? Did…Did you just kill them? Are they really dead?"

"Of course, they are, Becky," sighed Misty. "When I said I was going to kill you all, I was telling the truth, dummy. What part of this did you not understand? How else can I seal the pact?"

Misty gave poor, slightly-stupid Becky a frustrated shake of her head and walked over to Donna's body. She pulled the demonic knife from Donna's throat and quickly hauled the fresh corpse into the center of the pentagram, throwing Donna on top of the other two as if she were a side of beef.

There was blood everywhere now. It was all over the pentagram and on the floor. It was like a slaughterhouse down here, and yet the slightly-stupid girl next to Cindy was only now just figuring out what was going on.

"This…This is a joke, right?" asked Becky. "This is all a joke, right?"

The young woman began to cry, and Cindy immediately felt sorry for her.

"I'm afraid not," grinned Misty. "It's your turn, Becky. Now be a good girl like Cindy and just sit and wait to be slaughtered. Because you participated in the summoning, you'll be going to Hell to be tortured, but that's okay…It should be fine. I don't know exactly what they do down there, but you probably won't like it at all, but I have to complete the ritual, so that's not my concern. Now sit still so I can kill you."

Cindy watched the growing stain in Becky's grey sweatpants as the girl peed herself.

"NO!" screamed the slightly-stupid girl.

Becky stood and turned to run, but Misty ran her down with ease. The redhead plunged the knife into

Becky's exposed back, and the slightly-stupid girl went down hard with a loud scream. Misty stabbed her one more time in the back before pulling up the girl's head, only to slit Becky's exposed throat a second later.

Cindy stared down at the blood that covered her. She had been sprayed with these murdered girls' blood here and there, and she was only just now noticing it. It was on her night clothes and all over her face as well.

She could taste someone's blood, probably Janet's, because the mean blonde had been the closest to her upon death, but this simple awareness of that copper taste brought up something inside her, something that did not belong. She could feel a presence there, a dark and sinister presence, and she did not like it, but that presence delayed her crippling terror, giving her a weird and unnatural inner strength.

"That means you're number five, Cindy," smiled Misty. "Welcome to the club! Now just sit right there so I can kill you. It'll only hurt for a moment, and then you'll die and go to Hell. I'll get my power from Allerakth, and everyone wins…Well, I'll win, and you'll be tortured in Hell, but that sounds like a 'you' problem…You know what? I'll just stop talking and kill you now."

But Misty's annoying voice was drowned out by the pumping of Cindy's own blood in her ears. She could feel more than just an abatement of fear now. She felt energized, electric inside, those weird and unnatural feelings violating her once more, and she did not like it, but she didn't fight it this time, because this time they were giving her some disturbing form of sadistic courage.

The redhead ran toward her and stabbed downwards at her face, but Cindy reached up and caught Misty's offending wrist with her own left hand, stopping the point of the blade just before it reached the left lens of her thick glasses.

Misty grunted and pushed hard against her, but to no avail.

"You're number five!" hissed the popular redhead. "Just die already! I need your blood!"

"No…" said Cindy in a weird voice.

She felt different now, stranger than strange. Someone or something was whispering to her in the back of her mind, so she listened, not because she wanted to, but because she *needed* to. This voice was attached to her like some kind of parasite, but it was also giving her strength, more strength than she had ever felt in her entire life, far more strength than any human being had a right to possess.

Misty reached down with her left hand to pull Cindy's hair, but Cindy caught that wrist as well. The redhead standing above Cindy pushed and struggled against her, but Cindy stood on two confident and solid legs to fully confront her would-be killer, standing tall to face the popular girl.

Misty grunted, pushed, and strained to stab her, but to no avail. The sadistic redhead could not move the deadly tip of the ebony knife one fraction of an inch closer to Cindy, and this frustration of delay played out upon Misty's pretty face in the form of a swiftly growing rage.

"Why are you so strong!" she screeched. "No one is this strong!...Die already! You're the fifth! I need your blood!"

"No," repeated Cindy. "No, I'm not the fifth. That's not what my paper said."

"Wh…What?" asked Misty.

Her previously enraged face changed to genuine surprise at this confession.

"My paper said I was the sixth," said Cindy matter-of-factly.

"That's not possible!" shrieked Misty. "I'm the sixth! I have to be!"

"No," said Cindy in weird excitement.

She felt absolutely charged all over her body, as if soft fingers were running up and down her most sensitive parts. It was perverse and disturbing, but it was also giving her an unholy strength that could not be denied, certainly not by the likes of Misty.

"No, you're the fifth; I'm the sixth," she said in a shaky, tremulous voice. "I'm supposed to kill you. In fact, you're the one going to Hell…You're going to Hell, Misty, and they're going to peel off your skin and do terrible, terrible things to you down there…How do I know this?…Well, here, I'll show you."

Cindy pulled down hard with both hands, gripping Misty's wrists tightly, and the popular redhead's arms came off at the shoulders, tearing off her body by means of some unholy, impossible strength, the arms coming off along with the rose-pink sleaves of the sadistic young woman's knit sweater.

Misty screamed in absolute agony as the stumps at her shoulders sprayed blood everywhere around the basement like some horrific lawn sprinkler.

Cindy dropped Misty's disembodied left arm to the floor, gripped Misty's detached right arm with both hands, turned it around to where the fist was facing away from her, and then swung the limb like an axe. The unholy knife that was still gripped within Misty's fingers plunged itself straight through the popular redhead's forehead, right through her skull, and directly into her brain.

Misty's green eyes rolled upwards and stared at nothing as she stood and wobbled for a second, and then she fell backwards into the center of the pentagram to land upon the other bodies there.

Cindy stared down at the pile of bodies and shook, trembling in place from the demonic power within her, because this horror was not yet through with her.

"Complete me," came a sultry voice inside her head.

She struggled against this voice, this dark force inside her, but she staggered along anyway in a stop-motion walk of clockwork jerking that led her to poor dead Becky's body. She gripped the dead girl's legs and dragged her toward the pentagram without wanting to.

"No…No, wait…" struggled Cindy.

The words "SEAL THE PACT" formed in blood all over the stark grey floor, that phrase everywhere, blood just congealing into those words, as Cindy dragged Becky backwards without her own volition, though she fought this otherworldly control with everything she had.

"Seal the pact," came the sultry voice inside her head.

"I don't want to!" cried Cindy.

She deposited Becky's body in the pentagram, but she refused to step inside it. It was a monstrous struggle of wills, as the bodies of all five girls were now within the confines of the evil circle. She had to fight with everything she had inside herself in order to keep from stepping into that terrible center.

"But you do," came the sultry voice.

"N…No…" struggled Cindy.

She was crying now, a stream of tears that would not stop flowing. She wanted out of this basement. She *needed* out of this basement. She needed to leave this place far behind her. If she really was going to Hell because of this ritual, maybe there was some way to undo that curse, but first she had to leave this awful murder basement.

"You want to be popular," said the voice in her head. *"You want to be famous. You want to be beautiful…Don't leave, Cindy. I love you."*

An image popped into her mind's eye, a picture of a beautiful woman in a gorgeous blue dress, and this woman was indeed as beautiful as anyone in those magazines Cindy had spent countless hours ogling over. This woman was everything she had always wanted to be, this woman with an hourglass figure and long, flowing, curly, black hair.

The woman in her mind's-eye vision rivaled the one in the smoke, an unbelievably gorgeous, magnificent star of a woman, bright and shining like a nova, and beneath her dancing figure was a Hollywood Walk of Fame Star, and Cindy's name was on that star.

It came to her all at once.

"Th…That's me?" wept Cindy. "Is that me?"

"Yes," came the sultry voice. *"With me, you'll have everything you've ever wanted…Join with me. Seal the pact…Bind us together…Don't leave me trapped down here…You know what you really want…Join with me, Cindy. Let us be one…No one will ever pick on you again…Don't be like Lauren Grouper…alone and without friends…*

"Together, we will take everything that belongs to us…Those other girls weren't your friends…I'm your only real friend, Cindy…I saved you…I gave you my strength when you needed it…Misty would have killed you…You know this…You know I'm your only real friend…I love you…

"You can be beautiful…You can have any man you want…You can have dozens of men…I know all your secret desires…I know all your fantasies…I know what you do when you're alone with your magazines…I know everything about you…You don't have to be ashamed…Come to me, Cindy…We'll dance together…The whole world will be our ballroom…Come dance with me…Don't you want to dance?"

The beautiful woman in Cindy's vision opened up her arms in acceptance, unjudging, open-minded acceptance, and Cindy took a step forward, but this time she wanted to.

Part of Cindy wanted to run from this murder basement, but another part of her wanted what she knew she could never have…to be the most popular girl in school…to date Brandon Marsh…but more than that. In the end, high school was small change…If she stepped into this circle, she could actually be famous…a star…She could act and sing and dance in front of the camera…be on the big screen…have her own star on the Hollywood Walk of Fame…

She sobbed as she gave in to the dark pull and admitted to herself what she really wanted in life, finally accepting what it was that she needed, and through that acceptance, join as one with her new friend.

There was nothing more to think about.

She stepped into the center of the pentagram to join the bodies of her classmates.

The blood of the slain girls sprayed upwards from the bodies to bathe Cindy in a sanguine fountain, springing from the floor here and there and everywhere, spraying her until there was nothing left of those bodies but dried and withered husks, desiccated mummies that looked like they'd been dead for decades.

The blood ran down her skin and soaked into her once-white T-shirt and her grey sweatpants, and she felt it draw into her, all of it, drawing into her skin and clothes until it vanished, but not just into her clothes and skin, but into her soul, deep down into her soul, and she loved the dark power it granted.

She drank all of it in, drinking it in through her skin and hair, and her mouth opened in a gaping smile, gulping in what entered her mouth, gulping it down as fast as she could.

The lights popped above her as the concrete walls in this large and empty basement set aflame, burning without heed to the laws of thermodynamics, the heat and flames everywhere around her.

She fell to her knees to the concrete floor to perch precariously above the withered husks that had once been her classmates.

Her hands shook as she brought them up to her face. Her vision was suddenly blurry, so she removed her thick glasses, and then her vision was perfect.

"I…I can see…" she stammered.

She looked down and gaped as her almost non-existent breasts instantly swelled beneath her shirt, growing out to a perfect size, and then her hips widened, granting her an hourglass shape, the ecstasy of this transformation overtaking her.

She was like a closed flower that looked ugly underneath, but then those closed petals had opened, and now she was showing all her beauty to the world. She knew her face was gorgeous now, because *she* was beautiful now, *her*, the skinny dork with the soda-bottle glasses.

She was beautiful in the sense of what *others* considered beautiful, and she would have held a tinge of regret over this in the past, because it was a loss of identity, a loss of who she was, but now?…No, this was what she wanted, what she had always *really* wanted, and she fully accepted this.

But there was more to come, much more, something horrifying yet bewitching all the same, for her other half had her own secrets.

Cindy could see her own future now, and she could see all the secrets only her mutual "friend" could see, dark secrets that were now part of her forever, so she let out her other half. She let out Allerakth the Dancer because she knew now that this dark force was her only *real* friend.

Black nails grew upon the tips of her fingers as she felt the skin on her forehead burst open with sudden pain. She reached up to feel the two long black horns that had grown out from there, and then black wings erupted from her back and through her shirt to unfold outwards, large, ebon bat wings that spread out in an eight-foot span. She felt a long and black, barbed tail poke up and out from her sweatpants as it snaked up and around to show itself in her surprised vision.

Cindy laughed long and loud as the tears rolled down her face and the fire spread around her, her mouth wide open with that crazed laughter, her new fanged canines glistening in the light of the demonic flames roaring away in this terrifying murder basement.

The withered bodies before her caught aflame, and yet she did not feel that fire, for it could not burn her, and she laughed as she cried at the same time, a dual spike of conflicting emotions that was her life and always had been.

Nothing could stop her now. No one could hurt her, and she would never be unpopular again.

*****

Misty's home burned away as the fire department was busy trying to put out that blaze, but there was not much left of the house…or anything in it.

Cindy stared up at the paramedic as the man placed an oxygen mask over her narrow face.

"It's going to be okay, sweet heart," said the paramedic. "You're going to be all right. It's a miracle you escaped without any burns. You've just got a little smoke in you. You've been breathing in smoke, but you'll be all right. Just a little smoke in you."

She silently nodded once at him as she was carried into the back of the ambulance on a stretcher.

Of course, she already knew things were going to be all right. In fact, they were going to be better than all right from now on, because she was finally beautiful, an undiscovered star waiting to burst her light upon the night sky. Yes, things were going to be incredible, because she was now a dancer, and the world was her ballroom.

#6…ARK LIGHT

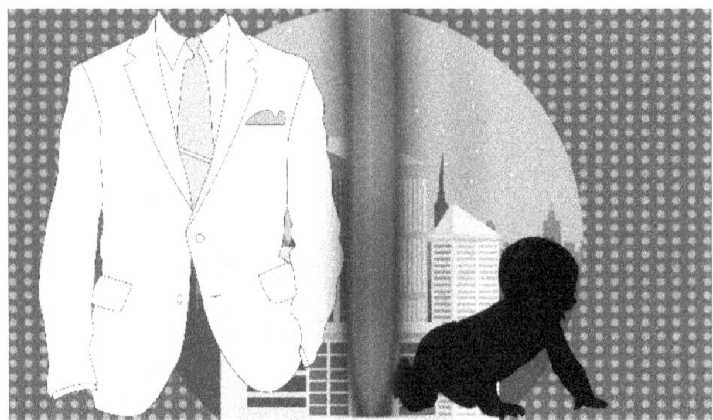

No crisis is too big for the superior man.

Pendleton Hartwood was the superior man. He was a multibillionaire, he was in his early forties, and he owned the largest company for cutting-edge technology in the world. He had acquired many smaller companies in his time, absorbing them into a greater whole like some amorphous, carefully-calculating, Ayn Rand amoeba, and now he led those companies as their admiral in his vast fleet of collections, therefore making him the superior man.

Unfortunately, one particular woman in his high-rise office was making his life quite miserable at the moment. He owned many high-rises and many offices around the world, but this particular office and high-rise happened to be infested with this annoying female at the moment. Honestly, there were times when he wanted to make his ex disappear on a permanent basis, but there were far too many eyes on him to make that happen, even with his vast wealth and power.

Nevertheless, he would deal with her, because he was Pendleton Hartwood, and he was, after all, the superior man.

"So, after your new bimbo graduates high school," said his ex, "then maybe she'll grow a brain that resides above the belt line. Then she'll see what a worthless piece of—"

"Leave Dotty out of this, Patricia," warned Pendleton.

"Or what?" asked his ex, Patricia. "I suspect the only reason you keep her around is as a life preserver in case one of your yachts sinks. I'm sure those fake boobs can float."

Pendleton could see Dotty shaking a little, but the young blonde wasn't going to say anything to his ex. No, Pendleton had deliberately instructed her not to, and unlike Patricia, she was well-trained not to argue with him. He'd handpicked Dotty as his girlfriend, making doubly sure she was an appropriate trophy that did not talk back…He'd learned the first time.

"There's no reason to go after Dotty," sighed Pendleton. "You're getting fifty billion in the settlement. That's more than enough for the likes of you."

Of course, this comment did not sit well with Patricia. Her face swirled into a pool of semi-confused rage, but she doused him with vitriol whenever he spoke anyway. She simply didn't get him.

"For the likes of me!" she hissed. "What is *that* supposed to mean!"

"It means you can take *my* money and go do your welfare philanthropy thing or whatever it is you like to waste working people's wealth on," he said dryly.

"Working people!" screeched Patricia. "*Working* people! You've never worked a day in your life, you worthless para—"

"Enough," sighed Pendleton. "What is it she really wants, Randall?"

Patricia's lawyer handed him the documents in question.

"Miss Hartwood-Morgan's interests lie in shares of Hartwood Technologies," said the stoic bald man in the grey suit.

"You're not getting any shares in H.T., Patricia," said Pendleton with a simple shake of his head. "I own the majority of shares in *my* company that *I* founded, and there is no court of law that will hand you any in the divorce settlement. And in case you want to mention parasites, you're being generously rewarded with a good chunk of *my* money simply for me putting a ring on your finger. Fifty billion is more than enough to satisfy any judge."

"You smug, son of a—!" she began, but her lawyer interrupted her with his own observation, something that cut straight to the chase.

"We know about your research in para-dimensional energy, Mr. Hartwood," said Randall. "We know about the testing facility in Beijing."

"So that's what this is really about," sighed Pendleton. "You want in on the ground floor, do you?"

"There is supposed to be some sort of energy test today?" asked Randall.

"Yes, but this has nothing to do with Patricia," frowned Pendleton. "The testing facility is running a small test to see how well our new energy generator performs. Our D-energy generator taps into a previously untapped energy source…other universes…*I've* made this happen, *I'm* the one who pulled this beyond science fiction, and it's *my* vision, something that will win *me* the Nobel Prize. As I said before, this has nothing to do with Patricia, so she is not entitled to any credit."

"No, you meathead," replied Patricia in visible disgust. "I don't want credit! No, you need to have some common sense! What you're doing is incredibly irresponsible and dangerous! I don't want credit; I want you to stop delving into things that could destroy the entire plan—"

But she was cut short yet again, this time by Pendleton's new other-half.

"Why don't you just leave?" asked Dotty. "Just go. Leave us alone."

The young blonde had leaned forward slightly upon the white couch she was currently sitting upon, and now she had opened her mouth in spite of Pendleton's training. He couldn't blame her for wanting to tell off his ex, though. Patricia had that effect on pretty much everyone.

His ex once again turned her ire upon his girlfriend.

"Oh, so it speaks!" she said angrily. "I'm surprised your lips haven't been welded shut by injections!"

This was pointless. It was clear Patricia's rage was currently fueled by jealousy, because he was, after all, Pendleton Hartwood, richest man in the world, and he was now positive that his ex-wife was fuming over his acquisition of a new girlfriend. That's what this was really about. It wasn't about shares in Hartwood Technologies or his research in D-tech.

Of course, he didn't understand what all of the fuss was about. He'd waited an entire week after the breakup before hitting the dating scene again. That was an acceptable length of time, right?

"Dotty, you don't have to talk to her," said Pendleton. "I have an army of lawyers for that."

"You can't hide behind them for—" began his ex.

She was cut short again by the solid ringing of a phone, specifically Pendleton's phone, and considering the nature of the ringtone, it was a call he could not afford to miss. That tone was one of dire warning, a kind of "DEFCON" alarm for his own company.

He held up one index finger before picking up his phone and swiping it in order to answer the call. This stalling gesture of a single digit further enraged Patricia, but her anger would have to wait.

"Yeah, go," he spoke into his phone.

"This is Anita Carlson, head of the Energy Research Dep—" came a female voice.

"I know who you are," replied Pendleton. "The better question is obvious. Do you know what this phone is for?"

"Yes," said the woman quickly. "I don't have any time to explain. You have to head to the Lot-B bunker now. I and lead scientist Uwe Herrmann are already here. It's the only shelter that we've completely proofed against radiation."

Pendleton turned white at this. He had no idea what was going on, but his first thought was an incoming nuclear strike. Whatever the case, there was no time to waste.

"On it," he said, and then he hung up.

He studied the three people in his office for a few seconds. He needed to get to his Lot-B bunker right away, but the call had shaken him, and for the first time in his life, he did not know what to think.

"What's the matter with you?" asked Patricia. "You look like you've seen a ghost."

He looked up at his parasitic ex and shook his head in order to clear his mind. He had to get to the Lot-B bunker, but he certainly didn't need her tagging along.

"Something's come up," he said in a shaky voice. "Dotty, darling, we have to go. We'll have to continue this meeting later."

"Oh, no, you're not bolting on me now!" cried Patricia. "I'm not finished with you yet!"

Lot B was across from this building, a short drive or a brisk walk depending upon how you looked at it, but that meant the clock was ticking, so he did not have time for this.

He reached forward and hit his intercom button.

"Security," he said quickly.

"Hey!" cried Patricia. "What are you doing!"

"I don't have time for you," he said firmly. "I'm leaving. Either leave this building now or be dragged out."

"Mr. Hartwood, I think we can come to a more civil—" started Patricia's lawyer, Randall.

He was also cut short, but not because of any verbal interruption. No, Pendleton was quite sure that the bald man in the grey suit would have finished his statement were he able to.

A bright red light shone down from nowhere, penetrating the ceiling from above, and it speared through the top of Randall's bald pate, immediately ending the man's sentence. Randall closed his eyes and cried out in both fear and pain as that light seared straight through him, and all Pendleton could do was watch in surprised horror.

Patricia's lawyer de-aged...enyouthened?...He became younger and younger by the second, those seconds less than ten—Pendleton couldn't tell—but Randall became a squalling baby in nothing flat, just a babe covered by a suit way too big for him, and then that naked babe was sucked right up into the light, leaving just a pile of empty clothes behind.

Pendleton, his ex-wife, and his new girlfriend all stared at the pile of clothes in blinking disbelief for a brief moment, and then Patricia screamed, and then Dotty screamed as well, and their inane shrieking finally jolted Pendleton back into some working semblance of reality.

Two burly security guards in grey shirts burst through the office door, guns drawn, ready to blast away, but they didn't make it five feet in before two beams of light speared through the roof to strike them both through the tops of their heads. They were babies in mere seconds, and then they were gone, mere infants drawn up through the roof to pass through solid ceiling as if they were ghosts.

"MOVE!" shouted Pendleton.

He yanked up Dotty and pulled her toward the door, stopping only briefly to snatch up one of the missing security guards' pistols. This was the mistake people always made in the movies, never arming themselves when in a bizarre crisis such as this, and Pendleton, being the superior man, did not wish to make such a mistake, so he snatched up a pistol and bolted, bolting exactly as Patricia had originally warned him not to.

Of course, in light of the circumstances, her original decision had changed.

"Don't you leave me behind!" screeched Patricia from behind him, and she *was* behind him, exactly where she belonged, because truthfully, he wanted to leave her there.

He had a quick flash of cruelty, an ember of thought dedicated to turning around and putting a bullet in one of her legs, but he tossed that thought out as quickly as it had come. He couldn't afford to slow down anyway, so it was best to just ignore her. He'd deal with her later if necessary.

He pulled Dotty along as the young blonde cried out in terror for a few brief seconds, mostly at the beams of lights searing through the ceiling to catch employees running around the three of them in a chaotic panic, spearing through these headless chickens in order to de-age?...enyouthen?...babify?—yes—*babify* them.

By some strange miracle, Pendleton had not been struck as of yet, and this was a good thing, because he did not know what was going on, and he did not know if those affected and taken were dead or just abducted…He'd never seen anything like this, not even in science-fiction tropes.

"We've got to get down to the street!" he barked. "We'll have to take my personal elevator and hope we're not babified on the way down!"

They dashed across several large office spaces filled with cubicles in order to get to his private elevator. Only he had the keycard for that anyway.

A woman in a dark-blue, tight-fitting business skirt and vest, her shirt a white button up, stumbled in front of them as she was pushed from behind by another panicking employee. Pendleton was going to tell this nameless corporate tool to move, but he never got the chance to.

The woman had her smartphone up to her ear, but she stumbled as she was pushed from behind, and she dropped that phone as a beam of light speared her right through the head. She closed her eyes and screamed, shrinking and shrinking in on herself until she was yet another mewling babe, and then she was gone, just like Randall, the security guards, and everyone else he'd seen get zapped up.

Still, it was an off-putting sight to see, even for a superior man like Pendleton Hartwood.

Nevertheless, opportunity was opportunity. The more people in the water, the less chance the shark would eat *you*.

He hopped over the vanished woman's clothes and yanked Dotty along, briefly turning to see his ex trailing after them, a look of stark terror upon the woman's normally stern face. This gave him a slight chuckle, as he had never seen that look upon Patricia's acerbic face before, and this reminded him that she was, after all, only human and not entirely the caustic altruistic parasite she normally displayed to the public.

Beams of light seared through the ceiling to zap people and babify them as Pendleton weaved to and fro through desks and around victims in a desperate dash to make it to his own personal elevator. He didn't actually know any of these people's names, so he simply made them up as he went along, tagging fake job positions to them as well.

There went Portly Dan Gearman, head of regional sales, face like a clock…There goes Boring Bob from accounting, R.B.F. Margaret from advertising, Bouncing Breasts Betty from—No, wait…He knew Betty. She was actually one of his secretaries, Sara…Had been anyway. She'd been hot, and no surprise, she'd turned into a pretty cute baby. Hopefully, the process hadn't hurt her too much. If she wasn't dead, she could always grow up with that big beautiful rack again…He had some sympathy after all.

He pulled Dotty along to the elevator, Patricia trailing behind them. He quickly swiped his keycard through the pass lock and waited on baited breath as the elevator doors slid open.

"What are you doing!" yelled Patricia. "Get moving, you idiot!"

His ex pushed past them both in a mad rush, entering the elevator before the doors were completely open, but this caused Pendleton to stumble into Dotty.

"Patty, you bi—!" he began, but a beam of light cut him short.

A bright spear of light seared through Dotty's chest, right between the lowcut top of the expensive white dress he'd graciously bought for her, right between her gorgeous and quite squeezable breasts, one of the qualities on a short list of qualities he'd chosen her for in the first place. Patricia had been wrong about Dotty's bust, of course…They were all natural, home grown without a hint of silicone.

Pendleton cut short his own protest upon this new development. He pulled Dotty into the elevator out of sheer protective instinct, though why he had done so, he did not know. It was certainly unlike him. It was survival of the fittest in the business world, and making mistakes that put you in the line of fire was definitely an occupational hazard he could not afford, especially now.

Nevertheless, he pulled Dotty out of the beam of light and into the elevator, hitting the ground floor button in one fluid motion of semi-perfect timing. The doors shut, there was a brief pause as the elevator began to move, and then they were on their way.

"Pendy?" asked Dotty in a horrified voice, but her voice sounded off, higher-pitched than normal.

He looked over to his new girlfriend, but she was shorter now, her clothes loose upon her skinny frame, her face that of a young teen, probably thirteen or fourteen.

"Geez, Pendleton, I knew you liked them young, but this is ridiculous," said Patricia.

Naturally, her comment did not sit well with him, not after this, so he glared at his ex, a stare of imminent death that would have stopped a charging rhino…Oh, yes, he'd definitely had enough of her.

"This is all your fault!" he yelled.

Of course, Patricia looked completely taken aback.

"We're under attack!" she said in flabbergasted reply. "I didn't send down these beams of light, you moron! What is the matter with you!"

"You stampeded past us like a dumb animal to get into the elevator!" cried Pendelton. "Because of you, Dotty got hit!"

"You were just standing there like an idiot!" yelled Patricia. "What was I supposed to do! Stand around and wait to die!"

"Yes, you stupid hag!" yelled Pendleton in return.

"Stop!" cried his now ex-girlfriend.

Yes, Dotty was now his *ex*-girlfriend. It wasn't like he could date a teenybopper, so it appeared his short stint with Dotty was now over.

He and his ex-wife turned to stare at the now de-aged young lady.

"We can't fight right now!" said Dotty. "We have to find somewhere safe to go."

Patricia's normally stern face worked its way through a storm of visibly conflicting emotions before settling upon a look of focused determination.

"You're right," she sighed. "And for what it's worth, I'm sorry this happened to you, Dotty; I really am. I am so, so sorry…Look on the bright side, though. Now you get to be young a few years longer. That's something no one else gets to do."

"If we even make it out of this alive," said the young blonde.

"We'll make it," said Patricia. "We have to try."

"I…I don't know," said Dotty. "Let me just say…I just wanted to say that I…I'm not a bad person, Patty."

"Oh, I know," sighed Patricia. "Don't worry about that. I wasn't mad at you. My anger was misplaced. It's not your fault what's going on between Pendleton and I."

Dotty's young teen face shriveled up in despair in spite of Patricia's encouraging comment.

"What's the matter, hon?" asked Patricia.

"I don't know what to do now," said Dotty. "I'm not even old enough to vote anymore…What should I do? I don't know what to do!...You'll help me, won't you, Pendy?"

"I'll…think of something," he said after a few seconds.

"I'll help you, hon, even if he doesn't," said Patricia.

"I said I'd think of something," said Pendleton in a flat tone.

Boy, was this awkward. He was going to have to break up with Dotty, but he had liked her a lot, especially that perfect body of hers, so…he didn't want to just send a text or an email or a tweet or something. It was going to be a real letdown for her anyway. He didn't want to break her heart, but she wasn't even old enough to drive now, so what could he do?

God, she didn't even have real breasts anymore.

Of course, she'd be back to a legal age in a few years, so there was no reason to leave her behind. He had considered her the perfect dating material anyway, so five or six years, though a wait, was not unreasonable…No, come to think of it, he did not need to leave her behind.

But that was not important right now. No, what was important was the obvious: he had to get to his Lot-B bunker. He now knew *why* he needed to be somewhere radiation proof, even though his researchers had not filled him in on that little detail, but…yeah, that mystery had been solved.

The elevator stopped on the ground floor.

By yet another miracle, none of them had been hit with a beam of light on the way down, so now the real race could begin…

They had to make it to the Lot-B bunker, and considering the chaos of what was going down, they were probably going to have to travel on foot. It would take too long to get to his car in Lot A just to drive over to Lot B. That didn't make any sense, because the lots were not connected. Otherwise, he'd just cut through Lot A.

"We're going to have to make a run for it," said Pendleton in grim realization. "Get ready to follow me, Dotty. We've got to make it to my Lot-B safehouse. That's the only one I've got in this area that's radiation proof."

The door opened, and he poked his head out to view yet more of the chaos surging out of control as people ran in a mad panic. Whatever was going on was not just limited to the top floors, no. No, down here people were still like ants under a magnifying lens. Beams of light were still coming down, still spearing down through every floor to babify and snatch people up.

"Come on!" he yelled as he pulled Dotty forward.

He and Patricia surged forward from the elevator, but Dotty's narrow wrist slid from his grasp. He and his ex-wife had already moved ten feet forward before Pendleton realized he did not have Dotty with him.

He turned to see what was holding her up, but the very young blonde was still in the elevator, unmoving, not budging an inch.

"My clothes are too big for me," said Dotty. "I don't think I can make it, Pendy…Not like this."

He looked down at her sad and skinny, quite unfilled-out figure. Her adult clothes were hanging off of her narrow frame in a bare semblance of dress.

"Come on, honey!" exclaimed Patricia. "We'll think of something! We've got to try!"

She stepped forward to go back to the elevator, but the now young teen Dotty quickly pressed the up button on the elevator.

"You go on without me," said Dotty. "It's okay, Patty…I wish we could have been friends."

And then the doors closed.

Patricia banged on those doors for a few brief seconds before Pendleton pulled her away.

"We have to get her!" she screeched, but he knew it was too late for that.

"There's no time!" he barked. "She made her choice!"

Of course, he did not know why he was arguing with Patricia at this moment anyway.

He decided then and there to ignore and/or abandon his ex-wife, preferably both, so he made a run for it, but she followed him, doggedly pursuing him without mercy.

"You coward!" she shrieked. "How could you leave her behind!"

They weaved around more screaming people as beams of light razed down from the ceiling. It was hit or miss now, a bingo parlor of babification, and Pendleton did not want to be caught by a winning number. It was one game he did not want to win.

He made his way to the glass doors that were the exits and entrances to this cyclopean building.

"Pendleton!" screeched Patricia. "You're going to pay for every selfish decision you've ever made!"

"Oh, shut up," he grunted.

He pulled open one of the sets of glass double doors and ran out onto the walk, but Patricia was still right behind him.

"Pendleton!" she yelled. "You come back here!"

He ignored her. He had to get to the Lot-B bunker, and he did not have the time or the patience for this shrieking harpy.

The sky was unusually dark for this time of day, but that was irrelevant, because he still had more than enough light to see the pure insanity raging out of control around him. There were people in a panic all over the street, cars crashing everywhere as people were de-aged and sucked up through their car roofs, and just mayhem in general. Honestly, he didn't have time for any of it.

He made his way down the street, his ex-wife right behind him. She was like a toxic glue you couldn't rub off no matter what you tried. It was really annoying, but he couldn't even deal with that at the moment. Right now, he was just trying to survive. If the world didn't have the superior man, what did it have?

He ran his way to Lot B, and it was a good thing he was in decent shape. He'd kept up his athletic health simply to foster his own image, but it appeared that this physical waste of time had not been such a waste of time after all. It was all cardio now.

This off employee parking lot held some secrets, and his underground bunker was one of them. He had a bunker installed in every location he owned, and he had three here, but Safehouse B was the only one that was up to code for this situation…

If he lived through this attack, he was definitely switching contractors.

He ran into the darkness of the parking lot, that underground garage lit by dim fluorescent lighting. He knew where to go, so he cut across parked cars to make a beeline toward the red doors that led down even further, doors that mimicked a service room, because he did not want others to know he had a safehouse here.

There was just one problem as he came upon that set of double red doors…There was a homeless person in his way.

The filthy old man in stained rags saw him coming, too. He was just going to have to ignore this parasite on society and make his way in. Besides, he still had the gun he'd picked up.

"I told everyone they were watching us!" yelled the old man. "I warned them! They've been watching us, and now they're here!"

"Out of my way!" cried Pendleton.

He pushed past the filthy bum and pulled out his keycard. He never did understand why people chose to live without homes when they could simply be wealthy like him. It just didn't make sense.

"They came from the stars!" said the old bum in agitated excitement. "I've seen them! They've been watching us for years, and now they're here! They've come to collect us! That's what they're doing!"

Patricia jogged up behind them just as Pendleton swiped his keycard through the security lock.

"They've finally come!" said the homeless man. "They've finally come to take us away! They're saving us from our own foolishness!"

Pendleton eyed the old man, shook his head in disgust, and then said the first thing that had come to his mind.

"Why aren't you living off your investments?" he asked.

"Seriously!" exclaimed Patricia.

Pendleton yanked open the red doors, and naturally his ex-wife dodged underneath his arms to enter into the sloping tunnel beyond. He was going to say something to this obnoxious and intrusive hag, but he was grabbed from behind by the filthy old bum.

"Didn't you hear me!" cried the homeless man. "They're going to save us!"

"Get off me!" yelled Pendleton.

"You can't run!" exclaimed the old man. "There's nowhere *to* run!"

They struggled for a bit, a tug-of-war between safety and crazy, but Pendleton did not have the time or the patience for this. He still had the gun he'd picked up, so he pulled that pistol from his suit pocket without any further hesitation.

He fired two rounds into the old man's guts, a "BANG! BANG!" that reverberated around the lot and hurt his ears.

The filthy old bum went down with a muffled cry, his weathered lips partly open, blood seeping from those cracked twin lines.

Patricia was at Pendleton's side in a heartbeat.

"You…You shot him…" she said in stark, audible surprise.

"It was either him or me," said Pendleton grimly.

A light speared down from above and lanced through the old man.

Pendleton watched in morbid fascination as the bullets he'd just put in this disgusting old man popped out of the wino to roll across the pavement, and then the old homeless man was babified, shrunk down to yet another mewling babe. He was gone a second after that, sucked up into the light to phase through the ceiling, onward and upward to…wherever, who knew.

There was no time to waste. It was clear these assailants could reach down anywhere in order to snatch people up, so he had to double time it in order to get down to the bunker.

Pendleton pushed aside his ex and ran for a parked red tram at the side of this long and wide hallway that sloped down into the darkness underneath this city. He hopped in the tram, turned the key that was still in the ignition, and started forward just as his ex hopped into the seat next to him.

He pushed down on the pedal to get this little tram moving, though its speed was far slower than he'd have liked.

"You shot him," said Patricia in a dazed tone. "You shot that poor old man, Pendleton."

"And?" he asked. "That crazy bum would've gotten us both killed. You're lucky I shot him, Patricia."

She winced at the mention of her own name, but she said nothing more, and he considered that silence a godsend.

They headed down the sloped tunnel and into a longer tunnel, and at the end of that tunnel was the bunker door. He just hoped he could make it there in time.

His bunker was more like a vault for humans, a safe storage space where he could wait out any disaster, precisely why he'd had it built. If this attack didn't count as a threat that was bunker-worthy, then nothing did.

They rode down the hallway at a comfortable golf-cart speed, as fast as his stupid tram could go, but definitely faster and less tiring than if he had made a run for it.

He stopped in front of the bunker door and hopped out of the tram, Patricia right behind him, stuck to him like that toxic glue he had so appropriately thought of as a descriptor for her just minutes earlier.

Pendleton swiped his keycard through the electronic lock and waited as the seals on the door hissed open.

"What is this place?" asked his ex.

"Not for you," he muttered.

"What was that?" asked Patricia with alarm in her eyes.

He ignored her as he stepped into *his* radiation-proof safehouse.

The door to the bunker sealed shut behind him as Patricia made her way in alongside him, and despite the fact that his ex was with him in here, he finally felt some modicum of relief over the strange assault on humanity that was currently taking place outside. He felt much safer in here. Whether it actually protected him or not was another story, but for now, he would believe it would.

The bunker first consisted of the main room, which contained a circular area of monitors and tech equipment meant for viewing the outside world. Then there was the rest of the bunker, and that rest of the bunker started with a hallway, a hallway that led off to bedrooms, a small water storage and purification plant, an underground greenhouse garden, a power room for electrical generation, and a food storage room, along with a normal shower and toilet/sewage area.

These bunkers were all the same, all designed the same way, but the problem was in the contracting, because it was clear this one was not quite finished, mainly because he had "upgraded" it recently to be perfectly radiation proof. This new radiation protection had just been developed last year, but his company had not had time to upgrade all of his facilities, so he had placed priority on bunkers like this one. At least that little feature was completed here.

Nevertheless, he would figure out the status of the place in a second, because that was priority number one.

He was met by two of his employees as he entered the main room of his bunker, the ones who had contacted him via his hot-phone, Anita and Uwe, though he could not remember their last names off the top of his head.

Anita was an overweight black woman, while Uwe was an elderly German gentleman, but why they were here in his bunker and how they knew what was going on, he did not understand, nor did he care. Pendleton wanted answers, and he wanted them now.

"What in the hell is going on out there!" he demanded. "Do you know! Does either one of you know!"

"We've been here since we arrived just before the call we made to you, Mr. Hartwood," said Anita. "This bunker isn't completely finished, so the feeds are down. We don't know what's going on locally, so we've just been waiting for your arrival…We do have an assessment of the situation on a USB thumb drive—"

"A USB thumb drive?" asked Pendleton. "What is this, 2005? Just lay it on me. What's the status of this bunker? Where are we at in terms of survival here? How long can we stay down here?"

"As you know, this bunker is still in the process of being stocked," said Uwe. "I'd say we have six months down here at the most with five people."

"Mmm hmm, mmm hmm," nodded Pendleton. "I think I can stretch that length of time."

"How so?" asked Anita.

Pendleton withdrew his acquired pistol, pointed it squarely at his two technicians, and motioned toward the door.

"I think reducing the number of people within this facility should, in fact, lengthen the survival time within it," he said firmly.

"What!" cried Anita.

"Out the door," he sighed. "Don't make me shoot you. I've already had to put a couple of rounds in someone else on the way here."

"You can't do—" started Anita.

"I own this bunker, and this is about survival now," said Pendleton. "I suggest you leave now before I shoot you. You might have enough time to find somewhere safe."

"Pendleton…" said Patricia in an anxious tone.

"Wait!" said Uwe. "If we can just get the feeds running, we can see how advanced the leak is from Beijing, and then we can—"

Pendleton aimed center mass at Anita and then pulled the trigger. The gunshot was ear shattering within the enclosed space of the bunker, Patricia shrieked, and then the heavy-set black woman that was Pendleton's employee fell to the safehouse floor while clutching her right side.

It took a few seconds for their hearing to return, and of course, after those few seconds, there was no other sound than Anita's shocked and terrible moans of pain.

Pendleton leveled his gun at the old German technician.

"I suggest you pull her through that door and go look for help," he said. "Otherwise, I'll have to put you down as well."

There was no more argument from Uwe.

The older gentleman hefted the heavy-set black woman from up underneath her armpits and dragged her to the door. He took a few seconds to open the door, his old face etched with both fear and anxiety, and then he pulled the hefty woman through that ominous aperture.

Anita's cries of pain did nothing to sway Pendleton. He had already made up his mind at this point. It was survival now, and he was the superior man, so all subordinates were expendable.

"You can't do this!" said Uwe. "We'll die out here! There's no more time!"

"Not my problem," shrugged Pendleton.

Lights speared down from the ceiling just outside the door. One seared straight through Uwe, and the look on the old technician's face was one of genuine surprise as he stared down at his own shrinking hands in strange wonder.

"What is thi—?" was all he got to say before he began to babble in baby speech.

Pendleton watched the invasive light simultaneously de-age and heal Anita at the same time. His bullet popped out of her, she shrank down to nothing, and then she was gone, leaving behind nothing but a set of plus-sized technician clothes.

He stared at the two piles of clothes left behind and shook his head in both confusion and disgust. Whatever was going on was beyond him, but it was clear the lights from above could not reach down into this bunker, so that was all that mattered right now.

"Why did you do that?" asked Patricia, her voice filled with audible horror.

"Because it's either them or me," sighed Pendleton. "I thought we went over this already."

"That's so heartless…" trailed his ex.

It was clear she was in shock. Things were different now that she didn't have her lawyer or her own social-media circle to back her up. That was going to make what he was about to do next so much easier.

He put his acquired pistol in his pocket, pulled back on Patricia's carefully styled hair, reached down beneath her business skirt from behind, and pulled up on the top of her white panties. He pulled in two different directions at once, ensuring that he had both a good grip and an exceptionally painful wedgie at the same time.

She shrieked in both pain and surprise as he dragged her to the opening of the bunker, but she had no sense to defend herself before he had pitched her through the opening and onto the two piles of empty clothes.

She landed hard on the pavement outside the bunker door.

"Pendleton!" she screeched. "You son of a—!"

A beam of light speared right through her, right through her back, right through her spine.

Pendleton watched in supreme satisfaction as his parasitic ex shrank within her own clothes, squealing all the way, squealing like the money-sucking sow-pig she was, squealing until she was squalling as a baby, and then she was gone too, sucked up into the light.

He shut the door, brushed his hands together as if rubbing off dirt, and then smiled. Life was truly satisfying sometimes, especially if you were the superior man.

He stared over at the line of monitors and spied the small USB thumb drive resting inconspicuously upon a computer table. Honestly, though, he was tired, exhausted all of the sudden, so he'd look at it later.

He took his time to wander back toward a bedroom, grabbed some night clothes made specifically for him from a wooden dresser—this was *his* bunker after all—and made his way to the shower room. He quickly took a hot shower, dressed in his night clothes, and made his way back to a bedroom where he collapsed in bed, his worries, for the moment, behind him.

✱✱✱✱✱

He snorted himself awake, looked at the electronic clock on the night stand next to him, and realized that six hours had gone by.

He hopped out of bed, took his time dressing, and then walked back into the main room of his safehouse. It was time for him to activate the feeds.

His technicians had made the mistake of believing the feeds were already supposed to be up, but only he had the activation code for them, as he did not activate the full functions in any of his safehouses until they were completed. Now that all undesirable factors were removed from the equation, it was time to fully activate this bunker.

He sat down at one of his computer desks, booted up the PC, and then typed in the necessary code, a random string of numbers and letters that only he knew, and then he typed in his secondary password, "I AM THE SUPERIOR MAN."

The feeds over the last twenty-four hours popped up onscreen. Pendleton watched in awe, fascination, and slight horror at the various news reports detailing the end, the end of the human race.

Huge ships had appeared out of the sky, appearing without warning, appearing in spatial blips of warped time and space from out of nowhere. These massive juggernauts were so large that they darkened the skies here and there, and all attempts to stop them had failed.

Fighter jets from every nation had engaged them, and even nuclear missiles had been launched at these invaders, yet the beams of light that exuded from these huge ships eliminated all threats to them. These beams of light disintegrated hostile inorganic material and subsequently de-aged organic material. It had been a slaughter, if babifying and sucking up people into these ships was considered slaughter.

Honestly, Pendleton had no idea why any race, even an alien one, would use such a strange weapon. Personally, he would have disintegrated the people and left everything else untouched. That would have been the efficient way to acquire resources from an enemy.

Now, of course, there was nothing on any recent feed. There were just empty streets, empty everything, in fact. It appeared that Pendleton had outlasted the human race itself.

"Well, that's a bummer," he sighed.

In retrospect, perhaps he shouldn't have tossed out Patricia. She'd been a little old for reproducing, but at least he could have had some company…If only Dotty hadn't been hit by that ray…Oh, well. C'est la vie.

But a thought occurred to him. Uwe, the old technician, had mentioned something about a leak in Beijing, and that's where Pendelton's energy research facility was located. His team in Beijing was working on para-dimensional energy tapping, and they were supposed to have run a test earlier today…Perhaps that's where these alien invaders had come from, another universe. They certainly weren't local.

"What was he talking about?" muttered Pendelton.

He spied the USB thumb drive out of his left peripheral, snatched it up, and popped it into a USB port. He brought up the one and only file on it, a video of something, and then he played it.

At first, he watched in fascination as his Beijing scientists and technicians started up the first test run for his para-dimensional energy generator earlier in the day. His fascination, however, turned to stark concern as the generator produced a blue light that atomized and burned away organic tissue, that sapphire light erupting in a half-sphere, and that half-sphere grew as it consumed some of the staff. It passed through solid structures with ease, creeping outward at a slow and steady pace.

"I fear this is the end," came Uwe's voice, a latent recording across the file. "This D-energy will consume the Earth within twelve hours, eradicating all life as we know it. The Beijing facility did not use the new radiation proofing Hartwood Research perfected earlier this year.

"We have only just begun to upgrade our facilities, so only a few of our locations have the necessary protection against this disaster. The generator in Beijing has opened a tear in time and space that has been slowed by what little proofing was in the generator room, and the math shows that this tear in space and time…It has a threshold…I believe this tear will close on its own, but not before the human race has been annihilated, not before the Earth itself is destroyed…Only a miracle will save us now…May God help us all."

It occurred to Pendleton that the alien invasion had nothing to do with this energy leak. The invasion was something entirely different, but then his superior brain put all of the pieces together, and those pieces led to a perfect picture of distinct horror…

The aliens had not been abducting the human race on a massive scale.

No, they had not been slaughtering everyone. In fact, these invaders were not invaders at all. They were good Samaritans that had rescued a dying people destined for sudden extinction. The old bum Pendleton had put two rounds in had said these aliens had been watching Earth, so the outsiders from space must have decided to save the human race at the last minute, their eleventh-hour good deed.

What that meant, of course, was that Pendleton had been the one and only human being left behind, a poignant fact that was becoming clearer by the second.

"No…" hissed Pendleton as he flipped through his dead feeds. "No, no, no, no, no, no, NO!"

He flipped to one of his still active feeds for this city. The aliens were long gone, their ships no longer darkening the skies above.

His heart caught in his throat as he viewed the blue light on the horizon, that hellish azure light that was slowly and steadily turning every living thing on Earth to ash.

#7…AND TO ALL A GOOD NIGHT

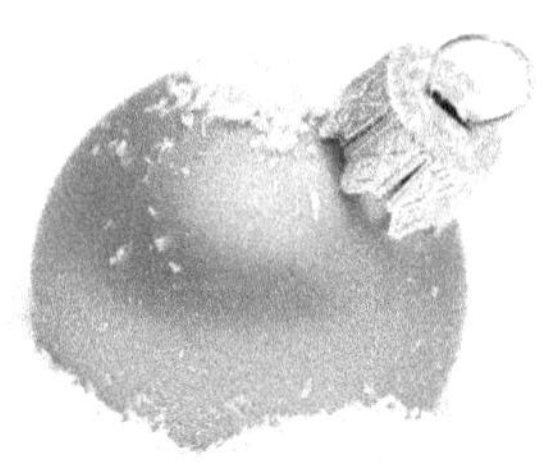

Ah, spreading Christmas cheer.

Dennis crunched through fresh snow, the soles of his thick black Santa boots leaving heavy imprints in that new ivory powder.

Snow always made him think of heroin, but the bitterly cold flakes beneath his feet were much cheaper than the controlled substance and not nearly as fun. Even so, he'd make this alabaster crust run red with blood tonight, staining it a nice sanguine crimson, and *that* would make this winter crap from the sky much more entertaining.

He was dressed as Santa, but the truth was and always had been that he hated Christmas. This holiday was a travesty, a sick joke created by the powers that be, so he railed against whatever divinity might exist, and he would do so with a body count. If God existed, then he was a sadist, so it was only fitting that Dennis laid down some punishment in return, a payback in the form of body parts.

It had been three days and three nights since he'd escaped the Hollister-Kemel Home for the Criminally Insane, but he'd been planning this foray for a long time, for years now. This was *his* time to shine, *his* time to make his mark on the world.

He'd come across an old red fire axe, so he'd stolen a Santa suit right away, smashing through a department store window to get it, and that stupid holiday suit fit him more or less. Now, with his suit and his axe, he was ready to start the bloodshed all over again.

Really, it came down to people being less than nothing. They were a cancer on the Earth, bugs to be stepped on, and so he would, and so it would be done…This was his creed. This was his commandment. He was the new Bible now.

He could still see the faces of the family he'd slaughtered, but those faces didn't haunt him, no. He had reveled in the pain and terror as he'd chopped apart the Mister and Missus, and he had celebrated as he'd buried the axe blade in the skulls of the children, hearing their sweet lamentations before the very end. Those memories, those visions bathed in blood, had kept him going throughout the years.

He'd played possum. That's how he'd escaped. He'd pretended to blend, to be a good boy, but that was the mistake the doctors and nurses and orderlies had made, the mistake in believing him. He was evil, and he wholly embraced that fact, and you could never trust evil, not ever.

But now it was Christmas Eve, and it was nearing midnight. Soon it would be Christmas, and then he would give the greatest gift of all, the gift of carnage, because that was the only thing these mouth-breathing wastes of flesh deserved.

He'd stolen a '54 Buick Estate, made just last year, and he'd driven out to the country, driving out to some back country road that would allow him some privacy before any cops showed up.

Oh, he'd thought about just laying down some havoc in town, but the police would be quick on the ball if any neighbors of his chosen victims spotted him staining the walls red. They'd definitely notice brains on the upholstery.

It was this accursed time of year, this madness of happiness and cheer that drove him even more insane than he already was. No, he absolutely despised Christmas, and he was going to make sure the relatives of this soon-to-be-deceased family were going to hate it too, but not for the same reasons.

That's why he'd picked this house. It was the lights on the outside of the house and the decorations on the winter lawn, the carefully crafted snowmen outside, the warm glow of 60-watt bulbs on the inside, pretty much everything about this two-story house out in the middle of nowhere that ticked him off.

He'd parked down this long gravel road surrounded by thick trees. Yeah, it was cold outside, but it was worth the walk down snow-laden gravel to get here, to get inside this Yuletide derivative, to let the slaughter begin.

The first thing he did was cut the phone lines outside. Obviously, he didn't want anyone on the horn to call out for help, so the first logical step was to eliminate the most expedient way to do that.

The second thing he did was kill both of this family's cars, a simple matter of popping the hoods and removing the spark plugs. He'd made sure not to slam the hoods of the cars shut, though. There was no sense in warning anyone. That would give the Mister of the house time to grab a gun.

He marched up to the front door after that. He was prepared to jimmy the lock if necessary, but as luck would have it, the door was not locked. These rural families felt safe and secure in their isolation, a lie that Dennis knew better than to trust, mainly because of people like him…No one was truly safe. If the Devil wanted you, the Devil took you.

He slipped inside the well-lit living room and looked around. The place looked like every stereotypical Christmas card ever, so burning this place to the ground was becoming a more viable option by the second.

This spacious living room was bedecked by off-white walls and a wood floor, and there was a single off-white couch in the center of that room strategically placed to face toward a TV set. Behind the couch and next to the outside windows was a Christmas tree, presents already beneath it. There were shelves with knickknacks here and there, and there was even a brick fireplace, a cozy fire burning within it, stockings hanging above it.

This place was an affront to the eyes. He was seriously thinking about burning the house to the ground once he was finished here, but then again, that would ruin the screaming art of blood and offal he was about to lay down, so he put that particular thought on hiatus.

He turned to stare at the Christmas tree. It was the standard, family, postcard crap, an atrocity to the mind, so he walked over to it and plucked off one of its red glass Christmas baubles.

He held the gleaming red bauble up to his face and stared into its reflection.

The glass ball brought back a memory, a dark memory, a dark but enjoyable memory from many, many years ago, back when he was a child. He had enjoyed smashing a ball just like this one, smashing it hard with a rock, just like he'd smashed in the skull of the child he'd taken it from.

Another memory floated to the surface, a memory of what he had done to the Missus of the family he'd murdered, a memory of what he'd done to her with a Christmas bauble just like this one.

These were fond memories.

He could see his own warped image within the crimson glass, but there was someone else within the room, another reflection, someone who had somehow and in some way gone unnoticed before.

He chucked the bauble within the stack of presents beneath the tree, making sure the ornament did not break upon anything rigid, because he needed to deal with whoever had suddenly appeared within this eyesore of a room, and he did not want anyone else to awaken yet.

He swiveled to view the man standing near the fireplace, and Dennis readied his axe, his intent steel-clad in his vindication of blood.

There was another Santa in here. There was another Santa in here, probably the Mister, so it was time to supplant that other Santa in the most horrific way possible.

But this Santa was a winner. If he was the master of the house, he was fairly old, older than Dennis would have pegged him to be. The fat man in the red suit was the spitting image of dear Saint Nick, because aside from the outfit, the old man held a jolly round face with a full-white beard, a true ringer for the ancient North Pole elf.

"Up to your old tricks again, Dennis?" said the other Santa. "I think, perhaps, there is a lesson here to be taught, though I fear you will not learn it."

His voice was easy, a strange warmth to it, something Dennis had not been expecting, that voice untinged by fear, unaffected by caution and woe. Furthermore, this Santa had called him out by name, so that settled it right there. The fat stranger in the red suit was going to be first on the dismembered list.

There was nothing more for Dennis to say. No, he simply raised his axe and charged.

There was a flash of light as the other Santa glimmered away into nonexistence. The old ringer exploded in a burst of myriad sparkles, green, red, and white specks that fluttered up the chimney above the heat of flames in the fireplace.

Those flames roared high for a brief second, the heat so intense that Dennis had to back away and shield his face. It was a good thing he was not wearing a fake beard, or it would have caught aflame.

He staggered backwards as the heat forced him to retreat a few steps.

Dennis blinked as he swiveled to stare around the room, searching for the other Santa, but there was no one to be found. There was no one else in here, obviously, so his mind came to the one and only possible conclusion for this new madness.

"It was those drugs," he growled.

It was the new "medication" the doctors had given him at the asylum. Had to be. There was no other explanation. Nevertheless, a seed of doubt planted itself within his chaotic psyche, a flipping switch of sudden and strange belief that he could not seem to ignore.

He walked back to the front door and exited the house. He needed to make sure his head was screwed on straight, such as it was. He could not lose focus now, not now when he was so close to slaughtering his way into the papers again.

He walked out onto the front lawn, that lawn a crisp winter land of alabaster snow, and he stared up at the roof, specifically where the chimney smoke was billowing from the brick exit up top, but there was nothing there, no reindeer, no sleigh, no fat man, nothing.

It was too bad, too. If Saint Nick had been real, Dennis would have reached legend by taking the old man apart at the seams. That would have been something for the little kiddos to cry over.

He was about to reenter the house when he spied the red gleam of glass in the snow, right in the center of the three snowmen ungraciously befouling the front yard of this travesty of a home. That red glass sparkled and taunted by its mere presence, a glass Christmas bauble just like the one he'd tossed into the pile of presents inside, just like the one he'd killed for as a kid, just like the one he had used to torture the previous Missus.

He grunted for a brief second as he walked over to the wayward bauble. He stepped on it with his left boot, feeling the satisfying crunch of red glass as he did.

He noticed movement too late as he started to look back up, the twig arms reaching for him, sharp digits of fire-blackened wood that strained for his unprotected face. He gave a shout without meaning to as lifeless fingers raked across his right cheek, swiftly drawing blood.

He turned to see the warped face of the snowman on his right, the coal eyes bent downwards in rage, the gaping mouth open and full of jagged teeth, like shark's teeth, triangles of serrated white, an impossibility that ravaged his already unstable mind.

Dennis backed away swinging. His axe plowed into the malicious snowman's head, exploding it in a storm of frigid white. The other two snowmen were upon him after that, already moving, their faces wicked caricatures of the holiday cheer normal people were so used to.

He shouted again as his left arm was raked open, his cheap Santa suit rent above the elbow, rent by blackened twig digits sharpened to deadly efficiency at the tips.

He brought the axe head down upon one of those terrible arms and snapped off the twig limb at the elbow.

He chopped and swung with his axe until all three snowmen were piles of white dust, coal bits, carrots, twigs, and old scarves. There was nothing left of them by the time he was finished.

He stood there in the snow for a few seconds, breathing hard, his breath a hot mist that crystalized upon exiting his chapped lips.

Dennis stared down at the mess he had created. There was no Christmas bauble within his vision, no crunch of crimson glass beneath his black boots. It was just him and three piles of wrecked snow.

He could feel the hot blood trickling down his right cheek and the sting of pain within his left arm where his suit was rent.

"Those drugs!" he hissed.

This was all those doctors' fault. Those quacks didn't cure insanity…They created it.

He must have injured himself within his momentary psychotic break. It was clear he was going to have to get it together in order to dish out his own form of Christmas cheer, or his window of opportunity would close.

He trudged back to the front door and walked back inside the house. Hopefully, the Mister and Missus had not awoken due to his inane shouting outside. Now he could only count on them being heavy sleepers, because he needed to catch them off guard.

He quietly shut the front door and listened to the satisfying click of the lock snap in place as he closed the bolt. No one was getting out now, not without unlocking the door first. Oh, they'd struggle to open the door without realizing it was locked, but he'd bury his axe in their backs before they could actually leave.

He chuckled at the thought of this, but that enjoyable thought was swiftly interrupted.

He heard the jingle of little bells and the giggle of a child, and then he turned to view this new intrusion, intent on dealing with it quickly. He had not wanted to start with one of the children, no. He had wanted to start with one of the parents. He'd wanted to butcher them in front of the kiddos…Merry Christmas, you little brats.

He saw the quick image of a child dressed in green and red, a small thing not three feet tall. He watched the child dash through the archway at the other end of the room, opposite the Christmas tree. The little tyke had on a long and pointed stocking hat with small bells upon it, little green tights on him, but this only enraged Dennis further, stoking his bloodlust to vicious levels.

To hell with saving the kids for last. This little abomination was going down first.

He made his way across the room and into the kitchen, following the small child that had ducked out of his vision.

The floor in here was all black and white, checkered in an obscene manner and make, but the kitchen itself was a throwback to another age, a collage of two thick oak tables and a stone oven, something no one anywhere had anymore.

There was dough and gingerbread men laid out upon one of the tables, and the other held a feast fit for a king, a collection of roasted meats displayed like fine treasure across it, including a huge roast turkey, that turkey surrounded by figgy pudding, Christmas cake, and various other foods of holiday make.

"What is all this?" he grunted.

The oven had a hot fire going beneath it, but in front of the oven was the child, or what he had thought was a child.

The little person in front of the stone oven was no more than three feet tall, a tiny thing with pointed ears and a rosy face, this new insanity dressed in the green and red of holiday colors, yet another Christmas delusion he was going to have to deal with.

"Dennis the meanie! He's a big fat weenie!" taunted the little stranger.

Delusion or not…this little sucker was going to die.

Dennis roared in rage as he rushed forward to deal with this new insanity, but the little person stepped away from the oven opening, and flames roared forth from that aperture, a blaze of hell-spawned heat that forced Dennis back toward the table laden with dough and gingerbread.

He cried out as the gingerbread men that were spread across the table sprang upon him. They swarmed him like rats, their little mouths biting into him, tiny fangs of hardened gumdrops sinking into his unprotected flesh.

Dennis flailed and screeched as he tore the demonic gingerbread men from him, but he only had the use of one hand, his right, as his left was currently clutching his axe.

He clumsily tore them off one after the next, but in his struggle, he stumbled toward the other table, the table laden with a feast fit for a king.

That feast was now a nightmare. Everything upon the table was a rotten and slimy mess, the once delectable holiday provision now nothing more than a waste of absolute and foul decay.

The centerpiece upon the table, the great roasted and finely-basted turkey, was now a dried husk of what it had been, and that husk burst open to reveal a sharp array of small bones pointing up toward the ceiling.

He stumbled and fell due to the swarm of unholy gingerbread men currently gnawing on him. Dennis turned his cheek just in time to have it speared in three places upon the ascending turkey bones, three nasty holes in his left cheek, but he had saved his eye, so that was something.

He screamed in rage as he pulled his face up and off the desiccated turkey. His face was a bleeding mess, yes, but one thing was very clear…He was mad now.

He was finally forced to drop his axe so that he could pull off and crush one gingerbread man after the next, and he did just that. It took him a minute of wild flailing, but eventually he crumbled them all to dust.

Well, almost all of them.

One last gingerbread man appeared out of his blind left, the little demon of brown spicy dough appearing upon the first table, this little nightmare wielding a chocolate-chip cookie in its little fingerless right hand. How it could hold a cookie without fingers was beyond Dennis, but that was unimportant. What was important was that it flung the cookie like a deadly disc, and that disc was razor sharp.

Dennis screeched out another yelp of pain as the cookie buried itself in the muscle of his right arm, the small disc tearing right through the fabric of his Santa suit. He pulled out the cookie and charged the little gingerbread horror, snatching it up off the table in a grand sweep of raw fury.

This time he was truly enraged. Dennis bit down into the gingerbread man's upper half, beheading the animated terror in one clean bite. Unfortunately for him, he felt the crunch of glass in his mouth, and then more pain assaulted him.

He spit out blood along with shards of crimson glass, that glass thin slivers of crunched Christmas bauble.

"Dennis the meanie!" came two little voices this time.

He looked up to see two strange little people in green and red tights, their dark hair covered by funny stocking hats, their pointed ears a mocking symbol of the holiday he so hated. These two little gremlins of Christmas cheer had his axe held between them. Yes, they had his axe, that murderous weapon he loved so dearly, and that would not do.

"He's a big fat weenie!" taunted the two thieves.

They ran out the kitchen archway with his slaughtering tool, absconding with it like it was some kind of trophy for a game that only they were playing.

"Come back here!" yelled Dennis in a voice garbled by blood.

He charged after them, ignoring the pain from all of the wounds he had previously suffered. He was bleeding from all of his minor injuries, but those didn't matter. All that mattered was his axe, and he was going to get it, and then he was going to dish out the pain, bringing down the first of that pain upon those two little delusions that had just robbed him.

He ran into the living room again, but the two thieves that had taken his axe were nowhere to be found. In fact, the room was empty of its couch and TV. There was only the Christmas tree now, that accursed Christmas tree with its presents and…

He skidded to a halt at the line of soldiers before him.

A line of at least thirty toy wooden soldiers, each a good six-inches tall, marched forward from in front of the Christmas tree. Dennis watched in strange fascination as these little wooden men in black and red lowered their tiny black rifles and took aim at him.

There was a "PAK! PAK! PAK!" sound as little puffs of smoke erupted from the rifles of the toy soldiers. Dennis felt the sting of tiny musket balls impact him in various places, but this only drove his fury to new heights.

He roared yet again as he rushed forward and stomped with thick black boots upon one soldier after the next. He kicked them across the room here and there, and he even scooped up a couple of them and pitched them into the flames of the fireplace.

He did not stop until every last soldier was a broken and twitching mess.

Dennis fell to one knee and stared at the wood floor beneath him as he felt all of his wounds catch up with him.

He was in severe pain now, weakened from who knew how many injuries, but he did not want to give in. He did not know if what was happening to him was real or not, but he did not want to give in. He hated this holiday with a passion, but he hated the people who worshipped it even more, and those people needed to be slaughtered, chopped apart in a carnage of blood and bone.

"It's not quite as fun when the shoe is on the other foot, is it Dennis?" came a voice, a voice that Dennis had only heard once before.

He looked up at the other Santa and grimaced. This old fat man was standing in front of the Christmas tree, a sad smile on his jolly and bearded face.

"You…" said Dennis as he spat out a wad of blood.

"You were always a dark little boy," said the other Santa. "Your parents were good folk, but you? Yes, you were a disturbed little thing, a dark soul with your dead birds and dead rats you collected and the cats you tortured and killed."

"How do you know that?" grunted Dennis.

"It wasn't until the little Anders boy disappeared that you had finally crossed the line," said the old man in the red suit. "He brought that Christmas bauble in for show and tell, that little red Christmas bauble you wanted so dearly…so that you could smash it…and you did…He's still there, the little Anders boy, his bones covered with slivers of glass, still in the deep woods outside of Green Lake, still waiting to be found."

"You can't know that," said Dennis as he shook his head in denial. "This is a trick…It's those drugs!"

The old fat man in the jolly red suit touched his own plump reddened nose twice with one big black glove.

"I'm the real Saint Nicholas, Dennis," said the man. "This isn't some delusion, nor is it an aftereffect of any medication…No, I'm real, and you know I'm real."

"This is a lie!" yelled Dennis. "This is my own mind playing tricks on me!"

"That would imply that your guilt has finally come to the surface of your psyche, Dennis," smiled this "Santa." "But that can't be, so we both know I'm real."

Dennis shook his head no. He refused to believe in any fat magic man from the sky.

"You're a lie," he growled. "A lie!"

"No," said the other Santa with a shake of his old head. "No, we know I'm real, Dennis. We both know I'm real because of one sad and solitary fact."

Dennis decided to play along. This delusion would eventually end anyway, especially after he chopped it apart. He just needed his axe.

"And what's that?" he grunted. "What fact could possibly make you real?"

"Why, you have no guilt, Dennis," said Santa matter-of-factly. "There's nothing in there *to* come to the surface."

"Is that right?" grinned Dennis. "Then you should know what's coming next."

Delusion or not, he was going to end Christmas for everyone tonight. Chopping apart Santa was going to be fun…Once again, he just needed his axe.

"Did the Coggins family know what was coming?" asked the old man. "No, I think not. You hid your real self away for years after what you did to the Anders boy, but that old bloodlust consumed you over time…as the Coggins, unfortunately, discovered in the most horrific way possible."

Dennis smiled. He'd shoved a red Christmas bauble in the Missus' screeching mouth and had watched her crunch down on that glass, blood running down her chin and lips, and then he'd ended her. Splitting open the Missus' skull and splattering her brains all over the two children's screaming faces was his fondest memory.

"I have no power to mete out divine punishment, Dennis," said Santa with an even sadder smile. "All I have is the power to give gifts to those who are deserving…but there are loopholes to everything…even with the powers that be."

Dennis smiled and gave the old man a slight nod.

"I'll give you a gift," he said with a slight chuckle. "Once I get my axe, you'll get it."

"You hear, but you don't listen," said Santa with a shake of his wizened head. "I'm giving you the only gifts you deserve, Dennis…ones, I think, you will put to immediate use with your 'unique' talents…My first gift to you, of course, is a new axe."

Dennis watched as the two little elves that had stolen his old red fire axe trotted back in from a side room and laid down another fire axe in front of him. This one was brand new, a big red bow tied around the unworn haft, that haft painted white with red stripes in the manner of a candy cane. The two little thieves that had stolen his first axe then trotted off, giggling as they disappeared from view, disappearing back into the side room from whence they came.

Dennis picked up this new axe, put forth a grim smile, and tried to stand. He cried out once from the pain that was coursing through him, pain due to his various injuries, but he managed to stand again through sheer willpower.

"You shouldn't have given me this, Sky Daddy," he grinned. "That was a mistake, Magic Man."

"There's no mistake, Dennis," said Santa. "You'll need that axe for where you're going…You see, my second gift to you is a new home, the home you need, and the home you deserve. I have been given the power to grant this, and it has been a long time in the making."

Dennis grinned and gave a short chuckle, and then he burst into laughter, a loud and insane laughter that he bellowed forth without care, and then he reigned in that insanity, because he had a figment of his imagination to butcher.

"You're done, old man," he said in a dark voice.

He raised his axe high in order to charge. He did not have much energy left, but he had more than enough to finish this farce once and for all.

This other so-called "Santa" raised a red Christmas bauble and displayed it as if it were a prize to be taken.

Dennis stopped his would-be charge as he stared at the reflective holiday ball within the old man's gloved right hand…He could not help it. There was something about that ball that called to him, something that mesmerized him in the mirrored glass.

"Remember this, Dennis?" asked the old fat man. "I believe it is yours."

Dennis stared at the ball. He could see the image of Gerald Anders within that reflective glass, and he could see the rock coming down to split open the boy's skull again and again and again.

"Do you want this, Dennis?" asked Santa.

Dennis could see the faces of the screaming Coggins children as he brought the axe down upon them, first the boy, then the girl. He could see the Mister's head split open, brains splattering, the Missus shrieking…

Dennis slowly nodded a couple of times in agreement of this holiday boon. This reflective bauble was actually a Christmas gift worth having.

"Give it to me," he grunted. "Give it…Give it to me now!"

"Then have it, you shall," said Santa. "A new home is what you need, one you are most deserving of, and this will grant that wish…Enjoy your new home, Dennis. I believe you'll have lots of fun with it…Look again, and you shall see it."

Dennis peered into the reflection within the red glass. He could see flames and distorted, wailing faces, darkness and despair, things both terrifying and grotesque that assaulted his vision.

"What is this?" asked Dennis. "Bring back the memories…I want to see them!"

"Your memories are where they belong," said Santa. "They're only in your head…And now for your second gift. Enjoy your new home, Dennis…Merry Christmas."

The old fat man tossed the glass ball at Dennis's boots.

"NO!" shouted Dennis.

The ball shattered at his feet, crimson shards of glass scattering in slow motion, and then a blaze erupted around him, an explosion of orange and yellow, a pillar of flame that turned him into a living pyre.

Dennis screamed as the pain attacked him all at once, and he fell forward, his new axe clutched within his hands, but the pain ended as he impacted solid earth, hard dirt without a hint of snow…

He did not know what had just happened, but at least he was no longer on fire.

He staggered to his feet as he stared about at the endless expanse of wasteland around him, that wasteland dotted by spigots of flame that erupted from cracks and crevices in the broken ground. The sky above him was a black night covered in roiling storms, and strange shadows flew overhead, those ebon shapes accompanied by the beating of large wings.

He could sense the despair of this infernal place, hear the wailing around him, and it took him no time at all to figure out where he was.

He could feel the intense heat that permeated this new plane of existence, that heat sending waves from the scorched earth beneath his booted feet, and then he saw them, misshapen and ghoulish nightmares in the distance, mockeries of life that had once been human. They staggered toward him with mottled, spindly arms and boney digits ready to tear and flay, naked and chained corpses with a hunger that he could sense so much as see.

Dennis was still in his rent and bloodied Santa suit, and he still had his new axe, his brand-new axe with the striped haft, so he gripped that haft tightly as he marched forward toward the residents of his new and permanent home.

Yes, he knew where he was, but he wasn't scared…No, quite the contrary. He was glad he was here. Now he could chop to his heart's content. He was going to butcher every last thing that moved down here, and that wasn't bragging; it was a fact.

He laughed again as he readied himself for carnage, gripping the haft of his new axe, that red-and-white-striped haft still adorned with a red-ribbon bow.

"MERRY CHRISTMAS TO ALL!" he shouted as he charged into the advancing horde, laughing all the way.

#8…JUPITER IS SEVERED

Being unattached has its risks.

Noah took out his books from his locker as his best friend, Alex Downs, sidled in next to him. Alex held up a science book in his hands, but it was the unrelated picture the boy had stuffed inside of it that caught Noah's attention.

"Is that another picture of Ava Winslow?" asked Noah.

"Uh, huh," smiled Alex.

The young man nodded in eager recognition of Noah's recognition, but this was not a happy moment. It was just weird.

"Dude, she's like eighteen," frowned Noah. "We're twelve. Give it up."

"Why?" asked Alex in visible confusion.

"You're like a stalker with that old camera of your dad's," said Noah. "I shouldn't even have to explain it…She's never gonna go for a boy. Girls like actual guys, specifically older guys. Everyone knows this…Besides, she's hot. She's got to have guys all over her."

"I heard she likes younger guys," said Alex with an eyebrow wiggle.

"That's just idiots talking," sighed Noah. "Even if she did date you, she'd get arrested...I'm pretty sure that's illegal or something."

His best friend shook his head with an adamant "no."

"I'm going to ask her out," nodded Alex.

Noah couldn't help but laugh over this one. This was too funny to pass up.

"She's never going to go out with a little kid," he chuckled. "You've gotta be kiddin' me!...Oh, jeez...What a loser."

"Hey," scowled Alex. "I'm not a loser!...I've got more guts than you. I'm gonna do it."

Noah rolled his eyes and shook his head. He could already see the problem with this one.

"You?... Have guts?" he asked unhappily. "You faint at the first sight of blood!...Plus, she's your neighbor, dummy. Once you do this, it's going to ruin what little relationship you have with her...She's babysat you before!...Are you nuts?"

"She's stacked and packed!" argued Alex. "Look at those boobs! Look at that butt!...Are *you* nuts?"

Noah could see that his friend was not going to back down. It was written all over Alex's narrow face.

"Okay, okay," sighed Noah. "You go right ahead and ask her...But you know what? Don't come crying to me when she turns you down, and she *will* turn you down. Mark my words."

"Whatever," said Alex as he waved off Noah. "I'm gonna do it."

"This is just some stupid crush," sighed Noah. "Do you even have a plan?"

"I gotta plan," nodded Alex. "I'm gonna show her my science project."

"That model of Jupiter?" asked Noah. "You're only doing Jupiter because of that stupid cola and that stupid vending machine outside of our apartment complex. That's dumb, but whatever. You do that."

Alex shook his head and gave Noah a fat thumbs down.

"Like you could do any better," frowned the boy.

"I don't have to do better," shrugged Noah. "This whole thing is stupid anyway, but since I can't talk you out of it, let's just meet up after school and talk some more then. We gotta get to class right now. Just give me the signal like you always do."

"Works for me," said Alex. "I know just the place."

"Cool," said Noah, and then he slammed his locker shut.

✳✳✳✳✳

Noah checked his phone after the message signal went off, the dulcet tones of that signal indicating that Alex was notifying him of where to meet. He knew this before actually checking his phone, considering Alex was the only kid in existence that actually texted him. Texting was an "old people" thing, but Alex liked retro stuff, so this did not surprise Noah. Besides, he, himself, had gotten used to texting thanks to his slightly-eccentric best friend.

The text read, "*Jupiter is severed.*"

Noah rolled his eyes and shook his head over this. He should have known.

"That stupid vending machine again," he sighed.

He put on his red coat and his grey wool hat in preparation for going outdoors. It was early January, and the weather wasn't doing him any favors.

He walked out of his bedroom and into the living room. His mom was there, home from work, her fat fingers already on the TV remote, fishing for whatever to watch.

"Where are you going?" she asked.

"I'm going to see Alex," he shrugged.

"Be careful," she warned. "They still haven't found that Jakobs boy."

"Mom, he disappeared six months ago," frowned Noah. "Besides, we're just hanging around the neighborhood. It's not like we're going anywhere."

"I don't like that new guy that moved in next to Alex," frowned his mother in return. "That one named Roger. He looks shifty to me."

"Well, if he just moved in, then he can't be the one who snatched Olliver Jakobs, can he?" asked Noah.

"Don't talk back to me, Noah," warned his mother.

"I'm not," replied Noah in exasperation. "I'm just saying…Never mind. I'll be hanging out with Alex, and we're not going anywhere. We'll just be hanging around his place."

"No going to the Busy All," said his mother. "It's too far down the street."

"I know, Mom," sighed Noah. "We're not going anywhere. It's too cold for that anyway."

"Call me when you're ready to be picked up," said his mother. "It'll be dark soon, and I don't want you walking home in the dark."

"Yeah, okay," said Noah. "I don't like walking home in the dark, either."

"No going into the woods," said his mother.

"Why in the hell would we go into the woods?" asked Noah in even more exasperation.

"Language, Noah," frowned his mother.

This banter had already gotten old. He needed to go, or he wasn't going to have any daylight at all.

"Mom, I gotta go," said Noah. "I'm losing daylight."

"Give me a kiss first," ordered his mother.

He gave the portly woman a kiss on the cheek and then took his leave.

It wasn't that he didn't love his mother; it was simply the fact that she annoyed him to no end. She could be really irritating.

He shook that thought out of his head as he made his way out the door and down the wooden steps to the concrete walk below. It was a brisk trot over to Alex's, but he could manage it, even in this awful cold.

He huffed it up the street and then down a hill in order to get to the correct location on Alex's side of the complex. Alex lived on the north side of their slew of apartment buildings, right next to the north woods, but it wasn't a long walk. Even so, it was a cold and gloomy day outside, so it wasn't like a pleasant walk, either. There was no snow as of yet, but there were plenty of browns, dead grass and leafless trees, to mark the sheer depression of a cloudy day.

Honestly, he hated January.

He continued his walk toward Alex's meeting place, but he did not have to walk for long. He saw Alex shivering in the cold, dressed in his dark-blue parka, standing right next to that "Jupiter Cola" machine the boy so loved.

The vending machine in question was parked next to the maintenance building wall, a slim, obnoxious, green eyesore with the planet Jupiter plastered across it, something, for some reason, Alex was enthralled with.

That boy was just weird sometimes.

"Hey," said Alex as Noah approached him.

"Hey," said Noah in return.

His hands were in his coat pockets due to the cold; he really needed gloves, but he hadn't gotten around to asking for them from his mom. His mom had bought him a pair of mittens, but who in the hell wore mittens at his age?

"What's up?" asked Noah.

"I'm gonna do it," grinned Alex. "I'm gonna ask out Ava."

"You're an idiot," said Noah with a roll of his eyes. "But whatever. Just don't drag me into it when you get squished like a bug."

"Nah, nah," said Alex as he waved him off. "It's all good. I'm gonna show her my Jupiter project, and that will break the ice."

"You'll be lucky if she doesn't break your face," said Noah.

"Why would she do that?" asked Alex. "It's not like I'm going to be a jerk or anything. Besides, she's cool. She likes hanging out with younger guys."

"Think about what you just said," said Noah with a shake of his head. "We're not guys, Alex, not yet. She's not gonna go for a boy."

"Whatever," shrugged Alex. "I'm gonna do it anyway."

"Okay," sighed Noah.

"Anyway…" smiled Alex. "Anyway, show me what you got. Let me see your Jupiter roll."

"This again?" asked Noah. "We're not space explorers, man. That's baby stuff. We did that when we were like…eleven. It's been a whole year since then."

"So?" asked Alex. "I think it's cool. Nobody else can pull it off in a winter coat. Show me you still got it…If you don't, I'm going to tell everyone you're a weenie."

Noah sighed yet again and rolled his eyes one more time.

Alex was the kind of kid that just didn't want to grow up…Well, considering what he thought about Ava, maybe he wanted to grow up too fast.

Whatever the case, Noah wasn't going to back down from a challenge, especially from Alex.

"Okay, okay," he breathed out. "Here goes…Hold my phone."

He took his smartphone out of his inner coat pocket and handed it to his best friend.

Alex held the expensive slab in his chilly hands, breathed out a trail of steam, and eagerly awaited the show Noah was about to pull off.

"Give me a double," said the young man holding his phone. "No, wait…Give me a triple."

"Okay," shrugged Noah.

He tucked his head in and rolled over his shoulder upon the hard concrete walk, popping up on his feet a moment later. He turned and did it again, the chill of the hardened walk edging into his bones, and then he did it one more time, this time with a loud "HIYAH!" as he popped up in front of Alex.

The young man in front of him backed up into the Jupiter Cola machine, and the slender vending machine wobbled for a second before settling back into place. Both of them backed away from that dangerous instability, if only a few feet.

"Man, that machine is too slim," said Noah in breathless alarm. "That thing isn't even bolted down. It's going to kill someone."

"Nah," said Alex. "It's not like one of the big machines. I don't think it's got enough weight to actually crush anyone…Funny story, but…that's how I came up with 'Jupiter is severed'. It's because of this machine…It's not held down, you know? I don't wanna be held down either, you know? I wanna live my life the way I wanna live it…I mean, you're right, it's not bolted down, but I don't think it will kill anyone if it tips over."

"It could kill one of us," said Noah. "It's got more than enough weight to do that."

"Maybe," said Alex. "Still, it's slim because the cans are smaller than normal."

"Yeah, because they're packed full of sugar and caffeine and ginseng and God knows what else," said Noah. "That stuff is full-body cancer, man. I wouldn't drink it."

"It's the nectar of the gods," grinned Alex.

"It's something, all right," said Noah. "I'm telling you, drinking that stuff will melt your—"

He cut his sentence short as a man walked up to them. They had been jibber jabbering away and having fun and simply hadn't noticed him.

"Hey, boys," said the man. "Loitering out here in the cold?"

This man was tall, around six-foot, broad-shouldered, and he was dressed in a tan overcoat with nice black slacks on him. This guy was around thirty years of age, ancient in Noah's mind, an age he couldn't even imagine. The man's face had the black ring of a beard and mustache to match his shaggy black hair, and he wore those big dorky black glasses that were popular nowadays.

Noah recognized him immediately. It was that "Roger" guy his mom was always going on about. For some reason, the woman just didn't like the guy, and Noah was beginning to see why. This guy gave off a vibe that spelled "creep." Plus, Noah didn't know what "loitering" was, but he was pretty sure it was an insult.

"We weren't doing nothin'," said Noah quickly.

"Oh, I don't care if you boys play out here," said the man. "Just be careful around that machine. I saw it wobble there for a second. You don't want it to fall on you."

"Yeah," said Alex nervously.

This man, this "Roger," moved past them, pulled out some quarters from his left coat pocket, and dropped them into the machine.

"Hey, you're Alex, right?" asked Roger as he gave Alex a strange smile.

"Y…Yeah," said Alex again, this time in a shakier voice.

"I talked to your mom yesterday," said Roger. "We came to a little understanding. She said you can hang out at my place whenever she's late from work. You don't have to be a latchkey kid vegging out on Tik Tok or anything. We can always watch TV or something; I don't mind…What do kids watch nowadays anyway?"

The man pressed the Diet Jupiter Cola button, and all three of them watched as the slim can of Jupiter Cola dropped into the delivery slot. Roger reached down, opened the plastic hatch, and picked up his can of Jupiter Cola.

Noah studied Alex's face. The young man looked cornered, as if he were a deer caught in the headlights.

"I…I usually hang out with Noah after school," said Alex.

"Well, I'll be around when you need me," smiled Roger. "I remember what it was like at your age…Ahh, I miss those days…I can understand all of the confusion with the hormones and changing bodies and body hair…Yep, I remember those days quite well. I never had a mentor with those things, so feel free to talk to me about any of that…Yes, I think we'll get along just fine…Anyway, your mom has my number. She'll let you know when to come on over."

"Umm, thanks," said Alex.

The man walked off after that, whistling some tune Noah had never heard before.

They watched him go, and then Noah shook his head as he turned and gave Alex a wide grin.

"What a freak, man!" he chuckled. "Changing bodies? Hormones?...That guy is a pedo if I've ever seen one! He's got 'stranger danger' written all over him. You go over there, and the next thing you know, you won't be able to sit down for a week."

Alex's face twisted from panic to instant anger.

"It's not funny!" he hissed.

"Did your mom even talk to that guy?" chuckled Noah. "What the hell, man?"

"She did talk to him," said Alex unhappily. "She wants me to go over to his place tomorrow after school, but he doesn't know that. That's why it's imperative, *imperative*, that I ask out Ava tomorrow. If I'm hanging out with her, my mom won't 'need' Mr. Braccio to watch me. She'll think Ava is babysitting me, even though we'll be out on a date."

"Living in your own little world there?" asked Noah. "The only way Ava Winslow is going to hang around you is if she's getting paid…Hope you like sausage, man. You might be getting a mouthful."

"Shut up!" hissed Alex.

Noah only laughed in reply.

Noah stopped his torment of his best friend and stood up straight and proper as someone else walked toward them, and he did so with good reason…The young lady walking toward them was Ava Winslow.

Ava Winslow was eighteen, five-foot-eight, and possessed piercing brown eyes set within her round, pretty face. She had long, light-brown hair that flowed down around her long brown scarf and down to the shoulders of her black winter coat, that look finished by blue-jeans tucked into the white-fluffed tops of her black winter boots.

She came walking up to them from the west, walking along their side of the street from the direction of Alex's apartment, but that was no surprise, as the young lady lived right next door to Alex.

Noah nudged Alex in the side and gave him a low whisper.

"Now's your chance, man!" he said eagerly. "If you're gonna do it, do it!"

Alex said nothing, but the look on his young face betrayed his nervousness. He was as pale as a ghost, and he shook a little, a slight tremble that Noah picked up on, something unrelated to the bitter cold out here.

"Hey, boys," said Ava as she walked up to them.

They parted to allow her access to the vending machine, and she took a moment to dig some change out of her right coat pocket. She inserted her change into the machine, pressed the Cherry Jupiter Cola button, and all three of them watched as the purchased can dropped into the vending slot.

She bent down and opened up the plastic hatch to retrieve her can. Her wide bottom filled out her jeans quite nicely, a beautiful and full heart that was impossible to miss.

Noah could see Alex's eyeline and where it was pointed, so he grinned, rolled his eyes, and shook his head. There was no way Ava was going to go for a boy. That was just ridiculous.

Ava picked up her can of cola, turned, popped the top on it, and took a short sip of it. She cocked her head to her right and gave them both a strange look.

"Were you boys staring at my butt just now?" she asked.

Either she was psychic, or she just knew guys. Whatever the case, Noah had developed a sudden case of laryngitis, because he had nothing to say in response to that. No, it was Alex who spoke for the both of them.

"N…No," said the boy nervously. "I was just…uhhh…just waiting to talk to you."

Ava took another sip of her cola and gave them both a flat stare.

"What about, little man?" she asked.

"I…uhhh…have been working on a science project about Jupiter," said Alex with a nervous grin.

"You have?" asked Ava. "Are you in the seventh grade?"

"Y…Yeah," smiled Alex.

"I did mine on the entire solar system," said Ava. "I made all the little models myself."

"Yeah," grinned Alex. "I've finished mine. It's a big model of Jupiter. Do you wanna see it?"

"You wanna show me your big model of Jupiter, little man?" said Ava as she took another sip of cola.

She rested her left hand upon her left hip and stuck that hip out a little, and Noah's eyes couldn't help but be drawn to that strangely seductive shift in posture. He could not fathom why she would show off for a couple of kids, but then it occurred to him that she was probably just used to doing it.

But his attention was snapped back to the painful reality of witnessing his best friend's awkward attempts to fawn over the older girl.

"Yeah," nodded Alex. "My mom's gonna be late from work tomorrow night, and I was wondering if…uhhh…if I could come over to your place instead of…of…"

This time Noah did interject. It was better than letting Alex drown in his own nervousness.

"His mom wants him to go over to that guy, Roger's, house," said Noah.

"Mr. Braccio?" asked Ava. "I've met him. He's…ummm…a little...Are you sure that's what she wants?"

"Y…Yeah," stammered Alex. "That's why I'd rather hang out with you tomorrow after school. Is…Is that okay?"

She gave him a strange smile right before she took another sip of cola, that smile something indefinable, two reddish-pink lines of unknown territory that deemed caution, if only because of its unfamiliarity.

"And you say your mom has already made plans with Mr. Braccio?" asked Ava.

"Yeah," frowned Alex.

There was a glimmer in her brown eyes, a spark of something, but Noah could not put his finger on what the older girl was thinking. There were gears turning in there, but what for, Noah did not know.

"I don't think that's a good idea," said Ava in a cautious tone. "Mr. Braccio is…I've seen him talking with the other kids before they get on the bus in the morning. I'd watch yourself around him…Going over to his place alone is a really bad idea…Hmmm…You know…you should definitely come over to my place. You can show me your big model of Jupiter, little man. I'd love to see it."

Alex grinned from ear to ear.

"I'd like that!" he said excitedly as he nodded emphatically in reply.

"Cool," said Ava as she took another sip of her cola. "Unfortunately, I have to go, boys. Why don't we talk about this after you come home from school tomorrow, Alex? We can meet up outside."

"Yeah, okay," grinned Alex.

"Bye, Alex. Bye Noah," said the older girl, and then she left them there.

She sauntered past them, and Noah raised one eyebrow at the young lady as her hips swayed slightly, right to left, left to right, sauntering on her way past, something he had not noticed her do before, something he had not noticed in any girl for that matter. It looked a little…deliberate…but that was weird, so he didn't know what to think about it.

He stewed over this new development, but his conclusion was, in fact, inconclusive.

Still, she had a great butt. He couldn't argue with that.

Of course, they didn't talk again until she was out of earshot.

"This is awesome, man!" said Alex in visible excitement. "I get to spend my time with Ava tomorrow night! Isn't that incredible! It's a date!"

Noah shook his head and rolled his eyes yet again.

"It's not a date, ding dong," he replied. "She's just babysitting you. It's not like she's going to let you touch her boobs. She just thinks she's babysitting you."

"You call it whatever you want," grinned Alex. "I am in heaven right now…Did you see her butt! Oh, my God!"

"Dude…" grinned Noah. "Those apples were some squeezies, man…It was impossible to miss…You know, it's weird, but I think she made sure of that. I think she was showing her stuff for us."

"Nah," waved off Alex. "That's just the way she is."

Noah thought about this and nodded once in agreement, reverting back to his original theory about her.

"Yeah, you're right," he said after a second. "Still, I'm glad she's that way…Hoo, buddy."

"No kidding," smirked Alex.

✷ ✷ ✷ ✷ ✷

Noah sat down on his bed.

He'd just come home from seeing Alex, so now was the time to kick back and relax, maybe play a game on his phone or on his Xbox. He wasn't about to do any homework yet.

He picked up his smartphone just as the text notification went off, so he swiped up to see what he had. It was from Alex, of course, because Alex was the only one that ever texted him…Nobody texted anymore. They used literally anything else.

"*My mom won't let me go,*" said the text.

Noah sighed and texted him back.

"She'd rather stick you with that pedo than Ava?" he asked.

"She said she's already made plans with Roger, and she doesn't want to change them," texted Alex. *"She says she can't afford a babysitter."*

"That sucks, man," texted Noah. *"I don't know what to say."*

"I'm going anyway," texted Alex. *"I want to live my own life. I don't want to be held down."*

"It's your funeral, man," texted Noah. *"You'll be retired by the time you're ungrounded."*

"It's worth it," texted Alex.

Noah shook his head a couple of times and frowned. This whole thing was going to end badly, and then Alex was going to get grounded, and then Noah was the one who was going to suffer for it, because with no one to see after school, he was going to be stuck at home, too.

"Great," he scowled. "Thanks a lot, buddy."

＊＊＊＊＊

It was Wednesday, two days later from when Noah had last met up with Alex outside of a school setting. Alex was supposed to have met up with Roger yesterday, and if he had or had not, Noah did not know. The boy had been absent the entire school day, so there was no way Noah could have talked to him about what had happened, if anything.

Noah had just put his backpack down in the living room when his mother walked out of their small kitchen. The portly woman's ear was to her own phone, and she was nodding to herself, though who she was talking to was anybody's guess.

"Uhh, huh, uhh, huh," nodded his mother. "I'll tell him."

She gave Noah a concerned stare and then frowned.

"Noah, I have Mrs. Downs on the phone," said his mother. "It's about Alex."

Noah groaned and silently cursed under his breath. He braced himself for the inevitable news that he was not going to get to see Alex for a while on account of the boy being grounded forever. Alex's mother was not forgiving when it came to this kind of thing.

"Hit me with it," sighed Noah.

"Have you seen Alex at all?" asked his mother.

"What?" asked Noah.

He wasn't sure he'd heard her right.

"He wasn't at home when his mom came home last night," explained his mother. "That 'Roger' fellow says he never showed up at his place, and he was supposed to watch him."

"What?" asked Noah again, this time in genuine surprise.

"Alex is *missing*, Noah," said his mother. "Ava Winslow called Mrs. Downs last night and said that *she* was supposed to watch Alex, but he never met up with her, either. That's two people who claim they were supposed to watch Alex, but he's just disappeared. Now, I don't know what's going on, but Mrs. Downs is in tears, so if you know anything, then you'd better say something right now."

Noah's breath caught in his throat. He had a terrible feeling sink into him, something he did not want to believe, but it was there inside him, and it was there in force. He didn't want to say it, and he hoped to God it wasn't true, but he needed to say *something*, or it was going to eat at him.

"Mom, I need to tell you something," he said as he swallowed hard. "It's about Mr. Braccio, that 'Roger' guy."

His mom turned pale as she lowered her phone and put her hand over the brightly lit screen as if to muffle it. That's what the mute button was for, but she didn't know that.

"What about him, Noah?" she asked forcefully.

"There are some things people have said," replied Noah. "He talks to the kids around here…He's…He talked to me and Alex on Monday after school, and…it was the way he talked to us…"

It did not take the shadow of a second for his mother to figure out where Noah was going with this line of thought.

"That's it," scowled his mother. "We're going down to the police station right now and filing a report. I want you to tell them everything you know about this 'Roger' guy. I knew there was something wrong with him…I *knew* it."

"Y…Yeah," stammered Noah.

It was good that they were doing *something* about this, but Alex had already been missing for an entire night and an entire day, so deep down, Noah had the sinking feeling that he was never going to see his best friend again, and that was a pill that was tough to swallow.

✷✷✷✷✷

Noah tossed and turned in his bed. He tried to sleep, but he simply couldn't. Alex was never far from his mind, and to make matters worse, there was nothing he could do about his best friend's disappearance. Even if he wanted to investigate it, he didn't even know where to start.

"Where are you, Alex?" he whispered in the dark.

He turned over to his left upon his small bed and sucked in his breath at the sight of the shadow on the other side of his room, right next to his bedroom door. The streetlamps from outside were shining a bit through his window, so he could make out the form of someone there, a shadow of a figure in that dim lighting.

"Who's there!" called Noah out of reflex.

He had not wanted to say that, but it had come out anyway, and it was too late to take it back now.

The dark figure in the distance raised one hand and pointed it toward Noah's window, that window parked upon the north wall. That dirt-smudged hand held a dark-brown twig, a root twig pointing north, the simple direction of north, right toward Alex's place.

Noah could see the narrow fingers and the pale, dirt-smudged, peach-brushed arm of a boy his age, and this disturbed him to no end.

Of course, his first thought over this eerie display was only natural, and he voiced as much.

"Alex?" he asked.

The boy stepped out of the darkness, and nothing but horror filled Noah at the sight of him.

The boy was not Alex, no, but Olliver Jakobs, Noah and Alex's classmate that had gone missing six months ago.

This was not what horrified Noah, however.

The boy was naked and dirty, his pale skin flecked with specks of earth here and there, and though this was disturbing, it was the fact that his eyes were a dead-white, an off-white that stared at nothing, an unseeing, unliving alabaster that stared into whatever void they were envisioning. Around his neck was wrapped a black cord, like a cord cut from an appliance such as a toaster or a TV, and there was an ugly purple and black bruising around the pale flesh of the neck where that black line hung.

Olliver Jakobs opened his mouth but said nothing, mainly because he couldn't. His mouth opened wide as his jaw dropped open, and nothing but dirt and dead leaves and large black beetles crawled out of that widened maw to spill upon the beige carpet of Noah's bedroom floor.

Noah woke up after that, but he was shaken to his core. It was Thursday morning, so he still had school, and though that was something he never looked forward to, he was only looking forward to it now in order to wipe the grisly vision of this nightmare from his brain.

He did not know what was going on, but he sensed that if ghosts were real, then one had just visited him in his dreams, and that ghost was trying to tell him something, something he really didn't want to know.

*****

It was Thursday after school, but the last time Noah had talked to Alex was on Tuesday during class. After that, he hadn't heard a peep from him. Now Alex was nowhere to be found, as the eccentric young man had never showed up for school that entire time. The last time he'd hung out with the boy was on Monday, out in front of that stupid Jupiter Cola machine.

The police had questioned Noah on Wednesday…His mom had dragged him down to the station as promised. A police detective had grilled Noah in a private room about Alex's whereabouts, and Noah had given the man all of the information he had known, especially everything he could remember about Roger Braccio.

Noah was kicking himself over the jokes he had made at Alex's expense. Mr. Braccio had been brought in by the police as a "person of interest," but that didn't make Noah feel any better.

He was afraid he would never see his best friend again…He should have just warned Alex's mother about the man…but he was twelve, and nobody listened to a twelve-year-old.

He shed a couple of tears over this as he picked up his smartphone in order to send a text to his best friend. He knew it wouldn't do any good, but he needed to do *something*, or this guilt wouldn't go away.

He had the terrible feeling that his guilt would never go away. It didn't make sense that he had guilt over something he couldn't have changed while there were plenty of people in the world who had no guilt at all regardless of what they did. It would take the hammer of God to get those people to change, something divine or supernatural to set them straight, and this ate at him, because he was kind of jealous of that, mainly because he did not want to feel like this, not over something he had no control over.

Sometimes, he just wanted to stare at the bad guy and watch in real time as they realized the error of their ways. It was a moment he'd been waiting for, because he wanted to believe that people could change, even the worst of people. Most boys his age just wanted to blow away the creeps and freaks, but Noah was different in that respect. He really wanted people to straighten up, or at the very least, feel some kind of remorse…Guilt was a pretty powerful weapon when it needed to be.

He tried unsuccessfully to ignore his anguish by texting his missing best friend, even though, as previously stated, he knew it would do no good.

"*Where are you, man?*" texted Noah.

He sent the text and then set the phone down. He knew in his heart he was never going to see Alex again, but he had sent the text anyway. He'd needed to.

It was not thirty seconds before the chime of his phone indicated he had received a reply.

Noah picked up his phone and stared down at the text reply in incredulous surprise.

"*Jupiter is severed,*" read the text.

This, of course, riled him up.

"I'm gonna kill him!" hissed Noah as he set his phone back down.

He was overjoyed that Alex was alive, but he was also furious that the boy had just up and vanished for a few days. That was not cool. For one thing, that meant an innocent man had just been fingered for a crime that had never happened…Oh, yeah…Alex had some explaining to do.

But first…Noah had to escape the confines of this apartment. His mom had him on lockdown due to the disappearance of his idiot best friend, so it was time for some ninja work to get out of this little place. The window in his bedroom was his best bet…but he had to get ready first.

He quickly dressed in his winter coat and boots, stuffed his phone in his inner coat pocket, locked his bedroom door, and escaped his bedroom via the only window in it. He quietly shut the window behind him and then made his way down toward Alex's side of the complex. It hadn't been that long since he'd come home from school anyway, so there was still daylight to burn, but it wouldn't be long before the sun went down, so he was going to have to hurry.

He walked down to the maintenance building and saw Alex standing in front of that stupid vending machine, standing there in the cold in that same dark-blue parka the boy always wore.

"What the hell, man!" hissed Noah. "Where in the hell have you been!"

"Shhh!" said Alex quickly. "Keep it down!...I have to show you something."

"Well, it had better be good, because you are in deep now," scowled Noah. "You've got a lot of explaining to do, especially to the police. Your mom is gonna have a fit when she…Wait…Does anybody even know you're back?"

"No," said Alex, "but that doesn't matt—"

"Of course, it matters, you monkey turd!" cursed Noah. "What in the hell is wrong with you!"

"I told you, I have something to show you," said Alex. "You have to come with me now, or you won't get to see it. The sun's going to go down."

"This is some bullshi—" began Noah, but Alex cut him short.

"There's no time to explain," said Alex. "You'll know when you see it, but we've got to go now. It'll make sense once you see it."

Noah jammed his hands into his pockets and shook his head no.

"And what am I supposed to see?" he asked.

"It's important," frowned Alex. "But we've gotta go. No more jibber jabbering. We're losing daylight."

"Whatever," frowned Noah. "Where are we going?"

"To the woods," nodded Alex.

"To the woods?" asked Noah. "Why in the hell are we going into the woods!"

"Just shut up and follow me," said Alex.

The boy took off after that, walking in a brisk trot, making a beeline past the houses across the street to head down into the gully that started the entrance to the woods behind their complex.

Noah had no choice but to follow. In fact, Alex traveled at such a good pace that Noah had trouble keeping up with him.

"Wait up, you dork!" yelled Noah.

They traveled for about five minutes, and Noah knew approximately where they were, but the sun would be going down soon, so whatever Alex was going to show him had to be quick, or they could get lost in the dark, even with such a short trek back.

He finally caught up to Alex after the boy had hiked down into a tiny ravine. In that ravine was the opening to a small cave, a little cave Noah was not familiar with. He was more than familiar with this ravine, but the cave...? He had never seen that before.

"What the hell, man?" huffed Noah. "Why are we all the way out here? What is this?"

"This cave opened up," nodded Alex. "It must have opened up when we had that huge thunderstorm, but that was months ago. I figure we never saw it because of some overgrowth. Anyway, it's winter now, so it's in plain sight."

"Uh, huh," frowned Noah. "This is stupid, Alex. We need to go back and tell everybody you're alive. Your mom is pulling out her hair right now."

"Just go inside the cave," urged Alex. "There's something in there you need to see…You *have* to see it. I wouldn't be here if I didn't think it was that important. It will explain why I disappeared…Just trust me on this, Noah. You know me. You know what I'm like. Why would I lie to you?"

"Whatever, man," said Noah with a shake of his head. "This is a terrible idea, but whatever. I'll go in there, but after that, I'm dragging your sorry butt back to your mom's whether you like it or not."

"Just go look," urged Alex. "I…can't go back in there…I just can't…Besides, it's not a very big cave…You have to see what's inside."

"Yeah, yeah," said Noah. "Go in the cave, blah, blah, blah. If this is a trick, I'm going to kick your butt. I should already kick your butt over disappearing anyway."

"Just go in," said Alex. "You'll understand once you see it."

"Right, right," frowned Noah. "I'm going."

He pulled out his phone, switched on its light, and used it to shine his way forth into the dark of the small hole. He crawled through that narrow tunnel and looked about as the dirt around him slowly expanded into a larger hollow.

"What in the hell is this place?" he muttered. "That boy wants me to crawl in the dirt after he up and ran away from home…I'm gonna kick his butt when I get out of here...I swear."

Noah crawled deeper in until he could see the dirt wall of the back of this small hollow. The small cave was not large enough for an adult to stand, but it was just big enough to sit up in.

"What's so special about this…" he started.

His voice trailed off as he stared at the shattered pieces of something in the east part of this rounded hollow. He could make out the various colors of orange and brown in this broken mess, but it was the large red dot on one particular piece that called out to him.

He picked up the pieces of papier-mâché and immediately realized what it was.

"This is your science project of Jupiter, you idiot," he whispered, though he knew Alex couldn't hear him.

No, the eccentric boy was still waiting for him outside.

"Why in the hell did you break this, Alex?" he asked himself.

His right boot kicked back and hit something, so he turned to see what he had jostled loose from the dirt.

He picked up Alex's dad's old instant camera and held it up for further inspection. The old tan camera looked slightly damaged, and turning it round revealed it to be open, the film removed.

"What the hell?" asked Noah.

This was getting even weirder. It was not like Alex to just up and break his own stuff. He was the kind of kid that treated his own things like gold. If you wanted to borrow something of his, you had to put it in three forms of writing.

Noah turned around in order to leave, because none of this made sense, so he was definitely going to have to question Alex about it, but his light shone upon something sticking out of the loose dirt in here, and that something stopped him cold.

There was a finger sticking out of the dirt. There was a pale-peach, slightly-bluish-from-the-cold finger sticking out of the dirt.

Noah sucked in his breath as the world grew very narrow in his vision…Alex had found a body…He must have. The boy had found a body and had dropped his stuff in here out of panic…

Oh, he knew his friend quite well…It did not surprise him in the slightest that Alex had run off and hid for a few days because of this. Where he had hidden, Noah did not know, but this was the most logical conclusion his mind could make over the discovery of something as morbid as this.

The nightmare he'd had, Alex disappearing, all of it together, it was all making sense now, so of course, only one name came to mind.

"Olliver Jakobs," whispered Noah.

Olliver had disappeared in July of last year, and no one had ever found him, so this…Alex must have come out here for some reason—why, Noah did not know—but the eccentric young man must have stumbled upon Olliver's body…Hoo, boy.

Alex was right, Noah knew him quite well. Noah knew that Alex had probably shrieked like a little girl and run like the wind…Of course, that didn't explain why the boy had abandoned his camera and taken the film out of it, but Alex was weird that way.

Point was, the boy had probably panicked.

Nevertheless, this wasn't about Alex; this was about Olliver.

It was really the dream of Olliver that sunk it for Noah. Maybe Alex had come out here because Olliver had visited him, too. Noah had never really believed in ghosts, but after that nightmare…he was a believer now. In fact, he was guessing Alex had been led out here by

Olliver, and when Alex had run like the chicken he is, Olliver had turned to Noah.

Still, Noah had to know if this body really was Olliver Jakobs, and that meant…seeing the face.

He did not particularly want to do what he was about to do, but he had to know. The finger in the dirt was about the right size for Olliver's, though Noah had not known him all that well. The boy would have been in the seventh grade just like him and Alex, but they really hadn't known him all that well.

Noah propped up his phone against the rounded west wall of the hollow in order to have some working light, and then he began to dig around the finger, scooping out the loose dirt as fast as he could, picking up speed as the entirety of the body began to form in his morbidly curious vision. His unprotected hands were cold, nearly freezing, but something inside him drove him to see the remains under the loose earth…He needed to confirm his suspicions.

The corpse in the dirt was naked, face down, definitely a boy—that much he could tell—but it was still in good condition, even after being buried in a shallow grave for six months. Whatever had happened to Olliver Jakobs had been terrible, and Noah really didn't want to think about it, but at least the whole world would soon know what had happened to Noah and Alex's classmate, and then maybe the boy's ghost could finally rest in peace.

"Sorry about this, Ollie," he said in tremulous anticipation. "I'm sorry, but I gotta know. I'm pretty sure it's you, so I'm just gonna turn you over and confirm it now, buddy."

He touched the cold stiff flesh with his bare hands and then gently turned over the body of the boy in order to look at his face. He was afraid he was going to see a mouth full of dirt, leaves, and bugs like in his dream, so he steeled himself and braced for the worst.

What he saw made him suck in his breath and crawl backwards in sheer horror. No amount of preparation could have prepared him for this.

The body of the boy was not that of the missing Olliver Jakobs…The body of the boy buried in a shallow grave under loose earth in a small cave in a tiny ravine in the woods outside their apartment complex was none other than his best friend, Alex Downs.

His best friend's sightless gaze stared up at nothing in the dim light of Noah's smartphone, the eyes dulled with death, the stiff and cold lips slightly parted, the tongue partially hanging out. There was a distinct line of bruising around Alex's neck, a black and red line that was impossible to miss.

Noah squeezed his eyes shut as tears came to them…This was not what he had been expecting…Not at all.

Alex's right arm was up above his own head, that arm laid out in the shallow earth, that dead finger pointing somewhere, that pale, bluish-from-the-cold finger that Noah had seen first, that ghoulish digit pointing toward the west wall of the hollow where Noah had propped up his phone.

Noah wiped his eyes clear, but he was still having trouble seeing, as his tears would not quite stop. He reached over and grabbed his phone, but he saw the white flash of something in the dirt nearby, a spot right where Alex's finger was pointing, so he pushed aside loose dirt to pull forth an instant photo out of the earth, one he was sure Alex had snapped at the last possible moment.

That's why the film in the camera was gone…The killer must have taken it.

Noah shook the photo free of dirt and then shone his light down upon it. His eyes widened in shock at what he saw, and then it all made sense, one giant epiphany of pure torment that suddenly rained down upon his twelve-year-old-brain. Oh, there was a pedophile involved all right, a terrible child murderer at that, and now he had evidence, one last gift from his best friend.

"Oh, no…" he rasped out. "Oh, my God, no…So that's what happened to Olliver. That's what he was trying to tell me. He was pointing towards this place, but it took Alex to lead me here."

He had to get out of this cave…He had to get the hell out of this cave. It was a good bet Olliver was buried in here too, so he needed to call the police right away. He needed to dial 911 as soon as he could.

He stuffed the picture into his right coat pocket.

He crawled his way through the dirt back to the entrance of the cave, crawling back out and into the dying daylight as his tears nearly blinded him. He wiped those tears from his face, smudging his cheeks with cold dirt as he did, but he needed to see, because he needed to get back home ASAP. He also needed to tell the police about this right away.

Alex was nowhere to be seen, nor would he be, but Noah had already known this, though he did not want to think on it. There would be time to deal with that otherworldly trauma once he was back in the safety of his own home.

He switched off the light on his smartphone and stuck the expensive slab back into his inner coat pocket. He couldn't call the police from here; he needed better reception, and that meant getting up and out of this tiny ravine. He could try a call once he was back up on higher land.

He climbed out of that pit, walked a few feet forward, and then sucked in a few breaths, his exhales steaming in the dimming light and the cold of January. He took out the picture and stared down at it for a moment, but this was a mistake, because it hit him all at once, the horror of it, and that left him reeling, but even that terrible sensation had to be put on hiatus…

He had a visitor.

He straightened up, wiped his face, and watched her walk out of the trees in front of him.

Ava Winslow appeared out of the tree line, the young woman dressed exactly as she had been on Monday, right down to the long brown scarf around her neck.

She took one look at Noah and stopped to stare at him just as he was doing at her.

Neither one of them said anything for a moment.

Her face twisted from surprise to confusion, and then it went from that look of perplexity to a calm and cold gaze of comprehension. She opened her lips to speak a moment later, but her voice was not kind.

"What are you doing out here, Noah?" she asked.

"N…Nothin'," said Noah in a shaky voice. "I…I…I was just taking a walk, that's all."

He was at a loss right now. He truly did not know what to do.

He realized too late that he was still holding the picture he had discovered in the cave. He still had it in his right hand, that picture that his murdered dead friend had pointed him to, the clue that had sealed everything, the clue that Alex had given him from beyond the grave.

Ava's piercing gaze slowly moved down to stare at the picture Noah was still clutching in his right hand.

"What's that in your hand, Noah?" she asked.

He did not like the way she kept using his first name. Her tone had a sharp edge to it, a brutal edge, and he did not like it.

Noah subconsciously looked down at the picture in his right hand; he couldn't help it.

It was a picture of Ava, her top half anyway, her bare and ample breasts in full glory within the photo, her off-brown nipples pert and erect as if from the cold, her brown eyes flashing, her smile a weird grin of strange inclination, the dark earth of the top of the small cave hollow just above her.

"It's j…just something I found," he stammered.

"Oh, *really?*" asked the girl in an accusing tone. "You just found a picture out here? It looks like a photograph to me. It *looks* like an instant camera picture, like one of those Kodak cameras."

"Y…Yeah," said Noah shakily.

She took two steps forward, and Noah took two steps back in response. He switched the picture to his left hand…He was going to need his right to reach for his phone.

"I think you found something, Noah," said Ava. "I think you found something important because I can tell you were crying. Why were you crying, Noah?"

Noah shook his head. This wasn't good…This wasn't good at all.

"I did find something," he said, but this time he felt his courage coming back.

It was an anger building up inside him, an anger over the fate of Alex and Olliver, and he could not contain that anger any longer. Still, he wasn't stupid, so he readied himself to run, but he needed to ask one question first, and this time, *he* was going to use *her* first name.

"I did find something, but now it's my turn to ask a question," he said.

"Oh?" smirked the young woman. "And what's that, Noah?"

"Where's Alex, Ava?" asked Noah. "I think you know where he is."

The young woman pulled off her long brown scarf and twisted the article of winter clothing in her hands, first in her right fist, then in her left. She pulled the scarf taught after that, a line of cloth that held no good intent.

"That's my picture, Noah," she said firmly, but there was a tinge of anger in her voice. "I came out here to get it, so give it to me."

But he was not backing down; not this time.

"Where is Alex, Ava?" asked Noah again.

She took another step forward, but Noah held his ground.

Her pretty face looked calm, but that face was nothing more than a mask, a mask hiding a demon behind it, a boiling pool of rage that was about to spill over.

"Don't you know?" she asked as she took two more steps forward. "Don't act like you don't know, Noah…You see, I gave him what he'd always wanted…I made a *man* out of him, Noah. I showed him what it was like to be a man."

Noah swallowed hard as his eyes flitted for an escape route. Yeah, he was angry, but he wasn't an idiot. He could literally run anywhere out here, but he needed to get past her in order to go in the right direction, and she was between him and the way home.

First though, he needed to ask another question, though he already knew the answer.

"What does that mean?" he replied. "How did you make a man out of him?"

The girl twisted the scarf until her knuckles turned white, and then she stepped even closer to him, but Noah's eyes did not leave the narrow line of cloth stretched tightly between her hands.

"Don't tell me you don't know," she said in a dark tone. "Don't lie to me, Noah. You already know what I'm talking about…You're twelve. You have the internet. Don't tell me you don't know."

"I…I don't," lied Noah.

Oh, he and Alex had definitely explored that territory online. That had only been possible, though, because Alex had figured out his mother's PC password in order to overcome the child lock on it. That, and Alex knew how to delete a search history. It wouldn't have been good if Alex's mom had caught wind of any spread legs and bare breasts they'd witnessed.

But that didn't matter right know.

"I don't know what you're talking about," he lied again.

"Oh, *really*?" asked Ava with a wicked smile. "Well, Ollie knew…Didn't anyone tell you?…I like younger guys, Noah…I can make a man out of you too, you know, just like I did Alex…just like I did Ollie…It *excites* me, Noah. It makes me feel alive…It's those cute little bodies and the looks on their faces as they go…Cutting off their air supply makes them detonate; it doesn't matter that they're twelve…They go with a smile…

"That's what sex is all about, Noah…It's about giving up a little piece of yourself each time…In the Middle Ages, they believed every wonderful explosion you had edged you closer to death…That's what I'm doing, Noah…I'm racking up a count…Doing it alone just wasn't enough for me, and older guys are *soooo* boring…I needed something *more*…and let me tell you, Alex and Ollie were *sublime*…

"Can't you see? I'm reaching for Heaven, Noah…So why don't you help me climb that ladder, huh?…It'll only hurt a little. You won't really feel the pain…You'll be too busy having your first *real* pleasure in life…Alex did…Ollie did…It's like nothing you've ever felt before, nothing at all…I can't explain it, no. You have to *feel* it. You have to *experience* it. Come on, Noah…Let's go make Heaven together. I'll send you there, and I promise you'll go there with a smile on your face…Come on…Let's go down to the cave."

Noah swallowed hard and shook his head no. He said the first thing that came to his mind, though he had not intended to.

"You're sick, Ava," he gulped. "You're sick…You need help."

"Don't you understand, Noah?" replied Ava with a weird grin. "Because I don't think you do…You're a cute little boy, and I *loooove* cute little boys to *death*."

She pulled the scarf in her hands until it was a brown, super-taught line of finality, something Noah could not take his eyes off of, but he had to, because now was the time to snap out of that snake's deadly hypnotic gaze.

So, he did.

He scrambled to pull his phone from his inner coat pocket, but she rushed him.

"Oh, shi—!" he started to say, but there was no time to complete even that short expletive.

Noah chucked his smartphone like a ninja star, throwing it out of sheer panic and reflex, and the expensive slab tagged the charging Ava Winslow right between her sinister brown eyes. She shrieked and fell to her knees in the dead leaves around them, her right hand clutching her forehead, but Noah was already running for his life.

He didn't have his phone anymore, but hopefully, its sudden departure had bought him some time.

He ran at top speed, his lungs burning from the cold in some weird paradoxical travesty of thermodynamics, and even though he was only five minutes from the complex, he knew this run was going to be the longest five minutes of his short life.

"NOOOOOAAAAAH!" screamed Ava from behind him.

She was as mad as a hornet now, and he knew this, so if she caught him…he seriously doubted she would take him to heaven in any sense of the word.

There was no time to cry at this point, no; he was past the event horizon, and there was no turning back now. He had to make it back before she got to him, so he booked it as fast as his twelve-year-old legs could carry him.

He scrambled up the gulley and hit the ridgeline that made it back towards people's backyards and back fences. It occurred to him that he could try to hop a fence or run around to the street to knock on someone's door, but Ava was right behind him, so there was no time for any of that.

The last of the daylight was fading, but he could see the green glow of the Jupiter Cola machine outside the maintenance office, and an idea formed in his young mind. It was a stupid idea, a very crazy idea, but it was the only thing swimming in his brain at that singular moment…Besides, he was sure Alex—wherever he may be—approved of what he was about to do.

"Come back here, Noah!" huffed Ava from behind.

Noah hit the street running, making a beeline for the vending machine. He knew what he was going to do, and he had one shot to do it right, but Ava was nearly upon him, her right hand reaching out for the back of his coat, her eyes flaming pinpoints that burned a distinct malice into his spine…He didn't have to turn to see her face, no. He could just feel that hateful gaze boring through him.

He jumped at the last second as he came upon the vending machine, Ava's fingers brushing the back top of his coat, her rage so palpable it enveloped him like a terrible heat, and then…

"You little shi—!" started Ava.

"Jupiter roll!" cried Noah.

He slammed into the top of the Jupiter Cola machine with a full running jump, slamming into it with his left shoulder, and that hurt, but that was only the first part of his plan. He rolled as soon as his boots struck pavement, rolling over his right shoulder to pop up again on his feet, deliberately out of line with the machine he'd just struck at full speed.

Ava cried out once as the Jupiter Cola machine pitched forward after it had rocked backwards from the hit, the slender machine pitching forward off its base, the bright green of its lights sparking off as the whole thing toppled over upon her.

There came a loud crash as glass and metal and plastic pinned the eighteen-year-old girl beneath the toppled machine.

Noah turned to view the damage he had done.

The pretty young woman that his best friend, Alex, had crushed upon was now ironically crushed beneath the machine that Alex had so loved. Ava struggled from beneath that machine, only her arms and head visible beneath it, and the young woman had blood leaking from her reddish-pink lips, her dark eyes squeezed shut in what had to be terrible pain, her teeth bloody and gritted from whatever internal injuries she had suffered.

Ava cried out and held onto the top of the machine pinning her to the concrete walk.

"Noah! Noah!" she cried out. "Help me! Don't leave me here! I'm hurt! I'm hurt really bad!"

He stared down at her for a moment, unsure of what to do.

"Get help, Noah!" choked out Ava. "We can just put all of this behind us, right? You won't tell anyone; I know you won't, and I won't tell everybody you just tried to kill me, okay?...Nnng!...I need help, Noah! Don't just stand there! Do something!"

It hit him right then…She wasn't repentant. She was sick in the head, so sick, so very, very sick, and that sickness had already killed two kids, one of them his best friend, so…there was only one solution to this supposed quandary.

She had to be turned in…He had the evidence…

Noah realized at that moment that the picture he needed, the evidence he had found, was no longer in his left hand. He panicked and patted down his pockets in a desperate search for the instant photograph, but he spied the white borders of it on the walk a few feet from him. He must have dropped it when he'd jumped into the machine.

He ignored Ava's cries of pain and help as he stepped forward to pick up the picture, but as he reached down to pick it up, a new hand in his vision picked up the photo before he could.

Noah stood up in silent shock as his best friend, Alex, held up the photo in the dying light of day. The boy was still dressed in his winter clothes, still dressed in that dark-blue parka he liked to wear.

Alex smiled once, handed the photo to Noah, and Noah took it, though he was shaking as he did.

Alex then stared down at the stunned and silent, bloodied face of Ava Winslow, and Noah knew right then that she could see him, too.

Alex turned and walked away after that, and with him was another boy, a boy that Noah instantly recognized as Olliver Jakobs.

Olliver was still dressed in the same forest-green T-shirt and white shorts he'd been dressed in the day he had disappeared, and he smiled at Noah as he walked away as well, and then they were gone, both of them disappearing, both boys vanishing like so much steam from a breath in the frigid air.

Noah held the photo in his hands, turned, and stared down at Ava.

The young woman's pained expression collapsed even further into a pool of despair and misery, and then she was crying, a loud and awful wail that cut straight through Noah like a stiff winter wind. It was the look on her face that got to him, that look of realization, that poignant and terrible realization that would live with her for the rest of her life.

What she had done had finally sunk in.

"There it is, the moment I've been waiting for," said Noah quietly as people from around the neighborhood opened their doors to see what all of the commotion was about.

#9…VERDANT AND VERDIGRIS

Some things should remain forgotten.

Michael squinted hard in order to see through the rain, but his efforts to see exactly what out-of-the-way road they were all on was quickly becoming a lost cause.

"Do you have any idea where we are?" asked Lexi.

The young woman he was currently sharing a bed with had only asked this question five times in the last fifteen minutes. It was annoying, true, but he had to admit that she had a point.

They were lost.

"Not really," sighed Michael.

"Typical," said Raymond. "We should have turned around a half an hour ago."

"Give the boy some credit," said Lance. "He's acting his part. It's what straight men do."

Michael muttered under his breath. Raymond and Lance were Lexi's friends more than they were his, and normally, he had no problem with them, but they were also currently getting on his nerves just as much as Lexi was.

Nevertheless, he had no right to complain. This trip had been his idea, a bonding experience in the form of a vacation away from the office, but things weren't going as planned, because things never went as planned in his life…He just had bad luck.

"Where are we anyway?" asked Lexi. "Does anyone have any reception? I'm not getting any on my phone."

"No, honey," said Raymond. "We're in the middle of a summer storm…That, and we're also out in the middle of nowhere."

"Great," muttered Lexi.

Michael felt for her. He understood the situation.

All four of them were packed in Michael's little dark-blue Toyota Celica, not a car designed for driving on some backwoods dirt road through the actual woods during a summer squall. Right now, though, he was trying to keep the car from hitting any debris or getting stuck in some pitted section of road that had filled with water. He needed to watch out for those things.

"So what's it gonna be, Mikey?" asked Lance. "Are we turning around?"

Michael swore under his breath and shook his head no.

"We can't turn around in this," he said unhappily. "We'd probably get stuck on this narrow road. I'm surprised we haven't been flooded out already…However, that doesn't mean we should just stop, either. This road has to lead somewhere. It has to lead to a house or the highway or somewhere. I'm not giving up just yet. Besides, we've got half a tank of gas. We're not in any danger of being stranded yet…And don't call me Mikey."

"Rowwrrr," said Lance as he made cat-scratch motions. "Feisty."

"We must have made a wrong turn going back to the interstate," said Lexi. "I think we're going south."

"Probably," sighed Michael. "It's not like we had reservations anywhere. This was just supposed to be a simple road trip, not an extended stay."

"Well, we may not have a choice," said Raymond. "At this rate, we're probably going to have to stay at a motel somewhere."

"Hope you like bedbugs," frowned Michael.

This trip was a disaster. He should have known this would happen, because this *always* happened to him on road trips.

He took a moment to think back on how all of this had started, and even though this had been his idea, his inspiration for this debacle was Lexi.

He had met Lexi at the office, at the IT firm the four of them worked at. Their firm contracted out to various other offices, but that was neither here nor there. The fact was that his new girlfriend was a beautiful brunette who had more than two braincells, a far cry from the bimbos he had previously dated. He had always gone for the luscious type rather than the cerebral type, but Lexi was a bit of both, and dating her had introduced Michael to a whole new world of women…one that didn't come with a headache.

Of course, interoffice dating was frowned upon at their firm, but considering Raymond and Lance were boyfriends and *no one* (no one in upper management anyway) wanted to break up a gay couple, Michael had crossed into the "grey" territory of interoffice romance with little trouble. The firm couldn't allow gay interoffice dating without its straight counterpart, or a massive lawsuit would be coming their way.

He'd met Raymond and Lance through Lexi, and he got along with them in a fair manner. Raymond was the dark-haired practical one, while Lance was the chatty blonde. Both of them were the gay-idol posterchildren for fawning straight women everywhere—good-looking, athletic, neat and clean cut—and that kind of annoyed Michael, but the truth was, they were both harmless, so he put up with them.

Michael, himself, was fairly attractive in his own mind. He was tall, six-foot, with neat black hair in a business cut and fair brown eyes…No, he had no trouble picking up the ladies, especially considering his disastrous past relationships with women who were hotter than their own tiny brains could handle.

Lexi, of course, was not one of those; she was the best of both worlds, and he was infinitely grateful for that. It gave him patience with her, which was something he had severely lacked with his previous girlfriends.

Michael was not abusive, no, but he had his limits, so he would walk away when the time was right, but he did not see that with Lexi. Maybe he was growing soft, but she had that effect on him.

Hence, why he put up with her complaints for the moment, and speaking of complaints…

"We've got to find somewhere to rest our heads," said Lexi. "At this point, I don't care if I sleep on one giant bedbug, but we are pulling over at the first motel or hotel we find…but first we need to get out of these woods."

"It's the rain, honey," said Lance from behind them. "He's got to drive carefully, or we won't be going anywhere, and without reception, we won't be calling for help, either."

Michael nodded his head in recognition. Apparently, Lance was not a total flake.

This little bit of alliance peaked Michael's resolve. He felt a little happier now that someone was listening to him.

"We'll get out of these woods," he said firmly. "They can't last forever, and we still have half a tank of gas. We'll make it, don't wo—"

"What is that?" asked Lexi as she cut him short.

There was the peak of a building in the distance, only noticeable due to a lightning strike from far, far south of them, though the building in question was much closer than that.

Raymond and Lance leaned forward in their seats to get a better look.

"That's a house; it must be," said Raymond. "We should stop there and ask for directions. They might also have a landline we can use."

Lightning struck again, but this time they could all see the great structure looming in the distance, and this backwoods road they were stuck on led straight toward it.

"That's not a house," said Michael quietly. "It has a steeple. That must be what we saw."

"Maybe it's a church," said Lexi.

"If it is, it's a really big one out in the middle of nowhere," said Raymond.

They drove toward the structure until they passed beneath a large stone arch, an arch of carved stone decorated with strange, concentric, spiraling swirls that Michael was not familiar with. Nevertheless, he drove onwards toward the huge building, a five-story construction that had to boast many, many rooms in it.

"That's not a church," said Lance. "It can't be. It's way too big. Country churches are tiny things."

"It's a hotel!" said Lexi excitedly. "It has to be!"

"I…I think you're right," breathed out Michael.

She had to be. There were too many floors to this place to not be a hotel, though the only visible lights were on the ground floor.

"Well, let's find out," said Lexi. "They might have rooms available."

That was the problem with hotels, of course. Many of the rooms were booked out months in advance, but still…people always canceled at the last minute, so…

However, upon driving up to the mansion-style building, Michael had an ominous feeling drift down upon him like a black cloak.

This large five-story building was of a design Michael did not recognize, with several steeples upon gambrel roofs carefully woven into the structure. There was even a huge brick tower topped by domed glass settled within the building, something Michael had never seen anywhere.

The construction was bizarre in general, and not just in the placement of the rooms; the bottom three floors were brick while the top two floors, save for the huge tower, were clearly made from wood.

It was a Frankenstein's creation of a thing, like a patchwork of architectural plans that did not make sense. Furthermore, it did not look like it was in good repair, and there were only three cars parked in a small lot out front, a lot marked by cracked pavement and reaching weeds.

The look of the place left a bad taste in his mouth, a sense of foreboding lingering at the back of his mind and at the tip of his tongue, so he couldn't help but protest.

"I don't know, Lex," said Michael. "I'm getting a bad feeling about this."

"We're stopping," frowned Lexi. "Don't you dare turn around, Michael. We at least have to check and see if this place will help us. I mean, it might not even be a hotel, but we at least have to try. We at least need some directions to a gas station, or we could get stranded. We only have half a tank of gas."

It was her insistence and the sincerity in her voice that speared through him. He wanted to please her, so he relented, though he still thought this was a bad idea.

"Okay," he grunted. "We'll stop and check."

"Oh, goody," said Lance. "We'll just park real quick and take a looksee."

The tires rolled over cracked pavement as Michael parked the car in the nearly empty lot. He turned the key and shut off the engine, and all four of them exited the vehicle.

The problem with this, of course, was the weather. The small group tried but failed miserably in a vain attempt to cover themselves from the pounding rain.

"Come on!" croaked out Michael as he ran toward the double front doors of the huge building.

All four of them hoofed it to the grand, yet decaying, structure's entrance.

Michael took hold of a large iron doorknocker, pulled up on the circular metal bar, and banged on the old wood of the righthand door.

The door creaked open after a few more attempts at knocking, and they were greeted by a man in his late sixties, a wizened fellow dressed in the formal attire that one would see on a professor from the 1950s.

The elderly man standing within the entranceway was tall and thin, Caucasian, with an angular face and a beaked nose. His eyes were a piercing dark brown that belied his shortcut white hair, and this gave him the appearance of a volatile temper.

Michael wanted to give most people the benefit of the doubt, but still…he did not want to tick this guy off.

This man was dressed in a brown suit with brown slacks and a matching brown vest over a white dress shirt, that dress shirt complete with a dark-brown tie. On his feet were well-taken-care-of dress shoes, brown dress shoes with angular tips, the shoes polished to a shine...He really did look like some kind of professor from the '50s.

Apparently, the imposing look upon the elderly man's face stunned even someone as forthright and as adventurous as Lexi, and this was surprising to Michael, because Lexi was the kind of woman who took no guff from anyone.

"H…Hello?" stammered Lexi. "We were wondering if—"

"Of course," cut short the old man.

"Excuse me?" asked Michael.

"We are not technically ready for guests," continued the man, "but since the weather is as such, we have been finding ourselves with strays this weekend. This place has a way of guiding people to it."

He had a refined British accent, something Michael had somehow expected him to have. Maybe it was the clothes or his bearing, but hearing the man's speaking voice surprised Michael only in the fact that his expectations of this man had just been fulfilled in the most stereotypical way possible.

Lexi shook her head and put on her "greeting" smile, something Michael was well familiar with. She used it when she wanted something from someone, and he had been the recipient of it many times.

"Oh…" said Lexi. "Does that mean we—?"

"It means we can accommodate you for the time being," said the old man. "The truth is, the Everwatch will not be ready for guests until some considerable repairs are made, but considering the weather, I can make an exception for now …Why don't you young people come in and dry off. We will discuss payment once you're inside."

"Thank you so much," said Lexi.

She immediately walked into the place as the host stepped aside, so Michael shrugged and followed her, Raymond and Lance right behind him.

"Thanks," grunted Michael as he walked past the old man.

"You are quite welcome, sir," said the elderly host.

The old man shut the door behind them, taking some time to ensure that both of the large wooden doors were properly closed.

Michael stood with the others inside the entrance area as he studied his surroundings.

This hotel had no foyer, or if this large room was a foyer, it was indeed a large one, larger than any foyer Michael had ever seen. There were four, large, brown leather couches seated in a circle as one would see in the relaxed atmosphere of a living room, and to the east was a huge stone fireplace with a roaring fire, four wooden chairs strategically placed before it.

There was a pair of large wooden doors next to the fireplace toward the southeast, something that stood out simply because the doors looked out of place. Each door had a carved symbol of a concentric swirl etched upon it, and this also caught Michael's eye, if only for a moment.

This place had a dim yet cozy air about it, a strange mix of gloom and comfort that somehow meshed together to perform a function, much like the Frankenstein appearance of the building's exterior façade.

The floor beneath them was made of layered dark-wood floorboards covered by large dark-brown carpets, those carpets unadorned of any decoration. Past the couches and to the south was the long wooden bar that comprised the admissions desk, and on the right side of that desk was a huge spiraling staircase also built of dark wood.

Upon the walls were tapestries of strange design, some green with odd circling swirls of silver within them, spiraling swirls that crawled in upon themselves, while other tapestries were royal red with the gold lettering "SPQR" within a golden laurel wreath, though Michael had no idea what any of them meant, if anything.

There were a few people lounging on the couches, four to be exact.

There was a tall and buxom blonde in a burnt-orange sweater and blue jeans relaxing upon the north couch, someone Michael would have hit on before he had met Lexi. She certainly fit the type he had liked to flirt with, blonde and curvy, though what she was actually like, he could only guess.

On the south couch was an elderly couple, this couple somewhat older even than the host of the hotel. On the left side of that couch was an elderly woman with white hair, her plump profile dressed in a print dress and a drooping tan hat, grandma glasses upon her nose, and on her right was an elderly man Michael could only assume was her husband, this man dressed in a tweed suit with a black turned-down bowtie, glasses perched upon his nose as well.

On the east couch was a portly man with a black mustache and short black hair dressed in a white dress shirt with short sleeves, a black tie around his neck, with black slacks and dress shoes to match.

There was no one on the west couch, but that was the spot their elderly host had chosen to stand, right in front of it.

"Oh, I'm getting a real *Clue* vibe here," said Lance. "I want to be Colonel Mustard."

"You are definitely Professor Plum, you nerd," said Raymond.

"Oh, quiet, you," said Lance in mock irritation. "At least I'm not Mr. Boddy…like you."

"Ha, ha," replied Raymond with an equally mock frown. "Keep it up, and you won't see any 'body,' that's for sure. Certainly not mine."

"Rowwrr, ffft, ffft," said Lance as he made clawing motions in the air.

Michael rolled his eyes and sighed.

Taking these two anywhere public was always going to be like this, but Lexi simply gave a subtle chuckle over their back and forth. They were funny sometimes, but they were also irritating at times, and right now, he just wanted to dry off and settle in, not put up with any minor annoyances. Nevertheless, he was here for Lexi, and she could keep them in check if she felt like it, so he would leave it up to her.

Michael decided to ignore them and head on over to the fire. He parked himself in a wooden chair, the seat nice and toasty due to the heat of the blaze in the fireplace, and he sighed yet again, only this time in some contentment.

"Why don't the three of you follow your friend and dry off first," he heard the old man say. "We will discuss payment after you've warmed a bit."

"Thank you, Mr…uhhh…" said Lexi.

"Mr. Armstrong," finished the old man.

"Thank you, Mr. Armstrong," repeated Lexi.

"Of course," said the host.

The three of them joined Michael by the fire and took chairs of their own.

"*Ooooo*…comfy," said Lance.

Michael gave a slight smile at Lance's simple observation. He was feeling better, less irritable, now that they were out of the rain.

He turned his attention back upon Mr. Armstrong. The man stood in the center of the circle of couches, his hands clasped together for emphasis that he would speak.

"For one reason or another," said the elderly host, "you have all found your way here. Though the Everwatch is not quite ready for guests, it shall be soon, so I suppose we can consider this a 'test run,' and this test has been a long time in the making, I assure you."

"Oh, I'm just grateful you let us in, Mr. Armstrong," said the blonde.

She had a soft and quiet voice, something Michael was immediately drawn to, but a pinch on his ear from Lexi made him realize he was staring, so he cast his eyes downwards out of respect.

"Of course, Ms. Pearl," said Mr. Armstrong. "What would a hotel be without guests?"

This conversation, however, was hijacked by the gruff undertones of another guest.

"So, what is it we're going to owe you?" asked the portly man with the mustache.

"We'll discuss payment when you check out, Mr. Coal," said Mr. Armstrong.

"Ms. Pearl, Mr. Coal," whispered Lance with a not-so-subtle snicker. "This really is right out of *Clue*!"

Both he and Raymond gave a short giggle, but one glare from Lexi shut them up.

"Be respectful, you hyenas!" she hissed.

Michael turned to see all of the other guests staring at them. Though he was eternally grateful for Lexi's ability to control his two coworkers, this did not lesson the embarrassment of the situation at hand.

He felt his face turn red.

Lexi, on the other hand, simply stared back at the other guests and waved them off.

"Continue," she said.

That was one of the things Michael loved about her. Nothing seemed to faze her.

The portly man on the east couch, the one with the rough, square face and thin black mustache, this "Mr. Coal," continued on as if nothing had interrupted him.

"I'd like to know what I'm dealing with here, Mr. Armstrong," he said. "What's the sticker price?"

"I don't quite know yet," said the host with a weak smile. "I don't believe I shall charge much, Mr. Coal. The hotel is not yet ready, but it would be inhospitable of me to turn down travelers under such conditions, so…I think fifty or so per night is acceptable."

The others murmured amongst themselves as Michael gave himself an approving nod. "Fifty or so" was incredibly cheap anymore…This road trip was beginning to look like a nice little vacation after all.

"Are you sure, Mr. Armstrong?" asked Ms. Pearl. "You've been so kind to let us in."

"If you insist upon paying any more than that," replied the elderly host, "I shall not turn away such an offer, Ms. Pearl. I would, however, experience what little there is here to offer before doing anything rash."

"Oh, it's not rash to reciprocate the generosity of a stranger," said Ms. Pearl.

"Yes…" said Mr. Armstrong.

The old man's lips frowned in response to that reply, a strange cast of guilt upon his refined face, a shadow of something unexplainable upon subtle observance, and Michael did not know what to make of it.

"Well…we are short staffed as of late," said the elderly host. "However, I shall see to it that some dinner is served before long; you are all owed that much. The dining hall is through the west doors there. I will see you each situated in a room on the second floor right away…I'm afraid our elevators are out of service, so it appears you will have to take the stairs…I apologize for the inconvenience."

"Oh, that's all right," said the old woman of the elderly couple seated upon the south couch. "We'll manage somehow."

"Thank you, Mrs. Corbin," said Mr. Armstrong.

The old host waved his right hand toward the admissions desk and gave his head a slight bow.

"I shall return momentarily," he said briskly. "For now, simply relax and enjoy the fire."

✳✳✳✳✳

Michael sighed and sat down on the south couch within the entrance hall.

Lexi was upstairs on the second floor in their shared room, Raymond and Lance were in their own room as well, and all four of them had decided to stay the entire weekend, more out of gratitude for Mr. Armstrong's generosity than anything else. Their road trip was at an end in lieu of this destination, but that was fine, because a vacation was supposed to be relaxing, and this place was relaxing, if not a little boring.

Michael did not know where the other guests were, but he had done the small service of helping the old couple, the Corbins, up to their own room. The stairs were hard on them, so he and Raymond had helped them up while Lance had carried their luggage.

Now it was just him and Ms. Pearl downstairs, the buxom blonde sitting across from him on the north couch.

"Hi," said the young woman. "You're Michael, right?"

"Uhhh…yeah," said Michael. "Michael Smith."

It was probably a bad idea to interact with her at all, but he still had to be friendly. She was definitely the type of woman he would have hit on in the past, but considering his commitment to Lexi, he was not about to jeopardize his relationship with his own girlfriend…He was, in fact, trying to be good.

"I'm Savanna," said the blonde.

He nodded and gave her a quick smile.

"Yeah," he said nervously.

"Did you just wander down that road out there by accident?" she asked. "That's what happened to me. I think that's what happened to everyone else, too."

"Something like that," said Michael. "I figured we'd hit the highway again or something, but I was wrong."

"My cell stopped working for some reason," said Savanna. "Isn't that weird?"

"A little," agreed Michael. "I've had the same problem…Huh…I never thought to check with the others about theirs."

"That is strange," said the blonde as she screwed up her lips in thought.

They sat there for a few awkward seconds of silence before she spoke up again, but the question she asked immediately made Michael cringe.

"Are you here with your sister?" asked Savanna.

And there it was…the bait. He knew this game. She was here alone, so she was hoping Lexi was his sister, and that way she could have a little "fun" with a stranger over the weekend. In the past, Michael would have jumped on that without so much as a by-your-leave, but he was trying to be dedicated to Lexi, so that's all there was to that.

"Lexi is my girlfriend," he said swiftly. "She's also the jealous type, but I still love her."

"Oh," said the blonde in sudden disappointment. "I'm sorry…I didn't mean to intrude. It's just that…it's so hard to meet good men these days. I mean, those two boys upstairs are good-looking, but they're as gay as a flaming rainbow. Anyone who isn't a complete space case can see that."

Michael chuckled and nodded in reply.

"Yeah," he said. "They irritate me sometimes, but they're all right. I work with Lance and Raymond in IT, and that's actually how I met Lexi. We all work in the same office."

"Interoffice dating, huh?" asked Savanna. "Isn't that a no-no?"

"Funny you should say that—" began Michael, but he was cut short.

The portly man with the black mustache, Mr. Coal, walked in and sat down on the east couch. He gave a nod for courtesy and then adjusted his weight upon the couch he was currently sinking into.

"Anyway, I guess that doesn't matter," sighed the blonde. "I'm just glad I have somewhere to park my butt out of the rain. That's why I'm going to pay Mr.

Armstrong one-twenty a night. That seems fair to me…What about you?"

She shot that question out there, something monetary that Michael really didn't want to answer, but he did anyway. In truth, he hadn't felt like paying more than eighty a night for the room he and Lexi were sharing, but if Savanna was paying one-twenty, then now he was on the hook to pay more. He didn't want to look cheap or selfish.

"One-twenty's fair," he shrugged.

"Well, I'm not paying that," grunted Mr. Coal.

The hefty man frowned and shook his head no as they turned their eyes upon him.

"Why not?" asked Savanna. "Isn't it the least we could do?"

"No," grunted Mr. Coal. "I've been in motels better than this. This place needs a lot of work. For one thing, it shouldn't even be open yet. Honestly, he should have just turned us away. I'll pay fifty, and that's it."

"Fifty is sufficient, Mr. Coal," said Mr. Armstrong.

The elderly host was standing between the south and west couches, standing just outside of the circle of that furniture. How long he had been standing there, Michael had no idea, but the older man's sudden appearance startled him a bit, though Michael was careful to hide his own surprise.

"Oh…uhhh…Mr. Armstrong…" said Savanna.

Michael could tell that the blonde was just as startled as he was.

"Yes, Ms. Pearl?" asked the old man.

"I…I guess I have a question," she replied.

"Of course, miss," said the host.

She was on the spot now. Michael wondered what she was going to say. It was the sudden appearance of the old man that had spooked her, obviously, but she appeared to have something she actually wanted to ask, so she did, and it was something that had been at the back of Michael's mind as well.

"This place has a lot of charm," said Savanna. "I was just wondering about a couple of things, like these tapestries on the walls. What do they mean?"

"The red ones are in reference to the ancient Roman Legion," said Mr. Armstrong as he nodded toward a tapestry on the west wall. "SPQR stands for 'Senatus Populusque Romanus,' which means 'the Senate and the people of Rome.' It is a symbol of ancient Rome's law over chaos and disorder."

"Uh, huh…" said Savanna. "What do the green tapestries mean?...The ones with the swirls?"

"The ancient Druids did not believe in an end, but rather that all ends are merely new beginnings," said Mr. Armstrong. "The circling swirls represent the endless cycle of nature, an endless cycle of death and rebirth."

"That's interesting," said Savanna. "Why have both types of tapestries here, though? Aren't they different themes?"

"It would seem as such to an outsider, yes," said Mr. Armstrong. "Both the ancient Romans and the ancient Druids believed in sacrifice, though they practiced such sacrifice in different ways."

That was an odd answer, or rather, it wasn't an answer at all, and Michael could not help but point this out.

"That…doesn't really answer her question," he said.

"I used to be a professor of ancient cultures, Mr. Smith," said their elderly host. "I moved here from the Isles some time ago, and when I did, I brought a very particular piece of history with me…two, in fact, and those two pieces can explain the duality of the tapestries."

"Oh, really?" asked Savanna.

"Yes, Ms. Pearl," said Mr. Armstrong. "In fact, all of you are invited to come see the pieces I had shipped in from overseas. Both are extremely rare and valuable. They are in the showroom of the Everwatch, and you will be the first people to see them outside of myself and my staff. Once you see what I've brought with me, you'll understand the duality of the Roman and Druidic 'themes' upon the walls, and you will understand why this place is named 'Everwatch.'"

"Oh, that sounds interesting," said Savanna. "I'm kind of excited now."

The old man gave her a short but sad smile, something off that did not quite match his supposed enthusiasm for ancient cultures.

Michael had to wonder what exactly was going on in the old host's mind.

"The showroom should be ready by tomorrow morning," said Mr. Armstrong. "I shall inform all of you when it is."

Michael had to admit that his curiosity was piqued. There was something about this place that was not quite right, a puzzle with most of the pieces missing, and he wanted to know what the whole picture looked like.

Plus, he was paying a hundred and twenty a night for this outing, and though Savanna was good-hearted in that respect, Mr. Coal was ultimately correct about the state of this place. Michael was forking over extra cash he had not intended to, and if he was going to do that, something extra had better be in the works.

"Was there anything else you would like to know?" asked the old man.

This time it was Mr. Coal who spoke up. The gruff portly man nodded once toward the large stone fireplace in response.

"What are those urns up there on the fireplace?" he asked. "They look like funeral urns."

Michael turned to study the so-called "urns" that Mr. Coal had pointed out.

Upon the fireplace were indeed seven urns, all of them large urns of carved stone, tapered things with wide tops and narrow bases, all with the same circular carvings he had seen on the stone arch outside and on the green tapestries within the hotel, and their look was not so disturbing as much as the fact of the sheer number of them.

"That's a lot of funeral urns," said Michael.

"Yes, Mr. Smith, Mr. Coal," frowned Mr. Armstrong. "I have had some…tragedy…in my life. Those urns contain the ashes of the ones I've lost."

"I guess we shouldn't ask, then," said Savanna. "It's terrible to lose a loved one. I can't imagine losing that many."

"Yes," said Mr. Armstrong in a downcast tone. "Time sacrifices everything. That is simply nature at play."

Michael lowered his head in thought. This place had "charm," true, but it had something else, something that truly bothered him…and that something was "secrets." Secrets had always eaten at him, and now the Everwatch's closet skeletons were doing just that.

*****

Michael sat down on the north couch, Lexi on his right, Savanna on her right. Raymond and Lance were on the west couch, Mr. Coal was on the east couch, and the Corbins were on the south couch. All eight of them had been ushered into the main hall right after breakfast, and now they were all waiting to be let into the showroom.

Lexi had come down the night before and had made friends with Savanna, so that was a thing now. Raymond and Lance and the Corbins had come down as well, and then all of them had been ushered into the dining room for a late dinner, that dinner consisting of Salisbury steak along with mashed potatoes, greens, and some wine, not bad for a hotel that wasn't supposed to be in business.

Michael had also taken a cursory glance at the skeleton crew of a staff here. There were a couple of young white men that were servants, a couple of young white women that were maids, an old black couple that served as cooks, and a fat, balding white man that was the janitor/handyman.

They were a solemn lot, speaking next to nothing, and they were more like shadows in the background than anything else. Mr. Armstrong did all of the talking for them, and Michael found this unusual, but he chalked that up to being a British thing, or maybe not…He had no idea. The only thing he knew was that their presence fit well with the overall mood of this place…gloomy and mysterious.

Last night had filled Michael with restless sleep. That, and Raymond and Lance's "activities" in the room next door had kept him awake for some time. He was a little tired because of their shenanigans, but breakfast had perked him up and had made him feel better. Eggs, grits, ham, and toast had put some energy back into his weary bones.

Now they were all out in the main hall once more, but this time they were awaiting the unveiling of the "showroom." Michael wondered just exactly what it was they were going to see.

Mr. Armstrong walked in and nodded once toward the sealed east doors of the main hall, that pair of double doors next to the fireplace, the doors Michael had ogled upon first walking into the Everwatch.

"If you would follow me," said the elderly host. "I shall show you all a grand piece of history within."

The old host walked in a stiff gait up to the double doors, unlocked them with a large brass key, and then opened the doors inward, waving them all forward in visible eagerness.

Michael walked into the "showroom" along with Lexi, and he had not been expecting much, but he was ultimately shocked at what he found within. In fact, he sucked in his breath out of fascination and shook his head once in amazement.

The showroom was huge, and it spanned all the way up to the top of the Everwatch, five floors of a round room lined with books upon books upon wooden shelves, those shelves carved to fit the circular formation of the walls. Each floor had a wooden guardrail surrounding it to prevent lethal falls, and Michael could only assume that each floor had a locked door that led into this strange library.

And strange it was.

The floor in here was made of pieced-together slabs of stone that fit within a winding concentric swirl, each individual slab etched with that winding decoration upon its stark grey surface.

At the top of the room was a glass dome of interlocking windows set in dark metal that made the shape of a concentric swirl as well, the ceaseless rain pattering down upon the panes, a neat but expensive design that just looked cool to Michael.

This showroom was actually the tower they had all seen from outside.

This giant tower of a showroom/library was something he'd only seen out of videogames or movies, but this was nothing compared to what was on the ground floor. No, the ground floor of the showroom took the cake.

In the middle of the room was a huge stone head, that head settled directly center within the winding stone slabs, a carving of a bearded, bald white man, that huge head resting upon its left cheek, the eyes closed, the "skin" bedecked with more concentric, circling swirls like strange, carved tattoos.

This thing had to be at least twelve feet long, ten feet wide, and eight feet tall. Michael's eyes widened upon viewing it for the first time.

But this was not the only sight to see.

There was the curious statue of a man facing the giant stone head, that statue facing east, placed just a few feet in front of the entrance doors, a bronze statue covered in the green of verdigris, and it was this statue that held Michael's attention. He did not know why, but it called to him somehow, so he stood before it as the rest of the group gasped and made their way over to the giant head, the others abandoning him to ogle and walk around that monstrosity of carved stone.

The statue before him was of a Roman legionnaire or general; the man had no helmet, but he did wear the strips of laminated armor that Michael so often saw in various depictions of legionnaires. In the Roman soldier's right hand was a long bronze torch with no flame, and though his left hand was empty, it was confidently placed upon his left hip as if nothing could shake the man. That sentiment and torch, coupled with the statue's bluish-green appearance, kind of reminded Michael of the Statue of Liberty.

"Hey, Michael, you have to see this!" called out Savanna. "Get your butt over here!"

Michael turned to see the blonde running her right hand along the statue of the giant head.

Lexi gave her new friend a mock frown and shook her own head.

"He's *my* boyfriend," she said firmly. "Get your own. Only I get to order him around…Hey, Michael, you have to see this! Get your butt over here!"

Both women laughed over their little joke, but Michael just rolled his eyes. Now he had two obnoxious couples to put up with.

"I'll be there in a bit," he replied. "I'm just checking out this statue."

"I had figured you for a man that would enjoy this piece of work, Mr. Smith," said Mr. Armstrong.

Michael jumped a little at the man's sudden appearance, but he quickly put himself in check. Armstrong was just quiet, and that's all there was to it.

"Y…Yeah," stammered Michael. "There's something about it I like. I can't put my finger on it."

"It's integrity, Mr. Smith," replied the old host. "This unnamed general represents the ever-watchful eye of law and order."

Michael did not exactly know what Armstrong had meant by that reference, but he hoped it was a compliment.

"Uh, huh," he breathed.

Mr. Armstrong, however, clearly sensed Michael's confusion over the matter.

"You have integrity, Mr. Smith," nodded Mr. Armstrong. "You've helped the Corbins up and down the stairs whenever you've seen them struggling. You've remained true to your significant other in spite of some outside temptation, and you've paid more for the hotel stay than what it is worth, even though you had good reason not to, so I would say you are the most suitable for this honor."

Michael had no idea what "honor" the old man was talking about, but what Armstrong had just said seemed a little too personal for a hotel host to acknowledge, especially when it came to Michael talking to Savanna without Lexi around.

"*Ooookay*," said Michael as he raised one eyebrow. "That's a little…That seems a little too personal for—"

"I meant no disrespect, Mr. Smith," said the elderly host.

The old man reached up and gently pulled the bronze torch from the statue's grip. The narrow and tapered torch slid from the clutching hand with a scraping sound, and Mr. Armstrong laid the bronze thing across his own open palms.

"This torch is lit every ten years for a very important ceremony," explained the old man. "We choose one guest at the Everwatch to do so, and I would like that guest to be you…but only if you accept such a monumental duty."

"Oh…" said Michael in stunned reply.

"You have integrity, Mr. Smith," said the old man. "Only someone with integrity may be the torchbearer. True, the Corbins have their fair share of such, but they're much too old to perform this duty. This is for…someone made of sterner stuff. I think, therefore, you are the right man for the job."

Michael studied the unlit bluish-green torch laid across Armstrong's palms. There was something about it that called to him, even more so than the statue itself. Still, something about all of this felt off, weird, though he could not figure it out no matter how he looked at this puzzle.

"What if I…What if I *don't* want to be the torchbearer?" he asked. "'Monumental' sounds a little more important than anything I'm ready for."

"Then I suppose the torch will not be lit this year," sighed Mr. Armstrong. "We will just have to wait another ten."

He reached up to put the torch back into the grip of the statue, but Michael stopped him.

"Wait!" he said suddenly.

The elderly host turned and gave him a questioning look.

"Yes, Mr. Smith?" he asked.

"Ten years?…That's an awfully long time," breathed Michael. "I…I guess…"

"Yes?" asked Armstrong again.

"I guess…" said Michael. "I guess I can do it."

"Excellent," said the old man. "Why don't you carry this with you to your room. It's quite heavy, so I would get used to the weight of it before the ceremony. That time is swiftly approaching."

"Swiftly, huh?" asked Michael. "Huh…"

He reached down in absentminded thought to grasp the haft of the torch. The moment his fingers touched the cool metal, the moment his palm slid around that dusting of verdigris, he felt a strange shiver run through him, a weird ecstasy of power that made him squeeze his eyes shut just to ride it out.

He opened his eyes, took in a breath, and clutched the haft of the torch in both hands, holding it up out of newfound respect. Armstrong was right; it was quite heavy, but hefting it made him feel…powerful.

"I…I like this," he said in strange wonder.

"Excellent," smiled the old man.

Michael took a moment to eye the statue of the nameless Roman general, feeling the power this man must have felt, but then he noticed something peculiar.

"He kind of looks like you, doesn't he?" he asked.

"That he does," said Mr. Armstrong. "It's one of the things that fascinates me about this piece. Perhaps he was a distant ancestor of mine, or perhaps he's me…You never know. It's a curious thing indeed."

"Yes…" said Michael, but he wasn't really listening.

He felt connected to the statue now, and maybe that was just because he had been selected to be the "torchbearer," but he felt different…He felt like someone really important, and that was odd, because he had always figured himself to be dead average.

His wondering was broken by Lexi's demanding voice.

"Michael, will you get over here!" called out his girlfriend.

"Yeah!" parroted Savanna. "Come give your girl some attention! If you don't get over here, I'm going to start dating Lexi!"

The two women laughed again, but Michael only sighed. Now that Lexi had found a "road friend," her behavior was almost as bad as Raymond and Lance's.

"Coming!" he said quickly. "Excuse me, Mr. Armstrong."

"Of course, sir," said the elderly host.

Michael walked over to the giant stone head, but he stopped as he neared within a few feet of it. There was a palpable aura swathing it, something sinister yet strong, almost as powerful as the feeling he'd had when around the Roman statue. It was a wave, a vibe, a…an *ambience* of malevolence that he could feel so much as see.

The others surrounded the giant head, that stone head lying on its own bearded left cheek, and even the gruff portly man, Mr. Coal, seemed fascinated with it, but Michael stopped just a few feet short of coming within physical contact of it.

Lexi, Savanna, Raymond, Lance, Mr. Coal, and the Corbins all walked around the thing in a circle, each laying a single hand on it, each sliding their collective hands across it, and Michael was not sure if what they were doing was even a conscious decision on their part.

"You *have* to see this, Michael!" said Savanna with wide blue eyes. "This thing is amazing! It's like nothing I've ever felt before!"

"It feels strange, but it's like…it's like it's talking to you," said Lexi. "It's really cool. You have to try it."

"Yeah, come touch this giant head where my hand is!" called out Lance.

"Lance!" warned Lexi as Savanna gave a short guffaw.

"What?" asked the young blond man.

Mr. Armstrong walked up next to Michael and gave a nod toward the statue.

"An equally fascinating piece," said the old man.

He turned his attention toward Mr. Coal as the gruff man ran his right hand along the statue's wide nose.

"Don't you think so, Mr. Coal?" continued Mr. Armstrong. "Isn't this worth a little extra money for your stay?"

The portly man with the mustache simply nodded in absent-minded reply, but Michael could tell that the gruff man's attention was upon the statue and not on anything Mr. Armstrong had said.

"What's the story behind this?" asked Raymond.

The young man ran his right hand over the carved stone of the bald pate of the giant head. His attention was also upon the statue, but his eyes were bright with wonder, a shine that beheld a curious hunger for the origins of said statue.

Michael was also curious about the stone head's origins, but not for the same reasons.

"There are some things that should remain dormant," replied Mr. Armstrong. "This is the likeness of an elder god worshipped so long ago that even his name has been forgotten."

"Fascinating..." breathed Raymond.

"Yes," said Mr. Armstrong. "This particular god was feared even by the ancient Druids. His sagely look belies his actual nature. He is a representation of the untamed power of wilderness, the full wrath of nature herself, though this creature is but a priest for such an uncontrollable force."

"Uh, huh..." said Mr. Coal.

"The Druids contained this power through sacrifice," said the elderly host. "They did so out of a need to survive and out of fear, because such a thirst, such a fire, can never be truly quenched...It was costly for the early Celts. Such a sacrifice demanded newborn blood, and that cost was paid…until a strange alliance was formed."

"Is that so?" asked Savanna.

They were like robots to Michael, walking around in a mindless circle, a group of ants following a trail that led nowhere. It disturbed him on a deep level, but all he could do was grip the bronze torch within his hands. That torch gave him some sense of safety, though he did not know why.

"When the Romans came and overtook their lands," continued Armstrong, "the Celts did not call upon this sleeping god for help, nor did their druids, nor would they, and all written records of this god were wiped from history, save one by the Romans, and what was written was nothing more than a warning."

"And what was that?" asked Michael.

He wanted to know because he needed to know. There was something wrong here; he could feel it. It raised his hackles and set his teeth on edge, though the others could not sense this like he could.

"That warning, roughly translated, was thus," said Mr. Armstrong. "It stated: *Such hatred of man and beast would make even lonely Diana weep, for it is boundless. The birds of song are silenced in its wake, the beasts of the field are no more, the oceans empty, the buzz of the bee stilled by the harsh growth of wild Terra…Come not here with open arms. Let sleeping giants lie.*"

"Interesting…" said Lexi.

"Yes, it is unique," said Mr. Armstrong. "These two pieces work in tandem, as it is clear the Romans encountered this long-forgotten god. They feared it as much as the Druids did, and so we have one singular instance of the two groups working together to contain such a thing, hence the statue of the ever-watchful Roman general.

"Each group sacrificed something so that a greater sacrifice would not be made. Yes, both groups employed sacrifice to achieve their goal, though each did so in different ways."

"Michael, you have to see this," said Lexi in a hushed voice.

But he did not want to go near it, much less touch it. He did not like the feel of the thing, and he was not a superstitious man, so for him to feel anything at all towards an inanimate object was strange in itself, and this raised all of his red flags.

But he did not have to worry about being cajoled into doing something he did not want to do.

Mr. Armstrong raised a small silver bell in his left hand and rang it, jingling the little bell in a swinging arc, producing a ring that was louder and clearer than it should have been.

The group around the statue awoke as if from a dream, and they released their hands from the giant stone head, only to wander off in different directions to study the various books upon the shelves of the showroom.

Michael, himself, clutched the bronze torch in his hands and would not let go of it. He did not want to put it down, because he felt that it was the one and only defense he had against…*something*, but he did not know what that *something* was, nor did he know why he needed to defend himself against it.

✱✱✱✱✱

It was well past ten in the evening.

Michael was in his black tee and black sweatpants, something he liked to wear in lieu of pajamas, a "just-in-case-he-needed-to-go-out" style of dress. True, this little venture was a road trip in essence, but all of them had packed extra clothes just in case.

Dinner had been served around eight, a very late meal, but no one had complained. No, everyone had gone back to the showroom and had spent their time in there, though Michael had simply sat out in the main hall and read one of Lexi's romances…He had not felt like going back in there with that giant stone head.

Now he was up in his room with Lexi, though his girlfriend was not being so hospitable at the moment. The young woman was in bed and in her underwear, in white panties and a white slip, reading the very same shlock that Michael had read for most of the day.

Lexi looked up at him from the pages of her book and shook her head in visible irritation.

"Will you put that thing down?" she asked. "You've been carrying it around all day long. What gives? Obsessed with playing with your stick?"

Michael stared down at the bronze torch in his hands. He had not even realized he was still holding it.

"I like it," he said stupidly, because that was the only answer he could give.

"You and your phallic symbol," said Lexi as she rolled her eyes. "That thing is gross anyway, Michael. You've got that green stuff all over your hands. You even have some on your face."

"I do?" he asked.

"Yes, you mutton head," sighed Lexi. "Go wash it off."

She reached down and scratched her right leg in absent-minded fashion.

Michael could see long scratches of red along Lexi's lower right leg, and upon closer inspection, she had scratches on her left leg as well. She had a growing rash on her normally perfect legs; the welts were a greenish red, and this caused him no small amount of concern.

"You're one to talk," he frowned. "You're tearing up your legs, Lex."

"I have some kind of a rash," she said unhappily. "We'll just have to stop and get a cream for it after we leave…Stop changing the subject. Go put that thing down and clean up. I don't want you kissing me like that."

"Fine," he sighed.

He walked into the bathroom and flipped on the light with his left hand, mainly because he was still holding the torch with his right. He probably should have set the torch down somewhere, but he didn't want to. He wanted to keep it close by, and try as he might, he could not set it down for one second. Even when he had been reading earlier in the day, he had set the torch across his lap. The weight of it did not seem to bother him anymore.

He shook his head and looked in the mirror. He did indeed have a long streak of bluish-green across his left cheek, his right in the reflection. He reached up to feel it, but then he noticed the green all over his right hand and fingers. He looked down to see that green across both hands, something that had most certainly gone unnoticed until now.

"Huh," he said to himself.

There was no point in trying to rub off the stain on his cheek when both hands were also stained, so he grabbed a white towel from off a linen shelf near the tub and ran the unsullied cloth under the running water of the sink. He reached up to clean off the stain on his face, fully expecting the water to run green from loose verdigris, but no matter how many times he rubbed his cheek, the stain would not come off.

He looked down at the wet towel in his right hand and shook his head in mild disbelief. There wasn't so much as a speck of green upon it.

"Huh," he said again.

He dried his face with another towel, but he never let go of the green torch in his hands. That bronze torch was his safety blanket for the time being, and somehow, he knew he was going to feel sad once it was taken from him.

He sighed and walked back into the bedroom, but he was met with yet another surprise, this time a guest, and that guest was Savanna. The young blonde was sitting at the end of the bed at Lexi's feet, and though Lexi was in her underwear, Savanna did not seem to mind.

"There he is, the green man," said Savanna.

Michael frowned and shook his head.

"I'm going to be the torchbearer for the ceremony," he said firmly, though he held some pride in that fact, and it showed in his voice.

"Listen to him," smirked Lexi. "He sounds like a little kid."

Both women laughed, and Michael could not help but feel the heat of embarrassment upon his face once more. The people in his life always did this to him, embarrassed him without seemingly any effort at all. Sometimes, he simply wished he had more control over them.

"Yeah, yeah, you harpies," he frowned.

"Get going, Michael," ordered Lexi. "Savanna and I are going to have some girl talk."

"Yeah," smiled the blonde. "Get thee hence. Go downstairs or something."

"*Ooookay*," said Michael cautiously.

"Shoo, shoo," said Lexi with a wave of her hand. "We're going to talk for a while. Go downstairs."

"Yeah," grinned Savanna. "Go play with your stick somewhere else."

Both women laughed, but Michael only frowned.

"All right, all right," he said unhappily. "I have to sleep sometime, though."

"We're on vacation," said Lexi. "We can stay up as long as we want…Go relax or something."

"Yeah," said Savanna. "Go to the showroom. I could spend all day in there."

The blonde scratched under her flannel shirt, and Michael could see greenish-red welts up and down both of the young woman's arms.

"You've got a rash, too?" he asked.

"Oh…I guess," said Savanna. "Huh…I just noticed that. How funny."

Michael did not think there was anything "funny" about a rash, but he knew she had meant "how strange," and that was something they could both agree on.

"You two need to get that looked at," he said unhappily. "That's not good."

"Says the man with green hands and a green streak on his face," frowned Lexi. "Go downstairs, Michael. Give us some space."

This irked him, mainly because of her tone, and his face momentarily twisted with anger, but he did not get a chance to say anything about it.

"I'm not trying to be mean," sighed Lexi. "I just wanted to talk to Savanna for a while."

He calmed himself enough to give a civil reply, but he was still unhappy about all of this.

"Okay, but I'm your girlfriend, not her," frowned Michael.

"You're my 'girlfriend'?" asked Lexi.

Michael shook his head at his own verbal error and silently cursed under his breath.

"Boyfriend!" he said angrily. "You know what I meant!"

But his hostility was only met with stark laughter from both women.

Of course, enough was enough. He waved them off and headed toward the door.

"Michael, it's just a joke," said Lexi. "Don't get angry."

"Yeah," said Savanna. "It's okay. We were just—"

"I'm going downstairs," he said abruptly, and then he left.

He shut the door behind himself a little harder than he'd wanted to, not quite a slam, but still…Those two were just as obnoxious as Raymond and Lance when they were together, and he needed a break from that. True, going downstairs had been Lexi's idea—more like a command—but it made him feel better to believe that he had made this decision on his own initiative.

He headed toward the stairs.

He stopped as a strange, musty smell assaulted his nostrils. It was the scent of decay, but more like the scent of dying foliage, not like a rotting carcass, and this confused him. He could smell that odor coming from the room right next to the staircase, the room the Corbins were staying in.

He walked up to the door to knock on it, but he thought better about it…He did not want to disturb the old couple. He figured the elderly deserved some rest in their old age.

He walked downstairs into the main hall, stopped in the center of the ring of couches, and sighed. Now that he was down here, there was nothing to do.

His eyes wandered toward the fireplace and toward its mantle, and then they lingered upon the row of etched stone urns resting quietly above the fire.

He walked over to the fireplace and inspected the urns. There was nothing particularly special about them— they were simply stone urns with winding swirls etched into their surfaces—but he could feel a sort of presence from them, an aura of sorts, a feeling as if they had a will of their own.

He was not superstitious, but this place had a way of bringing that nonsense out of him, and he did not know what to think about it.

He decided to shake it off, maybe sit down and relax.

"Huh," he said briefly as he turned to walk back toward the couches.

It was then that something most unfortunate occurred, mainly because he had forgotten he was still holding the bronze torch in his right hand, that heavy torch covered in the bluish-green of verdigris, and the accident was his own fault, but in his defense, the torch was like an extension of his own body at this point.

The head of the torch swung upwards and knocked over the left-most urn from Michael's point of view. The urn in question fell from the mantle and clattered across the wooden floor, leaving a trail of spilled ashes in its wake.

"Oh, crap!" he hissed.

He chased after the rolling urn and stopped it with his shoe, but doing so revealed the edge of something white within the top of it. He reached down and plucked an ash-coated picture from the urn, a small wallet-sized picture that he quickly dusted free of said funerary ash.

His eyes narrowed as he studied the fat balding white man within the photo, and then they widened as his brain made the connection between this photo and one of the staff, the janitor/slash handyman of the Everwatch. This photo was a dead ringer for the man.

"This must be his mom's urn or something," said Michael to himself in a hushed, nervous voice. "Oh, crap. He put his picture in with his relative's ashes…I…I need to clean this up before somebody notices."

There was a small ash pan and broom next to the fireplace, most likely for the fireplace ashes, so Michael grabbed those cleaning implements and got to work. He could not bear to let go of the bronze torch for some reason—he at least needed to be touching it—so he balanced it across his right shoe until he had restored as much of the ash to the spilled urn as possible.

He placed the picture back inside the urn and then returned the urn to its resting place upon the mantle. He then took some time to sweep the remaining stain of ashes from the floor towards the fireplace. He did not want any incriminating evidence.

He picked up his torch and stared at the other urns, but he was curious now, so he opened the lid of the next one on his immediate right and poked his fingers in it. He pulled out an ash-covered photo a second later, but then he stopped as he stared down at it, unsure of what it meant.

This one was of one of the maids of the Everwatch.

He had a strange anxiety growing inside him, something clawing to the surface of his mind…Something was not right here.

He replaced that picture, put the lid on the urn, and removed the lid on the next urn in line. He pulled a photo from that one, studied it, and then moved onto the next urn until he had seen every photo.

Each urn held a picture of one of the staff. There were seven staff members, and there were seven urns, and this seemed odd to him that they would put their pictures in a memorial urn.

"Must be some kind of a tradition here," he said under his breath.

Still, it was the sense of presence about the urns that sank into him. He could feel someone watching him, and this disturbed him a little.

He turned to walk back toward the couches, this time taking care not to slam his torch into any of the urns, but he did not make it two feet before coming to a sudden halt.

The staff of the Everwatch was there in the main hall…all of them. Each one of the staff members was wearing a dark-brown cloak with the hood down to reveal their faces, all of them in a semicircle around the couches, each one staring in silent judgement at Michael.

He did not like all eyes on him, and he certainly didn't like the implications of the staff dressed in…whatever it was they were dressed in.

"I…I…uhhh…was just looking at the urns here," he stammered. "I didn't mean anything by it."

The staff all raised their hoods at the same time. The motion was intimidating, like something you would see out of some strange cult, and Michael was speechless at the sight of it.

"Uhhhh…" was all he could say.

They burst into flames after that, each a pyre of green flame that became a roaring pillar of that ghastly color, fires without heat, no sensation of warmth from their passing at all, and then they were gone, turning to piles of ash that blew away in some phantasmal wind.

Michael shook in place as he stared at the empty spaces where the staff had been.

"Am I on drugs?" he asked himself. "Was I drugged?...I must have been drugged."

"Sacrifice, not drugs, Mr. Smith," came the voice of Mr. Armstrong.

Michael jumped a little as he turned to his right to see the elderly man standing there, a mere five feet from him, somewhere the old man should not have been able to get to without Michael seeing him.

"What's going on here?" asked Michael. "What have you done? Did you spike my food?"

"I'm afraid not, Mr. Smith," said Mr. Armstrong. "What you have just witnessed was a final release, a signal for the beginning of the end, or perhaps a new beginning; I'm not entirely sure. I was in your place ten years ago, as was my research team, and as terrible and as heartbreaking as it was, I made the right decision…Such is the nature of sacrifice…I should have never brought that cursed idol here to the States…

"The ancient Druids took many newborns before the Romans came to their lands, all to satisfy that bloodthirsty, vengeful thing. Once the Romans realized what they had uncovered, the Celts took the elderly, the sick, and the infirm instead. It was a trade the two peoples had agreed upon, because some things must remain sleeping. Even proud and able conquerors such as the Romans understood this.

"It cannot be fought head on. It must be lured into a trap, Mr. Smith. It demands sacrifice, so you will give it such, but that bait is poisoned, a fire that will burn within. When the time is right, the flames of justice will work against it, because it will already be vulnerable to them…Remember that.

"Such sacrifice is always painful, and you will lose everything, but everything depends on you now, so you must take this role. You are the only one here with the integrity to do so.

"Nevertheless, my role in this is done…Now we will see the end or the beginning. Whichever depends on you…Speaking of such, it appears my time here at the Everwatch is finally at an end…It is truly up to you now."

"Up to me?" asked Michael. "What's up to me? What are you talking about?"

"Circles within circles, Mr. Smith," said the old host. "All things must end in order for there to be any new beginnings. It is a basic premise of the universe, a foundation of our cosmos, and even forgotten gods must bow to this. It's the reason nothing ever truly falls into darkness."

"I have no idea what that means!" said Michael in exasperation.

The elderly host crusted over with green, first on his skin, then on his clothes, a fine cracking of flesh and cloth one would see in a painting withered by the sun. It caused Michael to back away in slight horror, backing away from whatever strange and otherworldly event was taking place right in front of him.

"You will, Mr. Smith," said the old man through green-crusted lips. "You are the torchbearer…"

He crumbled away after that, a large pile of particle verdigris, and then he, too, blew away in a ghostly wind, what was left of him scattering away to disappear altogether.

Michael gripped the unlit bronze torch in his hands and shook his head a few times, a shaking of disbelief to dislodge whatever drug-induced madness had suddenly invaded his brain.

He staggered to the south couch and sat down, but he felt stiff and ungainly, a strange sensation overcoming him, like he was being drowned in concrete.

"What is going on?" he whispered to himself.

He did not get a chance to ruminate further over the matter.

There came a stumbling cry for help and the sound of someone falling or sliding down several steps a moment later.

Michael peered over the south couch to see Raymond clutching the stairway rail upon Michael's right, the young man holding onto the rail with a desperate grip… There was clearly something wrong with him.

Raymond was at the bottom of the stairs, and as stiff as Michael felt in gait and motion, he hopped the back of the couch and was at his friend and coworker's side in a heartbeat.

"What's wrong!" he cried.

Upon closer inspection, Raymond did not look well at all. The young man was in his underwear, a pair of silk boxers dyed a stark grey, so his ravaged bare skin was more than visible. The left side of his body, from his shaved legs all the way up to his normally handsome face, was swollen and covered with dark-brown boils, as if he had been strangely burned or had suffered some kind of swift and terrible outbreak.

"Lance!" spat out Raymond. "Something wrong with Lance…Need help…"

"There's something wrong with you!" cried Michael. "I've got to get you to a hospital!"

"N…No…" stammered Raymond. "We got sick…Something happened…Don't have much time…I'm losing myself…It…It started out as a rash…"

He cried out and grit his teeth as the pustular skin on his left arm burst open to reveal a thick brown crust beneath it. Something was tearing out of him, *replacing* him, but Michael was too horrified to guess what.

"It was just a rash, but now…" gasped Raymond. "Now it's changing us…I can feel him deep down…calling me…He's calling me…"

"I…I…I've got to find a working phone," stammered Michael in hushed horror. "None of our cells work."

"No," choked out Raymond. "You've got to…to help Lance…He is…is first…You have to…release him…You must start…with him…"

The young man coughed up blood, and Michael retreated up the stairs a couple of steps as the rash that had previously covered one side of Raymond's body spread everywhere, covering Raymond's other half as well.

Michael was startled by the sheer virality of the spreading infection he was witnessing, but he was also stunned by the protective sincerity in Raymond's strange command along with the even stranger call to action he felt burning inside his own blood. He did not want to leave the clearly sick man's side, but he could not help but follow the path he felt his soul had just been thrust upon.

He turned and ran up the stairs toward Raymond and Lance's shared room, running at top speed out of heed from the calling fire burning in his heart and out of respect for Raymond's conviction toward his own partner.

He ran past the Corbins' closed door, but his nose was attacked by an even stronger scent of decaying foliage seeping from beneath that shut entryway. Nevertheless, he ignored that scent and continued past the old couple's room and straight to Raymond and Lance's temporary quarters. He was, however, still in for an odiferous shock.

He swung open the door, only to be assaulted by another strong scent, this time the strong scent of wet forest, something he had most definitely not been expecting.

He raised his left arm to cover his mouth in protection while he clutched the bronze torch in his right hand. His arms were all green now, a bluish-green that rode all the way up to the short sleeves of his black tee, but he was not concerned with that at the moment.

"Lance?" he asked as tried not to choke on the musty dampness that pervaded this small hotel room.

There were roots everywhere, roots of some tree growing along the walls of the little room, wet earth and dead foliage crunching beneath Michael's feet. Whatever trappings and draperies had bedecked this room were long gone…It was like a miniature deciduous biome during rainy season in here now.

The bed in this room had vanished; now the floor was covered with nothing but earth, dead leaves, and roots. On the back wall was a cluster of bark and branches like that of a tree, but how such a thing had grown in here, Michael did not know…until it moved.

The "tree" before him stepped forth from the root wall on two branching legs, and its bark-covered arms reached forth toward Michael, a yearning and seeking of hostility toward Michael's own face.

Michael stepped back out of reactive instinct and raised his left arm in some modicum of defense. The grasping, woody digits of the creature's right hand gripped Michael's left wrist, and he could feel a power there, a strength that belied its roughly man-sized form, but it could not damage him. It squeezed Michael's wrist with a terrible might, yet Michael felt little more than a mild pain.

Nevertheless, this angered him.

"Let go, damn you!" he cried out.

He raised the bronze torch in his right hand, and that strange accoutrement to an even stranger piece of art lit ablaze at the top, the eternally-unlit torch lighting at last out of sheer paradox, lighting ablaze with a vivid green flame.

Michael brought down the torch upon the creature's right shoulder, and the animated tree-thing went up in a green pyre, burning away in a pillar of emerald flame.

It staggered backwards as its branch-like arm came off at the shoulder, and Michael had to reach into the blazing green flame, torch still in hand, a half-grip between torch and the branch-like arm in question, in order to pull the burning limb off his own arm. The limb popped off of him with ease, but he felt the bark give way to the squishiness of flesh, and then he heard the screaming before the being in front of him actually died.

He could hear Lance's screams as the young man burned away to ash within that verdant mess of fiery bark and flesh, and then Lance was nothing more than ash upon the hotel floor, nothing more than a grey pile of what had previously been a living human.

It shook Michael, the whole of it, and he could do nothing for a few stunned seconds as he stared down at the green-flickering remains beneath his shoes. The emerald flame had burned the young man away to nothing, but it had not damaged anything else within the room; it had not spread like literal wildfire.

Michael staggered backwards himself, but not from pain. He was in shock, so he reached for the doorknob and quickly exited his coworker and friend's room.

He felt stiff in his joints, a side-effect, no doubt, from his immediate traumatic experience, but he was given no time to rest.

Raymond came at him from behind, the young man gripping him around the waist, and then Michael was flung forward into the wall next to the door he had just exited. He impacted the wall with a heavy thud, rattling the portraits upon it, but he felt little to no damage from that impact, so he turned and faced his new opponent.

"Raymond, no!" he yelled as the young man came at him again.

He knew with one look that Raymond was no longer in control of himself, either.

The young man was exactly like his partner now, all bark and branches, a walking tree-man, though the right half of Raymond's upper face was still human. In that dark-brown eye was nothing more than sheer hatred and madness, and that hatred and madness drove Raymond forward through some ancient and insane vendetta.

Michael raised his lit torch as Raymond speared himself upon it.

The young man before him lit ablaze in a green pyre, and that unconverted dark-brown eye of Raymond's widened in surprise just before it burned away as well. Raymond screamed in much the same manner as Lance had, and then he, too, was a pile of ash laced with flickering green flames.

But only one thing crossed Michael's mind at that moment, only one person came to mind as he stared down at Raymond's ashen remains.

"Lexi!" he gasped.

He needed to get to her. Whatever was going on, whatever infection was spreading amongst the guests, he needed to do something before she was taken from him as well. Both she and Savanna had the rash, so…

He tried to turn to run toward his own room, but he was ambushed yet again. Long tendrils of moss-covered vines wrapped around his waist and chest from behind, and then he was thrown bodily face first to the upper landing floor, just in front of the Corbins' room.

He turned his head as his nose was assaulted yet again, assaulted by a terrible smell of decay, and the source of that awful smell originated from the old couple's now open doorway.

"What the fu—!" he started to swear, but he could not finish that expletive.

More mossy vines wrapped around his waist, he was picked up in an effortless motion, and then he was unceremoniously tossed through the open doorway of the Corbins' hotel room. He had not even had time to see what had accosted him.

He landed with a loud huff on top of the stinking remains of rotting leaves, dead branches, and wet earth, a convergence of foliage and mud that had putrefied into a mire of sorts.

The air was moist in here, a perpetual fog permeating everything, a sickly and unholy heaviness that tried to bear him down.

He tried to stand, but he was struck hard in the back. He plopped face down in the mire, and then he was picked up by his black tee, but his shirt simply ripped off of him in one clean tear, the flimsy fabric shredding apart as if it were paper.

Whatever had struck him was momentarily confused by the tearing of Michael's shirt, so he stood while he still had the chance.

By some miracle of fate, his torch had not gone out. It had not been forced down into the earthy dampness beneath him, though it had flickered for a few seconds. Nevertheless, that weapon had worked before, and he knew it would work again.

He quickly turned to face the slick, mucus-covered form of the great mushroom with arms that had attacked him. He did not know which of the Corbins this particular creature had been, but at the moment, he did not care.

A thick, ivory-white arm swung toward him, but Michael danced backwards to avoid it. He saw the other Corbin coming at him from his left, a larger and darker shade of brown and white than the original, both mushroom people advancing upon him in a hostile shuffling through muck and mire.

They had no faces. They were simply stalks of fungus now, the wide brims of their tops dark-brown in color and slick with whatever clear slime exuded from them. Where their necks and faces had been were now frills, those alabaster, fleshy frills moving slightly as if pushed by an invisible wind, and the once old couple sprayed heavy spores from those frills, the spores' toxin filling the air around Michael in a noxious cloud.

Michael covered his mouth and nose with his left arm as he raised his torch in defense. The air lit up around him in a fireball as the spores set ablaze, but he did not feel that green heat, nor would he. He knew now he was immune to his own fire, though he did not know how.

He lowered his torch toward the shuffling terrors before him and willed his flame to extend. He could feel he could do this, push his brazen will forward, so he did. It was more out of faith than anything else, faith in something older and more powerful than him, but that was all he needed. He needed to lay down the law, the order which bound civilization together, the creed that burned away the chaos inherent in the savage growth of the wild.

The emerald torch he clutched so desperately within his right hand turned upon the Corbins in a stream of viridescent death, a supernatural flamethrower that caught the both of them in its raging wake.

The old couple did not so much as cry out as they burned away, both of them popping and fizzing within the stream of emerald flame. Their charred remains melted into flaming goop mere seconds later, and then they, too, returned to the earth, returning to the muck beneath them.

Michael stared down at his naked body. What remained of his clothes had burned away in the fireball that had ensued from lighting the spore cloud, so now he was without everything, even his modesty. His shoes had slipped from his feet within the muck beneath him, so he did not even have that to count on. He just had himself and his torch, and that would have to do.

Being suddenly nude did not surprise him. It was the fact that he was all green now, a bluish-green of verdigris, that surprised him, but he had no time to worry about that. Green or not, he had to get to his own room and to Lexi. He knew now that she and Savanna were also infected, and he did not know if he could save them, but he had to try. If he could not save them…

No. There had to be something he could do.

He steadied himself as he walked out of the pit that had been the Corbins' room. He was ready for ambush now, ready for whatever had attacked him and thrown him in here in the first place.

The first of the tendrils came at him from directly in front of his face, but he was quick to slash a green line of flame with his torch, and that moss-covered vine went up in a flash.

He turned to see the shambling mound of moss and vines coming at him. The tendril he had lit up fell to the floor in a withered blackening as more vines came at him from the amorphous blob that was trying to wrap him up again.

Michael slashed tendril after tendril, vine after vine, but they only detached from the mound as they lit ablaze, the appendages burning to nothing as the creature grew more and more of its own weird natural weaponry to attack him.

"Enough!" yelled Michael.

He lowered his torch and willed his law forward once more.

The torch he gripped in both hands now blazed forward in that devastating stream of viridescent flame. The shambling mound of vegetation blocking his path lit up all at once, all of it, every tendril and mossy piece of its obstructing blob, a green bonfire that burned nothing else around it.

He heard Mr. Coal's frantic screams as the man's fiery figure wrapped in emerald flame staggered out of the bonfire, that figure flailing only to pitch over the railing and fall to the first floor below.

Michael stared over the railing at the flickering ashes spread across the wood floor at ground level. He slowly shook his head in disgust at the sight, disgust that he had to do this at all, disgust that he had to execute people that had never done anything to him, had never harmed him in any way.

He felt stiffer now. It was becoming more difficult to move.

He looked down and realized that he was no longer naked. Around his waist, covering his lower parts, was half of the segmented armor of the Roman general he had been so fascinated with. He knew at that moment that he was becoming like that ancient and priceless statue, but this new development did not matter. Whatever was going on here, whatever madness had descended upon this wretched place, had to come to an end.

He made his way past Raymond and Lance's room, intent on getting to his own. He hustled up to his own room's closed door, turned the handle, and walked in.

The room was full of vines and leaves now, vines and leaves and blooming pink and red flowers covering everything, the heady musk of those vines and the sweet scent of those blooming flowers permeating everything, the empty space aglow with small specks of luminescent pollen that drifted within Michael's vision. The bed was gone, the room empty save for the wild growth and its two inhabitants.

They were in there, Lexi and Savanna, but they were…no longer human. He was too late, but if even he hadn't been, he had no idea what he would have done.

Both women were nude from their tops down to their waists, but their bottom halves were open blossoms of great and colorful flowers, the petals red upon Lexi and pink upon Savanna. The young and beautiful women were all green now, their skin a distinct stem green, their hair gone and replaced by delicate leaves and flowers. They were indeed beautiful in an alien way, but the sight of that beauty broke Michael's heart in an instant and nearly killed his resolve right then.

"Michael!" cried both women at once.

He sucked in his breath at the sound of their melodic voices and the warmth of their earnest smiles. He wanted to cry; that emotion of grief was within him, but for some reason, he could not…He just physically could not.

"Michael, come to us!" called out Lexi. "Everything is so much better now! Isn't this wonderful? We're so beautiful now! This is amazing! Come join us! You can have us both!"

Both young women reached out with open arms, a gesture begging for him to step forward into their wanton embraces. He loved Lexi, and he had to admit that he was attracted to Savanna, so he obliged them, though he knew it was a bad idea to do so.

He lowered his torch, walked into Lexi's open arms, and stared down at her beautiful face as she smiled back up at him.

"I love you, Michael," she said, her voice a haunting bell ringing within his stiffening green ears. "Give me your love. Give me all of you. I want you inside of me. Become one with me."

He bent down to kiss her, and their lips met for a few brief seconds, his stiff verdigris lines upon her soft and yielding red ones, her bare chest against his, their arms around each other in strange passion.

This was not meant to last, however.

Her gorgeous verdant face split down the middle to reveal a massive maw of fleshy interior and sliming tendrils intent on swallowing him whole. She wrapped her new "mouth" around his head and shoulders, the caustic digestive juices sizzling into him, but his skin was turning into bronze, so this was only a mild tingle to him, a discomfort and nothing more.

He could have allowed her to devour him, to take him all in, but this would have accomplished nothing. She would have died anyway in terrible immolation from the inside out, and to do such a thing was not within his nature. He would rather she die facing him.

She pulled off of him as her face closed shut, closing to reveal its original human beauty, that very human face revealing an expression of both surprise and horror. Acidic steam sizzled up from Michael's blueish-green head in puffs of caustic flow to mirror that expression; her eyes were wide with realized betrayal, the same betrayal he knew was burning within his own.

His torch had gone through her solar plexus and out her back, the green flame burning brightly as she burned to ash within his arms.

He stared down at his open, ash-covered arms and leveled torch and shed a single tear from his right eye. That was all he could shed anymore from those rapidly bronzing orbs, but that was more than enough to display his intense grief at that moment.

"You killed her…" said Savanna in audible shock.

He looked up at the once-blonde beauty but said nothing.

"You killed Lexi, Michael," said the young woman.

She shuffled toward him in a slow and deliberate fashion, strange white roots beneath her belled and petaled lower half pulling her forward.

"Stay back, Savanna," warned Michael. "I don't want to hurt you."

The young woman's face crumpled in despair as she continued to pull herself forward.

"You have to, Michael," she said sadly. "It's the only way."

"No, don't do this," he replied. "Don't be stupid!"

She opened up her arms and beckoned him into her embrace.

"I could have loved you," she said in a wavering tone. "You could have loved me. We could have been together."

"I know," he frowned. "I know that…That's why you can't do this…Don't make me do this…"

She continued forward, her arms wide, her bare green chest heaving as she wept.

He held his torch midlevel and shook his head no.

"Stay back!" he warned.

"He's calling me," said the once-blonde. "I have to do this while I'm still me…You have to stop him, Michael. You have to put him back to sleep. That's why you have to do this…Show me you have some love for me, Michael. Release me, and put him back to sleep."

There was nothing he could say. Michael could only stand in place as Savanna continued her deliberate advance, her arms open, her strange beauty striking at his very soul.

She turned into a pyre of bluish-green flame as she impaled herself upon his torch, the verdigris flame spearing straight through her midriff, her beautiful face twisting in pain for a brief second before it was engulfed as well.

"Thank you…" he heard her say, and then she was also ash, a scattering of that grey dusting upon the verdant floor.

It did not take a doctoral degree for Michael to figure out the meaning behind Savanna's last words.

He gripped his torch tightly and stiffly walked from his own room, the full set of his Roman armor now complete, a living statue of bronze and verdigris ready to combat a god that should never have existed in the first place.

He slowly made his way down the stairs and to the first floor.

It was time to end this. It was time to end this, and now he was mad, really and truly angry. There was no fear left in him, only vengeance and a need to lay down the law, the creed of humanity.

There was another group waiting for him at the bottom of the stairs, a group of robed and hooded figures, each dressed in the ominous dark-brown robes Michael had seen once before.

They walked, single file, into the showroom, the double doors flung wide, their hooded figures marching in slow procession through that dreaded opening.

Michael steeled his resolve and followed the robed figures into the showroom.

They stood in a circle around the giant stone head, and Michael stood in his position upon the now empty pedestal, the statue of the Roman general gone, replaced by him. Somewhere in him, he felt this was the correct thing to do.

The others knew what they were doing; he sensed this. They were performing an important role in this ritual, and his role was as equally important, if not more so, for he was the weapon of justice that would seal the fate of this long-forgotten god that had somehow rooted its vile presence here within the States.

They were all in a circle now, Michael and the robed figures, the circle closed and completed with the number eight, that mystical number that represented infinity, eight sentinels to overlook a much-needed imprisonment, an imprisonment that deserved no parole, nor would it ever.

Michael could see their faces now, all of them, and they were all there, all seven, Raymond, Lance, the Corbins, Mr. Coal, Lexi, and Savanna. Each of them held an etched stone urn in their hands, and each of them held up that funerary urn in recognition of this uncanny shared ritual.

All of them lit aflame in a weird unity of conflagration, a group immolation of green flame that reduced them to nothing more than their stone and etched funeral urns upon the showroom's own stone-slab floor. Those flames burned around the urns in a bizarre dance of virescent blazing, and then those same dancing flames turned into small globes of fire that were drawn into the giant head, that head absorbing the emerald flames through cold and bearded stone.

The massive stone head opened its eyes, two huge brown eyes burning with an inner-green light, those burning eyes staring with both malice and abject hatred at Michael, an animosity older than mankind could imagine. It opened its giant bearded mouth and gave forth a low moan, a call of inhumanity that spoke of a verdant world long forgotten, an empty world meant to be long forgotten.

But Michael would not be shaken. No, he realized now that he did have integrity, he did indeed have it, and now it was time to lay down that law, to show this thing why human civilization was the natural progression of the cosmic order.

"You have no place here," said Michael through quickly stiffening and creaking lips. "This world is ours, and it always will be."

He could barely move, but what he did have left in him was enough…It had to be.

The ground beneath him shook as the elder creature struggled to be set free; its freedom a mere precedence to the destruction of all men and beasts.

Michael lowered his torch and aimed with both hands, pushing his will forward, pushing forth the green flame that had already poisoned this ancient thing through its own demanded sacrifices. He felt the blaze pulse from his heart and out through the extension of himself that was his torch, that torch a symbol of law and order, that fire a symbol of justice, that viridescent hue a symbol of the innocents lost, of friends lost, of the woman he loved lost.

The verdigris flames washed over the enormous stone face as the elder god roared in one final defiance.

✳✳✳✳✳

Michael adjusted his brown tie. His brown dress shoes were shined, his good brown suit was pressed and ready, including his brown inner vest, and his white dress shirt was buttoned up to the top. He took a moment to spread out the creases in his good brown slacks, and then he turned to address his staff.

"It's almost time," he said firmly. "I want to make sure everything is prepared."

"We have a fully-stocked kitchen," said Mrs. Corbin.

The old woman and her equally-elderly husband were dressed in aprons and short chef hats, their withered hands ready to cook and bake.

"Got my good recipes up and ready," said Mr. Corbin.

"Good," said Michael. "Carry on."

He turned to address his handyman.

"Things are as good as they're going to be for now," said Mr. Coal.

The portly man with a thin mustache and a square face placed a screwdriver back in his toolbelt and then adjusted the straps on his overalls.

"That will have to do," replied Michael.

His attention swiveled toward his two servants. They were troublemakers, but they still knew their place. They knew how important their roles were, especially now when it was almost time.

"What's the word?" asked Michael.

"It's all good down here," said Raymond.

The young man nodded once and then elbowed his inattentive partner in the ribs.

"Ready as we'll ever be, I guess," spoke up Lance. "I think we're good, but I wonder if we'll have any cuties show up. I'm hoping for ones with a gym membership. I love those firm butts."

"Lance…" frowned Raymond. "Behave. You're only supposed to like mine."

Both young men were dressed in full servants' outfits of black suit jackets and slacks, that black attire completed by white dress shirts, and Michael had to admit that they looked good in those clothes, but they were still the same two obnoxious friends he'd always known. Even this bizarre situation had not changed that.

Still, he needed to lay down the rules one more time, just in case.

"No talking to the guests unless asked a direct question," frowned Michael. "Even then, don't embellish. We can't have them leaving early…Seriously. You know the rules."

"Yeah, yeah, 'Master,'" said Lance with a roll of his eyes. "We all skip to your rope now. While we're at it, Mikey, would you like me to suck your—"

"Lance!" warned Lexi.

"Oh, right," sighed Lance. "That's your job."

"Lance…" growled Lexi.

Michael turned his attention to the woman he loved and the woman he could have loved. In truth, he loved them both, though his feelings toward Savanna were complicated.

Both Lexi and Savanna were fully dressed in their black-and-white maid outfits, the outfits lowcut and revealing to show off their natural beauty. Just looking upon them gave Michael a start; the pair of young ladies were a source of natural human art he had never expected to see in this new and strange life. They honestly took his breath away.

At any rate, he needed to address his girlfriend.

"It's okay," smiled Michael. "You don't have to defend me."

"Michael…" frowned Lexi.

"We're all in this together," he said. "Everyone here. I consider everyone here my friend, and…the Everwatch is as ready as it's going to be."

"It's been ten years, Michael," said Lexi with a worried frown. "None of us have aged. We've been stuck here for ten years without any visitors, too. We can't leave, and it's just been us, and none have us have aged a day…I'm scared. I've gotten used to this life…We're only wearing these ridiculous outfits because we all want out, but I'm terrified of just that…What's going to happen to us when…you know?"

Michael stepped forward and laid his hands on the young woman's bare shoulders.

"I love you, so whatever's going to happen, we're going to be together," he replied. "We're leaving here together, too…It will all be fine; I just know it. I think everything's going to be fine."

"I sure hope so," said Savanna. "I'm worried, too."

Michael smiled at her and shook his head no.

"There's nothing to worry about," he said firmly. "All of us have gone through a lot. We all made the same sacrifice, so we'll all be fine. Nothing bad's going to happen to us. I can feel it. Like I said, I just know it."

The young blonde smiled and looked thoughtful. Her blue eyes held a warmth he could not indulge, but she knew this. She'd known this for the last ten years. Nevertheless, this did not stop her from confessing her feelings one last time.

"I love you, Michael," she said sadly. "Lexi knows that…and I know we can't have a life together, but even so, I…I hope I meet someone like you when we leave this place. I want what you and Lexi have. I want to be with someone like you."

Michael was truly touched by that honest confession, but he did not get a chance to reply. No, his other half spoke for him, and her earnest words might as well have passed through his own lips.

"You will," said Lexi firmly. "You know I think of you as my sister now, and I'll make sure my little sister gets her wish. We all love you, Savanna; you know that."

But that heartfelt moment was interrupted by a loud snort from Lance.

"Oh, my God!" said the young blond man with a roll of his eyes. "If there is a Jesus somewhere, just let us leave already! I don't even care where we go at this point. Reincarnate me as a poodle for all I care, because if you two keep up with the *Hallmark* moments, I'm going to die all over again."

Michael gave a quiet chuckle over Lance's unflattering comment, and the rest of the group followed suit.

Lexi smiled, and Michael smiled back at her, and then he turned to look outside the hotel windows. The rain had begun to fall outside, pattering drops at first, and then it came down in a deluge that rattled over their collective hearing.

"There it is, the storm," said Mr. Coal in a gruff but quiet voice. "They're going to come now."

"Oh, goody," said Lance. "Finally!"

"Yep," said Michael with a sad smile. "I hate to say it, and I really hate to do this to complete strangers, but…it looks like our replacements are on their way."

#10...NAMELESS

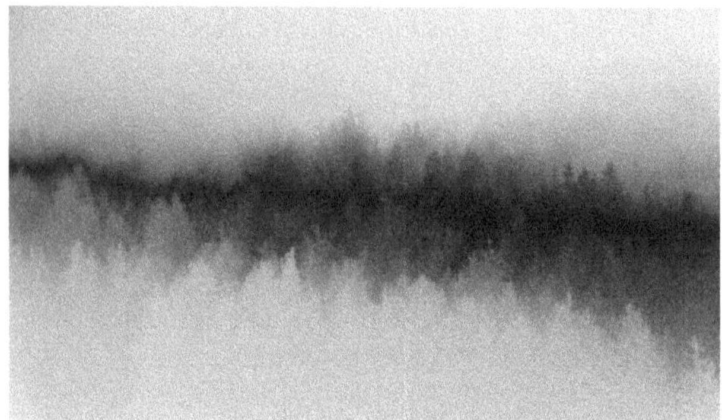

Sometimes there's a reason the unexplored remains unexplored.

"**Careful** with that sample," said Aurion.

Brell sensed at him for a second but said nothing, at least not at first. She simply took the foliage scraping and dropped the sample into a nearby containment tube.

"I have been doing this longer than you've been alive," she said firmly.

"But the foliage here—" began Aurion.

"Is extremely toxic, yes," finished Brell. "However, considering the gravitational force and atmospheric pressure of this planet, any rents in your suit...or mine...would instantly kill us. We'd simply explode, implode, or some combination of the two."

"I understand that, but—" started Aurion.

"Once we are back on the ship," continued Brell, "all protocols will be followed to the letter, and this sample will never make skin contact with any of us. As I have previously indicated, Captain, I have over forty cycles of experience in Xenobotany. If I didn't know what I was doing, I would already be dead."

Aurion wanted to put her in her place, but he did not argue with her; there was no point. Brell was the one member of his crew he would not argue with. She had that effect on him and…well…everyone else, for that matter.

"Carry on, then," he sighed.

He turned his senses to the strange alien forest around them. The foliage here was far, far larger than anything he had previously dealt with, as were the strange creatures inhabiting this rogue planet out in the middle of nowhere.

Technically, none of them were supposed to be out here, not out here in the Forbidden Zone, an arm of space few travelers ever returned from, but the scientific discoveries just waiting to be…discovered…were far too tempting to pass up.

"I just wish we'd had more backing," said Aurion.

He'd said that more for himself than for any wayward senses, but Brell had detected him anyway.

"This was an 'enter-at-your-own-risk' proposal by the council," she replied. "I chose to come because the opportunities for discovery and study were abundant and important. There's no telling what we may learn from this run. This field study may be the most important research of my life, or for that matter, anyone else's. Who knows what we might glean from this?"

"No weapons, no armed guards, nothing," muttered Aurion. "How are we supposed to defend ourselves?"

"The point of a scientist is to unravel the secrets of the universe," said Brell. "We're not supposed to destroy them. That's the military's job, and they are far too adept at doing just that. I, for one, am quite happy they are not involved with this trip in any way."

She was right in a sense, because this *was* a research run, not a scouting foray with military units, but still…he did not like being defenseless.

"If you insist on feeling competent, Captain," said Brell, "go investigate what the others are doing. You're wasting your time with me."

Brell always had a habit of making him feel inferior. In the end, though, he still had the final say when it came to anything on this mission, and he needed to remind her of that.

"Let me know if you find anything unusual," he said in a firm tone.

"Everything here is unusual, Captain," said Brell.

Well…she had a point there.

The terrain here was dangerous to the point of stupidity, the foliage was gigantic and quite thick, and the native fauna was to be avoided at all costs.

Aurion had already caught a glimpse of a creature through the clustered convergence of what passed for stalks on this planet, and the thing he'd sensed was three times the size of any of them. He couldn't even begin to describe it. Brell probably could, but he was not that old witch, and he thanked the gods for that.

He took his leave of the old xenobotanist and trotted off to find Bermoth and Campor. The two were not difficult to locate, however, as they were taking soil and mineral samples a mere tick away from Area 45.

Their xenocartographer, Irdan, had separated all areas within a circular pattern radiating out from their ship's landing site, each area spanning one tick. Irdan, of course, was currently exploring with Brettel, their only scout. Those two were the farthest out, somewhere Aurion wanted to be at the moment, mainly because neither one of them had reported in.

That made six of them, six researchers for this mission, and in the long run, six was not much for an expedition such as this. Aurion wasn't technically a researcher, but he did have some passing knowledge in xenoarchaeology, and that little fact had put him at the top of a long list of candidates.

Of course, where they had landed was just wilderness and nothing more. That was just his luck, though, and he couldn't help that.

There was the ship crew, naturally, but they were by and large irrelevant. The crew of the *Brazen* were still onboard the ship, and they were not to leave it, so he didn't count them. They were only there to pilot and maintain the ship, though Aurion was still the one calling the shots.

Nevertheless, the ship crew had explicit instructions to take off and abandon the research team if all six life-signals of the team's members were snuffed out. It was heartless, and it was cold, but it was also practical. Someone had to report back home to explain what had happened if anything were to happen, and Aurion was truly praying that nothing of that sort actually *did* happen, for it was not a pleasant thought.

Aurion made his way through the treacherous terrain and even more treacherous foliage to reach Area 46. He took it more slowly than he would have liked, but one could never be too careful in such a hostile environment. True, his powered exosuit was armored with maneuverable plates, and the suit was designed to self-seal in case of injury, but he didn't want to find out if that experimental feature actually worked or not. That brand-new benefit was still a work-in-progress.

For one thing, the gravity on this world was insane. The G-force here alone would kill any one of them without protection, but considering the atmosphere on FZ-189763G7 was more toxic than the ninth level of the underworld, the crushing gravity was the least of his concerns.

Right now, he had to find Bermoth and Campor.

Bermoth was a younger male than Aurion, but he was talented in his field, while Campor was somewhat older than Aurion, but she was also an incorrigible flirt, and Aurion was now regretting pairing the two together. They were best paired together considering their fields, but still…Aurion needed to keep them on track, not discover them doing…other things.

He discovered Bermoth and Campor with little effort. The two were indeed together, and they were not doing their assigned tasks, but their lack of work ethic was not due to any of Aurion's private fears. No, they were both staring off toward the outskirts of Area 46, but for what purpose, Aurion did not know.

"What are you two doing?" he asked. "Why aren't you collecting samples?"

"We were," said Campor, "but then we sensed an aerometric disturbance five ticks out."

"An aerometric disturbance?" asked Aurion. "What aerometric disturbance?"

"It was forceful," said Bermoth. "We sensed it all the way here. Didn't you feel it?"

"No," said Aurion, but he was unsure.

Perhaps he had, perhaps he hadn't. More than likely, his mind had been elsewhere due to his many duties, where he was, and that old witch, Brell. Of course, he had a more pressing matter at hand than whether or not he had sensed any aerometric disturbance.

"Was this in the direction of Irdan and Brettel?" asked Aurion.

"Yes…I think so," said Campor.

"Did you contact them?" asked Aurion.

"Well…" trailed off Bermoth.

"Well, did you or didn't you?" asked Aurion.

"We tried," replied Bermoth. "We tried to contact them, but we haven't been able to."

"Hmm," said Aurion in verbal wonder. "All right. I'll go and look for them. You two get back to work while I'm gone…and no funny business. This isn't mating season."

The hostile tone Campor exuded implied an expression of indignation upon her face that would have been humorous were it not for the fact that Aurion was being dead serious.

"What is *that* supposed to mean!" she demanded.

"It means what it means," said Aurion.

"You're communicating that to me, aren't you!" asked Campor.

She was sensibly upset, but Aurion didn't care. He knew full well what she was like.

"Of course, I am," he said firmly.

"This is because I'm female, isn't it!" accused Campor.

Of course, one look at Bermoth, and Aurion could sense the discomfort in the young male's posture. It was clear he wanted no part of this.

"It's because you have a reputation," said Aurion flatly. "It's in your file."

"That was one time!" said Campor. "It happened when I was younger, and it wasn't even my fault!"

"I will take that into account," said Aurion. "We can discuss this later…Just get back to work."

"Oh, we'll discuss it," said Campor in obvious disgust. "We'll discuss this with Central once we're back home and I file a formal complaint!"

"You do that," said Aurion. "Right now, just get back to work. I have to go find our missing xenocartographer and our missing scout."

He pushed past her and made his way through more thick foliage, but he did catch her parting comment before she disappeared from sight.

"Pompous, egotistical, self-important…" she blathered on.

She was definitely going to be a problem later on. This was concerning, true, but he still had a job to do. He still had to find Irdan and Brettel.

He trudged once more over treacherous terrain and thick alien foliage. He had to make it out to Area 51, the area he suspected his xenocartographer and his scout were currently located.

Irdan was around his age, but he was a giant nerd, a complete geek in the field of xenocartography, and Aurion had little in common with him.

Brettel, on the other hand, was older than Aurion but younger than Brell, and she was a tough, hardened, and weathered female with many years of experience in military survival. Aurion didn't particularly like her, mainly because of her gruff attitude. He preferred his females submissive.

He had made his way to Area 50 before he'd found them. He'd already known they were still alive because their life-signals had not been terminated, but what they were doing, he had no idea.

They were huddled down, lying flat within the dense shedding of foliage upon the wilderness floor, staring off toward Area 51. Naturally, he walked up to them in order to question them upon what kind of tomfoolery they were currently engaged in.

"What are you two—" he began.

He was cut short as he was yanked flat by Brettel. He didn't even have time to protest before she mashed his face into the foliage shedding, his only view her unflattering posterior as she turned back around to face toward Area 51.

"Quiet!" she hissed.

Discretion was the better part of irritation here. Aurion wanted to cuss her out, badly so, a long string of expletives that would put her in her place, but he needed to know what was going on first.

"What's going on!" he hissed in return.

"We were a tick ahead," replied Irdan, "but then we discovered other beings there."

"Other beings?" asked Aurion. "What do you mean by that? Are you saying—"

"Unregistered alien lifeforms," said Brettel. "They're unlike anything we've ever encountered."

"How so?" asked Aurion, but then he thought better about it. "I mean…No, wait…We scanned this planet before arriving. There are no sentient minds here."

"Is that so?" asked Brettel. "Tell that to them."

He was really getting tired of her attitude, but he decided to play along.

"How did we not detect them, then?" he asked.

"I don't know," answered the scout. "All I know is that when we tried to communicate with them, we received no reply. It was like communicating with a wall. There was nothing there."

"What?" asked Aurion. "Are you sure?"

"Yes!" hissed Brettel. "It's like they're dead inside."

"Plus, they're huge," said Irdan. "They're giants."

"What?" asked Aurion again, but this time in complete disbelief. "You expect me to believe that mindless giants—"

"It's the truth!" cut in Brettel. "They're huge, they don't communicate, and they must be natives to this planet."

"How can you tell?" asked Aurion.

He had asked that without thinking. All of this was unbelievable, but his mind had already wandered toward the "natives" part of her reply.

"They have little to no protection against the atmosphere," said Irdan.

"They're also armed," said Brettel. "They're armed with weapons that work specifically within this atmosphere."

If this was a prank, it was a well-thought-out one. This disturbed Aurion, if only because of its believability.

"What do you mean?" he asked. "We should be safe anyway. Our exosuits have reflective plating."

"They're not using beam weapons," said Irdan. "Their weapons cause some kind of aerometric disturbance, but the damage done is tremendous. Brettel suspects they're firing metal shards via some unknown propulsion source."

"Metal shards?" asked Aurion. "We don't have protection against that."

"I know," said Brettel. "We can't communicate with them, and they've already fired at us once… These things are nameless. We have no idea what they are, only that they're hostile. That's why we're leaving immediately."

"I give the commands around here," said Aurion firmly.

"You won't be giving any commands if we're all dead," said Brettel just as firmly.

"We need to report this to Central, Captain," said Irdan. "They have to know about this…if only to protect our people. If we don't make it off this planet, Central might send more ships for search and rescue. They'd be walking right into a trap."

"Look, you can take all of the credit for this," said Brettel. "You can be a hero back home, for all I care. Right now, we need to get off this planet."

Aurion did not like being ordered around, but they were right. If what they were saying was true, then all of them had to leave immediately. If what they were saying wasn't true…well, they could be court-martialed upon return.

"So be it," sighed Aurion. "Let's make our way back."

"Good," said Brettel. "I haven't sensed them recently, but they're difficult to sense anyway."

"Giant creatures that are difficult to sense?" asked Aurion.

He was really beginning to wonder if this was some sort of elaborate prank set up by his research team. He knew they didn't like him, especially the females. He would not put it past these bitter witches to do this, to make him look like a fool in front of Central.

He would have asked more questions about this, but his irritating scout would not allow it.

"Yes," said Brettel in flat reply. "I told you, we tried to communicate with them, but there was nothing there to communicate with. Plus, it's difficult to sense their presence in general. Irdan and I have narrowed down their movement indicators by sensing slight adjustments in aerometric vibrational changes…I'm telling you, it's like they're ghosts…

"But that doesn't matter right now. It's only a matter of time before they make their way here…We'd better return now…Follow me. I can cut short our travel time with a clearer path through this insane foliage."

Yet again with the orders. Aurion was the captain here, but he chose to defer to his scout anyway. Next time, however, he was not bringing any females along for the ride. Their sense of entitlement grated upon him.

"Let's go," he grunted.

Both he and Irdan followed Brettel along a new path toward Area 46. They had to inform Bermoth and Campor, though Aurion was seriously considering leaving Campor behind. In light of her loose mouth, she was going to be a problem when they finally returned home.

They trudged over unfamiliar terrain through thick foliage as Brettel led them back. Aurion could only hope she knew where she was going, but he had his doubts.

"Are you sure you know where you're going?" he asked.

"Yes," said Brettel, but her attitude was defiant. "This path should lead us back."

"*Should* lead us back?" asked Aurion. "Is this the path you first took?"

She traveled onward in more defiance, replying as she went. Aurion took this as a deliberate insult, but that insult was short-lived.

"No, it's not," she said matter-of-factly. "I'm taking a new route because it's a quicker—"

Her reply was cut short as large metal jaws erupted from the shed foliage upon the planet floor. These huge jaws sprang upwards and closed upon Brettel, crunching through her exosuit with ease, splitting her nearly in two. She popped a moment later from the crushing atmosphere, her internal fluids spraying everywhere as one of her legs flew past Aurion's face.

This, of course, initiated instant panic, but that was to be expected.

"RUN!" yelled Aurion.

He and Irdan ran for their lives without a second thought.

"That was a trap!" screeched Irdan. "They've set traps!"

"I know!" yelled back Aurion. "Just keep running, you fool! We have to make it back to the others!"

He sensed the aerometric disturbance before witnessing the damage it dealt, a shockwave of ambient power, and then Irdan exploded into bits right next to him. The xenocartographer geek's life-signal snuffed out without any warning at all, just like Brettel's, here one moment and gone the next.

Aurion scuttled and scampered as fast as he could. More aerometric disturbances vibrated the air molecules, but he made himself a tough target by putting dense foliage between himself and his murderous pursuers.

Bretell had been correct; he could sense them closing in as he weaved this way and that, because they did indeed leave behind aerometric vibrational changes when they moved. However, they were fast, much faster than he could have anticipated for supposed "giants."

In truth, he had not even caught so much as a sensory scan of them, but he had no desire to. He was afraid if he stopped for even one second, he would be a glob of exploded paste all over the planet floor, just like his two newly-deceased compatriots.

He dashed back toward Area 46, his legs moving as fast as they could, though his powered exosuit slowed him down somewhat. The servomotors simply could not keep up with his brain's commands to run and then run some more.

He came upon Bermoth and Campor, and they surely had to know by now that Irdan and Brettel were dead. They were probably waiting for confirmation and a lengthy description as to what happened.

And confirm that he did, though he did not elaborate on that confirmation.

"RUN!" yelled Aurion as he scuttled past them. "BACK TO THE SHIP!"

They ran along with him, but that did not stop them from asking questions, especially Campor. She was not about to let this go without an explanation.

"What's going on!" yelled Campor.

Aurion cringed at this simple question, but he replied anyway.

"Alien giants killed Irdan and Brettel!" he cried. "Just run! Duck and weave!"

"What!" cried out Campor.

Aurion ceased listening to her. No, he was intent on making it to Area 45, preferably alive and unexploded. Of course, this was compounded by the fact that giant, invisible, alien murderers were pursuing him, but that was the reason he was running anyway.

An aerometric disturbance kicked up near him, there was an upwards blast of shed foliage just in front of him, and then there was a cry of pain and fear from Bermoth.

Aurion turned out of reaction, though he had not intended to.

Bermoth was struggling forward, though he was missing a leg. His blood was splattered across the shed foliage, though his suit had sealed at the wound thanks to the new experimental exosuit technology they were all equipped with, and that was good (for Bermoth), but Aurion could tell that Bermoth was in great pain. That technology wasn't going to grow back the younger male's leg.

"Help me!" cried out Bermoth.

"Help me get him!" pleaded Campor.

It did not take two seconds for Aurion to come to a decision over this little dilemma. No, there was only one solution for this, and it was cold, but it was necessary.

"There's nothing we can do," said Aurion flatly. "He's not going to make it."

There was nothing else to be said, so Aurion took to running once more. Bermoth was already dead as far as he was concerned, and what little was left in the xenopedologist would serve as a distraction for the alien murderers, so the young male's death wasn't entirely in vain.

"Aurion!" yelled Campor. "Get back here!"

She chased after him, but neither one of them made it very far before the air molecules vibrated again from another aerometric disturbance.

Bermoth's life-signal ended. There was no longer any argument as to whether the young xenopedologist needed help or not.

Aurion ignored Campor's screams of rage. No, he took to running again, because unlike her, he knew the situation at hand, and also unlike her, he was a competent leader.

"You filth!" screeched Campor. "You trash!"

Aurion hit Area 45 without slowing down. There was no way he was going to let some self-righteous female hold him up, or for that matter, get him killed.

Brell stepped out before them, and Aurion was momentarily forced to come to a screeching halt due to the imposing presence of the old witch.

"Stop!" cried out the weathered xenobotanist.

"There's no ti—!" began Aurion.

"He left Bermoth behind!" screeched Campor. "Bermoth is dead because of him!"

"I didn't kill him!" said Aurion defensively. "The alien giants did that!"

"What alien giants?" asked Brell. "The only thing I know is that three of our research team are dead, their life-signals terminated."

"Something killed Bermoth," said Campor.

Her tone was watery, upset, and completely unprofessional. Her weak personality was just one of the reasons why Aurion was going to oust her the moment he got back home. That was a given.

"Something killed all three of them," corrected Aurion. "Brettel and Irdan claimed that nameless alien giants were hunting them and were somehow natives to this planet. They also claimed that these giants possessed unknown weaponry that we have no defense against, weaponry that fires metal shards."

"Giants native to this world?" asked Brell. "And how did we not detect them? We scanned for sentient life."

"Brettel claimed she had tried to communicate with them," continued Aurion, "but she said, and I quote,

'There was nothing there.' She claimed it was like talking to a wall, like they were dead inside."

"Were they artificial lifeforms?" asked Brell.

"I…I don't know," said Aurion nervously. "I've yet to actually sense one in its entirety."

He had not thought to scan for artificial lifeforms…Such a thing had never crossed his mind. As captain, it was his job to anticipate any and all hostile encounters, especially out here in the Forbidden Zone.

"You didn't scan for Artificials!" hissed Campor. "Bermoth is dead because of you! Brettel and Irdan are dead because of you! You didn't scan for Artificials, you moron! By the Thousand Rings, I should kill you, you incompetent piece of—!"

"Enough," said Brell firmly. "You two will report back to the ship. I will lead off these giants. Either I'll lose them, or I won't. Either way, I'll ensure you have a clear path."

"You can't do that!" said Campor in sensible surprise. "You can't just throw your life away, especially for him!"

"I'm old, and I've had my adventures," said Brell. "This trip to the Forbidden Zone was the last thing on my ascension list. I've made my peace already, Campor…Now, I want you two to go…Go now. Go before it's too late."

Aurion did not have to be told twice. He simply turned and ran.

"Coward!" yelled Campor.

The old witch, Brell, was not so much of a witch in his mind anymore. She had some real grit, some real and honest sense of priorities, something Campor clearly did not possess. Brell knew it was her duty to ensure the survival of her captain, unlike Campor, who had become a liability some time ago.

Speaking of which, the younger female was the real witch now.

Campor was after him, naturally. The younger witch of the two was not going to leave him be on the matter of Bermoth, but Aurion knew some sacrifices had to be made for the greater good. He had to get his crew safely home, and Bermoth's abandonment was just one of those cold but proper decisions that captains had to make in the heat of the moment.

"Trash!" hissed Campor as she followed Aurion through dense foliage. "Filthy, cowardly trash!"

Aurion attempted to ignore her as best he could, but her persistence in hostility wore at him. Nevertheless, he made it all the way to Area 40 before he sensed the distant jarring of an aerometric disturbance. This was followed by several more distant aerometric disturbances, but Brell's life-signal did not end until Aurion had entered Area 38.

Considering the distance between the disturbances and his location, Aurion slowed down to a much more acceptable pace. He was very tired anyway.

"You're a coward," said Campor, the hostility still evident in her tone.

"I am the captain," said Aurion calmly. "I have to make the tough decisions when called upon."

"That's an excuse," replied Campor. "You're nothing but a coward…a bigoted, self-centered, narcissistic coward."

"You are going under arrest and review for mutiny as soon as we get back," warned Aurion. "I think a stay in the brig will do until you can be transferred to a tribunal at Central."

"What!" cried Campor. "Oh, you are so done when we return. I'm going to let everyone know what happened. You are finished…Do you sense me! YOU…ARE…FINISHED!"

This settled the matter for him; her shouting simply would not do. She was a clear and present danger to the ship and the crew now, so there was only one clear course of action.

He picked up a rather large stone and hefted its weight, checking to sense just how hard and how dense it actually was.

"What are you doing?" asked Campor.

He could sense the nervousness in her. It was that sense of impending doom that was an instinct in all living things.

"I'm doing what's necessary," said Aurion matter-of-factly. "You cannot be allowed to jeopardize the safety of the crew. I am hereby terminating you for the good of all."

"Stop!" screeched Campor. "STOP!"

He came at her a second later. She tried to defend herself, and she shrieked quite loudly, but it only took two good hits to her suit's exoplating to rupture it.

She ballooned outwards for a second as he backed away, and then she exploded, her blood and guts spraying everywhere, absolutely everywhere, and he knew he was going to have to explain why he was covered in her brains and other parts, but he would cross that bridge when he came to it.

He took his leave of her corpse, though there was not much left of it.

It was a travesty, really, but this had been the alien giants' fault anyway. Yes, this wouldn't have happened if there hadn't been any alien giants on the planet. Oh no, this was not his fault. He, the captain, was not to blame for this insanity. And speaking of insanity, Campor had gone mad, and he'd had to put her down. It was the giants who were responsible for everyone's deaths anyway, so he would simply list her as killed by them in his report.

He made his way back to the ship, but he had no further issues. Brell's sacrifice had paid off, and he was no longer being pursued. He would make sure her sacrifice would not be forgotten, either. He would mention that sacrifice in a memo within his full report. Campor, on the other hand, would simply be listed as "killed by her own incompetence in response to a hostile alien threat."

Aurion shook off any other doubts as the *Brazen* came into view just up ahead. It was time to get off of this pit of a planet.

✶✶✶✶✶

Billy deftly maneuvered a stick through leaves and dirt in order to pick up what was left of the "leg" on the ground. It was long and spindly, about as thick around as a twig or a stick itself, a husk of a thing with a brown, chitinous exterior. It leaked a glowing goo from where it had blown open, a neon liquid of rainbow hues that shifted and shimmered in the dim light of dawn.

"What are these critters, Billy?" asked Jimmy Joe.

Billy dropped the hollow limb and stick, scratched his thick brown beard, and shook his head. He took off his hunter's cap after that and wiped his brow in confusion. In truth, he had no idea what he was looking at.

"Got no idea, Jimmy Joe," he said. "They look like big ol' ticks or mites, but they pop like zits when you shoot 'em. Can't says I ever seen anything like 'em."

"Maybe they're aliens," said Jimmy Joe.

Billy grinned and nodded a couple of times as he put his hat back on his head. He dropped his shotgun barrel off his right shoulder and gripped the weapon with both hands.

"That they might be, Jimmy Joe," he said. "If they are aliens, you know what that means?"

"Yeah…We gon' be rich, Billy," grinned Jimmy Joe.

"Yepper," nodded Billy. "We can get ourselves in *National Discovery World*. Hell, maybe we can even get ourselves in *Guns and Women*!"

"Aww, you're thinking too small, Billy!" said Jimmy Joe. "We can get ourselves on TV!"

"Yeah," breathed Billy as he thought about this. "We can be like those good ol' boys on that duck show."

"Now, you're talking," said Jimmy Joe. "But first we need to find the rest of these…critters…"

His voice trailed off as both of them stared in the distance at the long, almond-shaped object rising above the morning tree-line. It looked fairly large, even from the distance at which they were viewing it, and it was truly almond shaped, but it was definitely unlike any kind of nut either one of them had ever seen before. It was more like a giant pointed oval with a brown chitinous exterior that was segmented and banded like an insect, like the abdomen of a roach.

"They are aliens, Billy!" breathed out Jimmy Joe in excitement. "That's their ship… They must be some kinda alien bug hive!...They must be invading! They want to lay eggs in our brains or something…Oh, it's a good thing we got the ones down here, but they're gettin' away!"

"Not for long, Jimmy Joe," said Billy with a shake of his head. "Not for long…You hear that? Our boys just showed up."

They both turned to view several fighter jets streak through the dawn sky, the rumbling of the planes an indication that help was already on the way.

"How'd they get here so fast?" asked Jimmy Joe.

"Our boys have been shooting down those commie spy balloons," nodded Billy. "They been on high alert lately. They pro'lly already knew these critters was here…Ain't you watched the news?"

A number of missiles slammed into the alien craft in the distance, contrails of debris flying everywhere and in every direction as the strange ship exploded. There was nothing left of the weird alien ship after that, just pieces of it raining down upon the forest treetops some distance beyond their own position.

Billy and Jimmy Joe whooped and hollered as they jumped up and down in excitement.

"Yeah!" yelled Jimmy Joe. "That's our boys! Woohoo!"

"That'll teach them aliens not to mess with the good ol' boys of Earth!" cried Billy.

About the Author

Mr. Marlott has a background in psychology and classic literature, and he enjoys literature of all types and genres. Mr. Marlott lives somewhere within the United States, has two Gen-Z children, and enjoys telling stories to anyone who will listen.

Books and Sites

You can read new stories of mine for free at bloodytwine.com. This site is my workshop where I work on new stories and perfect them for publication.

For more twisted tales with twisted endings, you can purchase *Bloody Twine #1-4* wherever they are sold.

If you want the basic building blocks to writing genre fiction, you can explore my two cents on the subject in *The Quick and Easy Guide to Writing Genre Fiction*.

For great cosmic horror, you can read some awesome eldritch-horror tales by Bert S. Lechner. You can purchase Mr. Lechner's collection of cosmic horror, *The Roots Grow into the Earth*, wherever it is sold. You can also check out Mr. Lechner's personal website at bertwriteshorror.com.

For a mix of traditional horror and cosmic horror, check out some incredible short stories by James Dermond. You can purchase Mr. Dermond's Doorways to the Unseen series wherever it is sold. You can also visit Mr. Dermond's website at jamesdermond.com.

If you like this book, give it a good review and tell me what your favorite story was in this bundle.

THE BLOODY TWINE SERIES

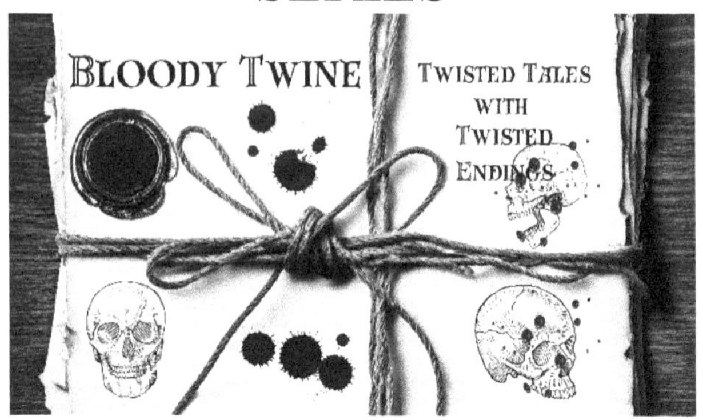

Welcome to the Bloody Twine Series, a collection of short horror stories written specifically for horror fans everywhere. These books contain a minimum of 10 traditional short horror stories for the collections and a minimum of 5 traditional short horror stories for the selections, all for your terrifying entertainment, so go someplace quiet, dim the lights, sit back, and enjoy some twisted tales with twisted endings.

Imagine walking into an abandoned storage room filled with old newspapers and magazines, all articles stacked in bundles neatly tied with twine, but then you discover other bundles, bundles not so neatly tied, ragged bundles of yellowed and partially-charred paper tied in bloodstained twine.

You see, some stories are meant to educate, and some stories are meant to entertain, but some stories…some stories are simply looking for a victim.

Enjoy.

Matthew L. Marlott

THE QUICK AND EASY GUIDE TO WRITING GENRE FICTION

Thinking of writing your own tale of love, redemption, and heroics? Writing genre fiction is an art, and *The Quick and Easy Guide to Writing Genre Fiction* provides the building blocks for being successful in this art. Learn all of the necessary techniques to get yourself started with writing in your chosen genre. Whether you're writing a mystery, a romance, a thriller, science-fiction, horror, fantasy, or any other genre, you'll have the foundation for writing great stories right here at your fingertips in this guide.

Included in this guide is a step-by-step instruction of what it takes to put together your creation in any genre. Also included in this guide is the complete creation process of an original short story by author Matthew L. Marlott, so you, too, can have an easy example of how to create your own stories, whether those stories are short stories, novels, or novellas. You'll be able to create your own worlds and your own universes, so learn the basics of writing genre fiction for the purpose of selling, for publication on a site, for fanfiction, or just for your own personal satisfaction.

Remember, if you want real life, you can just walk out the front door. Why not write down your own story on paper or screen instead? Get started with your journey into genre fiction by learning from this invaluable guide. Don't wait until you're on your deathbed. Get started today.

Matthew L. Marlott

THE ROOTS GROW INTO THE EARTH

"In the dark we found them…"

The Roots grow into the Earth. Unseen conduits of Power, growing through the darkness of the void; walkways for malevolent, eldritch things to travel, connecting their dead worlds to ours.

In this collection of nine short stories and novelettes, you will find tales of unfathomable predators, cosmic gods, dark magic, and the people who cross their path: from archaeologists, long on the search for the find of the century, ensnared by a being beyond their understanding, to a man who notices a detail on a wall in his house for the first time, unwittingly inviting the attention of a malefic force from beyond the stars.

The Roots Grow Into the Earth consists of nine of Bert S. Lechner's previously published works, including three stories available as standalone eBooks: Interstate, the Wall, and Joanne's Vault.

Bert S. Lechner

DOORWAYS TO THE UNSEEN

"The Doorways to the Unseen series is a collection of short story books from author James Dermond. The stories take the reader around the world and through time, with each tale offering a glimpse into a supernatural episode. Every volume in the series contains six short horror stories meant to chill the blood and inspire unimaginable terror in their readers.

"So, step inside and find that which has been hidden from you all along. Where the unknown and the unimaginable meet."

James Dermond

Until Next Time...

Bloody Twine #5
Twisted Tales with Twisted Endings